Courtney Ann McGrail is an Irish writer from Co. Tyrone. She is a media writing and production graduate from Bolton University and journalism graduate from Dublin City University. She is an atheist, animal lover, WWF sponsor, wine connoisseur, tattoo enthusiast, lover of leather, rock music and justified naughtiness. She can also be referred to as the Holy Grail.

Dedicated to the minorities fighting for freedom and equality. To those fighting against oppression and to those who keep fighting in the face of seemingly unconquerable adversity. Dedicated to all those who refuse to crack when the world seems dark and hollow and to all those fighting to make this world a better place.

C A McGrail

Alex Valentine: The Midnight Children

Austin Macauley Publishers™

London * Cambridge * New York * Sharjah

A CIP catalogue record for this title is available from the British Library.

ISBN 9781528978057 (Paperback)
ISBN 9781528978071 (ePub e-book)

www.austinmacauley.com

First Published (2021)
Austin Macauley Publishers Ltd
25 Canada Square
Canary Wharf
London
E14 5LQ

I acknowledge my mother, my father and my partner for sticking by me and thanks to Austin Macauley Publishers for giving me this opportunity.

Prologue

Dark blood congeals upon the alter.

The deed has been done, but this is just the beginning.

Screams fill the black sky as Giovanni soldiers drag struggling victims from their houses. Masses of Innocents are slaughtered in the streets. Those deemed not to be a threat are lucky enough to be put to the sword. The unfortunate are taken, beaten and hauled deep underground into cramped, dark prison cells. Here, these martyrs await their torture. Here they await their slow, agonising deaths.

High above this oubliette, the Hall of Vampires stands as a looming shadow in the blackness of the night. Its gothic pillars tip the dark sky wherein yellow lights burn.

The fortress towers on the Bodmin Plateau far above the desolate city below. Now, nothing stirs but the wind that drifts like a dying breath through the crumbling Moor Falls Cemetery and through the winding blood-stained cobbled streets.

The plateau is flanked by a mediaeval wall, where armed, ethereal guards man the border between the esteemed domain and the 'peasantry' below. Violence has given way to silence and their glowing green eyes scan for signs of life.

Within the hall, the Giovanni Authorities hold their court. Adorned in gilded motifs, engravings and tapestries, the gothic interior of the hall is palatial. In honour of their aristocratic inhabitants, servants carry out their duties, ensuring the antique furniture is set to nothing less than perfection.

A servant carrying decanters of blood glides up the majestic mahogany staircase and along the crimson carpet towards the Giovanni Authorities' conference room. Along the walls, hundreds of portraits reveal the lineage of the vampire clans in all their glory. Below the staircase on the back wall, all eyes are commanded to look upon the grandest painting, an enormous depiction of the First – the first angel to fall from grace.

Flanking this image are portraits of the grandmasters of each of the four clans. To the immediate right of the First is an image of the current Giovanni Grandmaster, Balthazar, who was the first vampire created by the angel. Further along, the wall is his second in command, Zanned Delin, who was the first vampire turned by Balthazar. He is a proud and self-righteous figure appearing as a politician wearing a sash emblazoned with the Giovanni Seal. Nailed to the wall beside him is his second in command, Caros, a creature who never knew a smile except at the expense of those beneath him. Dressed in the military uniform of the Giovanni Clan, on his left arm he wears an armband with the Giovanni Crest. Nothing would give these creatures any more pride than to call themselves a Giovanni Authority.

The servant timidly knocks the door to the Giovanni's conference room. "Come in." A voice booms from within. The servant enters and awaits instruction. Something is going on; he could sense it even before entering. The atmosphere in the hall had been putrid for weeks since communication had broken down between the clans. Hostility was ripe.

At a long mahogany table engraved with the Giovanni Crest, the Giovanni Authorities have gathered. They appear not as a conference of men. Not as politicians – but as a coven. The darkened room is illuminated by candlelight which flickers as the servant is instructed to approach the table.

He moves silently to the head of the table where Zanned has taken his throne. The coven of thirteen preternatural creatures does not make a sound. The servant fills Zanned's glass then moves to fill Caros' glass. No sooner has the servant filled the crystal to the brim that Caros snatches it away.

The servant crosses behind Zanned to where a female sits – Evelyn Delin – Zanned's wife, a rare female in her male-dominated world. She is an affluent female appearing to be in her late forties dressed in a regal dress and jewels with her green eyes glowing in the dim light. She moves her glass for the servant to fill. Her hand trembles lightly as she raises the glass to her pale, thin lips. She has already warned Zanned that his plot would start a war. Regardless of whether they succeeded or failed in this endeavour, much blood would be spilled.

Zanned exhales with frustration as the servant moves to the next. "Just leave it on the table." He commands in a grisly, thuggish voice – more Cockney gangster than a politician. The servant jolts instinctively at the sudden noise. He looks to Zanned, nods quietly and leaves the tray of decanters on the table. The remaining Authorities are left to satisfy themselves.

The servant quietly escorts himself out. Zanned takes a drink then turns to Caros, "We have made the first move. We cannot afford to waste any more time."

"I agree, most vehemently." Caros sits straight in his military regalia; his square jaw clenched bitterly. "We should have taken action a century ago. More. Our inactivity. Our patience shows weakness to the other Clans. The Teva and Lanuonin are controllable – they have no fight. The Ronakites, on the other hand will seize opportunity in a prolonged period of Giovanni idleness."

Zanned scans his Senechaux. All eyes are empty. Their pale faces are pained with troubled thoughts. Zanned turns to an Authority to the left of Evelyn. Farius appears as a priestly figure dressed head to toe in a black habit with its white tongue. Around his neck hang worn, wooden rosary beads.

"Farius, might you offer an opinion?" Although asked as a question, Farius knows better than to hesitate. Farius knows to answer quickly and supportively. "I believe, Zanned, that you will always choose the wisest path in the name of the Giovanni Clan. And, in that case, you have my full support." Farius raises his glass.

"And do I have your support also?" Zanned addresses his coven. Caros raises his glass without hesitation, "Until my dying breath, Brother." Zanned smirks and turns back to see all arms extended upwards, the crystal glasses shimmering in the candlelight. Inside the glass, its bloody contents appear black.

Zanned turns to Evelyn, taking her right hand, her left arm still raised in toast. "Are you sure you're content with this decision?"

"I would die for my Clan," she declares. Zanned squeezes her hand then raises his own glass.

"It is decided. The waiting is over. It is time to take matters into our own hands. The angel is dead. Now Balthazar too must die." Despite a number of weary glances at this declaration, the coven toast and drink.

Zanned lowers his glass to the table with a rough thump. A trickle of dark blood bleeds down his chin. He brushes this away with the back of his hand. On the table, a small crack creeps up the side of the delicate crystal glass.

The decision has been made. Little do the Giovanni Authorities know, they have just signed their death warrants.

Chapter 1

On a gilded throne at the end of a long mahogany table emblazoned with the Giovanni Crest, the sands run out inside a large gold encased hourglass.

As the last sands run out, a bullet blows the hourglass to pieces. The glass shatters and scatters into millions of shards and cascades on to the floor. The remaining sand pours as a pitiful trickle on to the cold mosaic-tiled ground.

At the opposite end of the table sits Julius Silverstone, always the gentleman. With his long brown hair tied back in a tidy ponytail, he is dressed neatly in black from head to toe except for a deep-green crushed velvet coat.

His hazel-green eyes watch the space where the hourglass sat just moments before. His expression is calm, contemplative. He appears to be in his late thirties to early forties although he could be centuries old – his eyes reveal his true wisdom, his presence, his composure tells his true age.

In his hand, he holds a smoking gun. On his finger is a ring bearing the Giovanni Seal. Once a loyal and respected member and a candidate for an Authority position, Julius Silverstone is about to embark on the most dissenting quest of his life.

Placing the gun within his coat he rises from the throne and moves to the end of the table, the heels of his boots echoing around the walls. He stops to stand above the remains of the broken hourglass and brushing away the sand he reveals a small key in the shape of an ankh. Holding the key up before his face he smiles, the time has come.

Ever since he learned of the Giovanni Authorities' plan to destroy what he believed to be the key to the survival of the vampire nation, he planned to destroy them.

When the Giovanni Authorities decided to intervene in an ancient prophecy, when they decided to take matters into their own hands to serve their own interests, Julius knew what he had to do. The Giovanni Authorities could not kill the Midnight Children. So, Julius would dedicate his life to protect them and to protect the prophecy.

It was foretold of the Midnight Children's arrival. It was foretold that the Midnight Children would be the undoing of the Giovanni Authorities, the Authorities who had long ago divided, conquered and tore the vampire nation to pieces. Julius knew what he had to do.

Leaving the evidence of his betrayal behind him, Julius marches from the room where he finds a handsome man in the black military uniform of the Giovanni Clan. He wears a long black leather trench coat revealing that he is of high rank. Shoulder length black hair drapes around his pale, sculpted features.

Julius pauses a moment at the sight of the soldier then continues towards him, passing him coldly. The soldier, Blaine, stops warily as he passes then pursues. Catching up, he speaks in hushed tones as they march together down the long corridor.

"Have you done it?" Blaine questions.

"I have." Julius does not flinch. Blaine appears shaken.

"You do know what this means?" Julius turns to him, expression stern.

"Yes. I am fully aware of the wrath that will be set upon me. I've made my peace with it."

Blaine shakes his head, "Julius. Why? Why risk it all for these creatures? What if they can't be controlled? What if the Authorities are right?"

They reach the top of the staircase, where Julius pulls Blaine aside. The luminescent light of a full moon shines in on them through a huge arched window.

"Blaine you have so much still to learn." Julius advises, "I need to do this." He checks his pocket watch – it is almost midnight. Blaine studies Julius with doubt. Sensing Blaine's disturbance, Julius rests his hand on his shoulder for a moment.

"Some people in this world know the difference between right and wrong but only a special few understand that sometimes we must do wrong in order to do right." The usually placid and collected gentleman speaks of impending anarchy that unnerves the young soldier before him.

Julius continues, "Corruption breeds anarchy, but often it is the anarchists who become the heroes. Our world is paradoxical and more than often the true criminals are those in suits who hide behind desks. I have witnessed this too many times. If I must become a dissenter, a betrayer of my own Clan, it will be for the cause of a greater good."

Blaine appears solemn as Julius' words settle upon his mind like frost and chill him to the core. "So the war has started?" He questions.

"It is just the beginning." Julius speaks softly, the future bears heavily upon him. His eyes meet Blaine's, "Can I trust you?" Blaine appears horrified to having been asked such a question. Julius sighs, "Blaine, Caros would have you executed for what you have already done for me and the knowledge you have concealed from him."

"I did it for you," Blaine states, "Your words are convincing."

"Know this, Blaine; I am grateful to have such an ally. And I believe your role in this quest will be much more difficult than mine." Blaine nods slowly, Julius' words causing troubled thoughts to clog his mind. But, deep down, he knows his part to play. He is a soldier at heart. He has discipline. He has morals. He will fight for the cause of righteousness and die for it if need be. He composes himself with dignity, "Sometimes killing the king is the lesser of two evils. If we should fail, I will have failed as a traitor of my Clan but nevertheless a traitor for the love of it."

A silence falls upon them. They have made their peace. Julius moves closer, clutching Blaine's hand tightly as if to make a pact. He speaks softly, "Remember, it is the anarchists who take the fall for the sins of the corrupt because they know the need for rebellion, for justice, for honour. And, they understand that if they want to make a stand, they must be the sacrifice."

Blaine's eyes become teary with emotion as Julius squeezes his hand tightly then releases with a smirk. Blaine steps forward, the light of the moon on his back, watching as Julius descends the magnificent staircase. His respected status is well established by the servants who acknowledge his genial presence as he passes through the entrance hall. The perfect gentleman in neo-Victorian dress he greets them by name as he moves towards the colossal wooden doors of the hall. Two sentries in military regalia unlatch the doors which they draw open like a long inhale. Julius thanks them and exits.

Behind him Blaine remains, silhouetted in the light of the moon. Having fought for his rank, for his respect within the Giovanni Clan, and indeed even among the Authorities, he can only imagine the struggle before him to win this fight and the fate that lies in store for him should he fail.

Julius descends the steps from the hall into the desolate, cobbled courtyard where a valet waits beside an elegant black car. "Mr Silverstone." The valet greets him. Julius moves quickly; there is no more time to waste. He quickly thanks the valet as he grabs the keys and jumps into the car. Little do the Authorities know that their favoured son has left them to ruin. Little do the Authorities know that their favoured son has become an agent of their undoing. Little do the Authorities know that the War of the Midnight Children has begun.

Before anyone discovers what he has done, Julius drives off into the darkness. With a glance in his rear view mirror he observes as the pale moonlight casts its icy glow upon the Bodmin Plateau. He can only imagine that if he ever sets his sight on the Hall of Vampires again, the Giovanni Authorities will have been jailed for their crimes or he himself will be in chains.

Chapter 2

The darkening blue sky of night falls upon the glowing streetlights of the bustling Irish city. The wide Liffey River that intersects the city shimmers like diamonds beneath the streetlights. Tourists take photographs by famous monuments in the city centre while by the statue of the famous socialist, James Larkin, a group of tourists stop to listen to a guide recite the history of the city and its people.

Locals go about their business, weaving through the crowds on their way home. Young people emerge from high street shops carrying bags while others pass to and from the cinema Men, women and children wait for and emerge from taxis and buses while men in suits with briefcases march through the crowds, their expressions stern.

In the darkness of the alleyways and side streets, those of unfortunate circumstance load up on various narcotics. And, beside shop doors, ATMs and bridges where tourists snap selfies, the homeless beg for pennies.

Far from reality, men in tuxedos and women in formal dresses and sparkling diamonds emerge from the city's most opulent and historic hotel. Greeted by a doorman in a tailored jacket, waistcoat and top hat they are escorted to their chauffeured vehicles. The illusion of Georgian style decadence for the rich provides comfort. Clearly the Celtic Tiger has been and gone with no lessons learnt from it.

On another dark street across the road, a gleaming black car pulls up outside a club where scantily clad eighteen to thirty year olds queue to enter. A group smokes on the corner of the street while another group of young men eye up two model type women in bodycon dresses and high heels.

Two suited men with earpieces emerge from the sports car and stand guard as the back door is opened by the driver. A middle-aged man with an authoritative belly covered by an Armani suit steps onto the pavement. This 'mafia don' is escorted to the club through the VIP entrance by his bodyguards, their gestures hinting at concealed weapons.

A loud rev of a car engine breaks through the street as a bright red sports car thunders along the road. Inside the car, Alex Valentine, a beautiful young woman appearing to be in her late twenties or early thirties with dark eyes and a fierce pout listens to loud rock music. Frustrated by the heavy traffic and crowds she checks her blood-red lipstick in the mirror. Her gaze diverts to her wing mirror where she sees the 'mafia man' entering the club. Scornfully she wonders, what happened to this place?

As the car crawls forward, Alex observes the commercial spectacle. Everyone is just a cog in the machine. The monuments of famous writers and activists are soiled in bird-shit and littered by posing teenagers. Just as she is contemplating her disgust a taxi pulls out in front of her. The gothic beauty is snapped from her brooding thoughts. Slamming on her breaks she blares her horn before gesturing what the taxi driver interprets as 'what the fuck?'. However, the taxi driver just waves it off and drives on. Then, just as she is about to continue, a middle-aged couple complete in black tuxedo and formal dress step out in front of her. Again she halts and repeats her gesture. The couple mouth apologies and hurry on.

Slamming her foot on the accelerator, Alex takes off on to a quieter street where Ar Novad's Institute the striking, ancient building dominates the city skyline, standing out from the crowd of modern buildings along the river that runs through the city. Despite being called an Institute, Ar Novad's is a military barracks – a fortress of hard graft, discipline and corruption.

Smoking out her window, Alex accelerates down Aston Quay past the thousands of tourists and locals swarming around Temple Bar. She glides along the road towards the formidable barracks singing along to the music, knowing fine well she was late for duty but deliberately taking her sweet time to get there. Just as she reaches the point at which she needs to cross the bridge a huge force knocks her sideways. "Fuck!" she exclaims, tossing the cigarette out the window. The loud crash of her car being rammed against the stone river wall causes her to jolt forward and sharply back. Alex immediately looks for an escape as a van relentlessly rams her car, pummelling it into the low river wall.

The steel of the car screeches as she attempts to pull away from the stone bridge shielding her from plunging to the river below, but the van rams her again. She scrambles to grab her military backpack from the footwell along with a beautifully crafted sword before kicking through the windscreen and escaping through it.

As her car is rammed again, she drops over the river wall, slinging her backpack on to her back. Clinging on to the river wall with her sword in hand she watches as her car plunges into the still, sparkling river disturbing the gentle flow with a roaring splash. The calculated collision takes the normal, busy city traffic by surprise, causing a chaotic pileup. From the attacking van, two men with glowing red eyes and corpse-like skin dash towards the river to observe their work. Have they succeeded? Have they hit the target?

Instantly, Alex jumps up onto the wall, decapitating both assassins with one swift swipe of her beautiful sword. The two headless corpses burst into flames which reduce them to shards of bone and dust. As the drifting wind carries their remains away, sirens wail from downstream.

Adrenaline fuelled and perched on the low wall above the river, Alex turns in the direction of the wailing sirens and flashing blue lights. The bright lights catch her unnaturally beautiful labradorite eyes that glow in the dark like a cat. Below her, she watches as her bright red car sinks into the darkness of the Liffey River. Her eyes finally leave the disturbed river and her attention turns to the mangled wreckage of the other car.

A driver emerges from a car that has been halted by the incident. Approaching Alex carefully – half in shock, he eyes her sword warily. "Are you OK, miss?" his thick Dublin accent shakes. He observes her black leather boots, her long leather coat and then realises she is wearing a military uniform. A badge on her clothing above her heart is the Ar Novad's Insignia – a military version of the Giovanni Crest. The old English Calligraphy style 'G' is subtly blended with the Ankh symbol. The Giovanni Authorities branded as much as they could with such. They had always been quite possessive and territorial.

The man relaxes somewhat as other civilians begin to approach the scene. "You're from Ar Novad's Institute? Are you injured?" the man approaches. Alex's fierce eyes lock on him.

"Don't come any closer," she warns, blood trickling down her forehead. She hops off the wall into the road, placing her sword in a sheath beneath her coat. As the Gardai's police cars race closer, blue lights flashing and sirens wailing, Alex slips into the darkness, dashing towards Ar Novad's Institute.

As the darkness obliterates the sight of the mysterious soldier, the man turns to another civilian standing nearby who has also observed the incident, "There's something not right about those soldiers." The two men share gestures of agreement. No one in this proud Irish city had ever really trusted the soldiers of

Ar Novad's Institute. A history of colonialism and British occupation had left these Irish citizens wary of a shady military presence in their city. The Ar Novad's soldiers didn't support the regular army. They didn't participate in ceremonial events. They didn't complete State missions. No one really knew what this army was stationed for and what their mission truly was.

Chapter 3

Bleeding and dishevelled, Alex arrives at the entrance to the barracks, where an administrative soldier observes her appearance with curiosity. It is obvious she is of Ar Novad's Institute judging by her uniform and the fact that her fingerprints match the scan, yet the soldier does not permit her entrance through the sealed bulletproof glass door. Alex eyeballs the soldier. Don't push me.

"Identification?" the Administrator requests. Alex rolls her eyes, "Are you kidding me?" the Administrator doesn't flinch. Sighing exaggeratedly Alex pulls her military ID with her photograph and symbol of the Giovanni Crest and slams it against the window. A scanner then scans the hidden code within the seal. On the computer before the Administrator, Alex's extensive records populate with red flashing letters on the top of the screen reading: MIDNIGHT CHILD.

Alex replaces the ID within her coat, "Satisfied?" the Administrator presses a button, and the bolts on the entrance door click open. Still, in fight mode, Alex provokes the Administrator, "Attitude problem much?" the Administrator chuckles, "That's rich." Alex flips the Administrator the middle finger then enters the building with a smirk. The Administrator returns to their duties, shaking their head with derision.

Admitted entry to the expansive barracks Alex storms through the portico and into the courtyard, blood smeared down her forehead and cheek. In the middle of the courtyard is an ancient, towering stone carved Egyptian Ankh – the pride of Ar Novad's Institute and hailed by all vampires as a sacred relic.

Beside the Ankh, a section of Alex's platoon have assembled, Danielle her 2nd Lieutenant, Trente, her platoon sergeant, Ten, her sergeant, Noelle and Catherine her corporals and Holly and Elaina her lance corporals. They stand chatting, however, in full pristine regalia, they have obviously gathered awaiting orders. At the sight of Alex, they are astounded. They immediately rush to her as on-looking young recruits and cadets eye the rebellious and mysterious lieutenant with curiosity.

Concerned for Alex's wellbeing, Elaina also being the medic is the first to comment on her appearance, "Oh, my God! Alex! What happened?" Alex shoos them off, frustrated by their fussing.

"It's nothing. It's fine. It's fine."

"Where were you?" Catherine queries worriedly, seeing a few high ranking female soldiers approaching behind Alex.

"Nowhere." Alex refuses to elaborate as she wipes at the drying blood on her head.

Behind Alex Stephanie Mesmit approaches, a well-groomed, by the book know-it-all. Being competitive to the core, she somehow had become Alex's superior; however, this woman is all book and no blood.

"Lieutenant Valentine. I must have a word with General Delin about standards at this Institute." Mesmit's cohorts appear amused by her ridicule but Alex is in no mood. Keeping her back to Stephanie she flips her the middle finger – Alex's go-to gesture of 'fuck up' when words are dangerous. However on this occasion, really not in the mood, she follows the gesture with a threat.

"Fucking bite me, Mesmit." Stephanie expects this and decides to push her luck.

"Honestly, I don't know how any of you freaks made the cut," She smirks. Alex's group are sickened by Stephanie's remarks, but while they bite their tongues they sense Alex is about to lose it.

Turning with a smirk, Alex welcomes the confrontation, "Mesmit, your daddy bought you in. Everybody knows it. You might look the part because you're wearing the uniform, but you'll never be a soldier. Although if we ever go to war and the Giovanni decide, 'You know what, we've tried that fightin' craic before. That's got us nowhere. How about we just stand and bitch at them this time? That'll show them!' You've got that covered." Alex's group try to stifle their sniggers; they know this will not end well.

Stephanie's gaze turns from the sadistic amusement of a gloating bully to the daggers of a woman scorned. "We'll see how much you laugh when I'm the one giving your orders. I think you'd look great on your knees scrubbing toilets." She sneers.

"Better than what you'd be on your knees doing." Alex fights back inciting Stephanie to square up to Alex, eyes locked and face close.

"You think you're untouchable, Midnight Child. You think you have Delin and the Authorities wrapped around your middle finger, but the truth is you're just a freak. You're a mistake. You're nothing. And, someday soon, they're all going to learn that." She pauses to let her words sink in. Alex doesn't flinch. Both groups eye the hostile situation timidly. Lower-ranking spectators observe from the porticos flanking the courtyard.

Having savoured her moment, Stephanie gives Alex a shove forcing her at least a foot backwards. She threatens Alex and her group, "Don't fuck with me." She starts off with her lackeys in tow.

Elaina notices Alex's simmering rage, "Alex, no." But Alex sees red. Ignoring Elaina completely, she shoves her rucksack into Elaina's arms.

"Hold this." She storms off after Stephanie. Sensing trouble, Alex's squad chases after her.

"Hey, Mesmit! Stephanie Mesmit! I'm talking to you!" Alex roars. The eager onlookers move closer – shit is about to kick off. Stephanie and her section turn to Alex with amusement.

"It's Captain Mesmit'," the vile bitch smirks.

"Who the fuck do you think you are?" Alex stops before her. Stephanie pulls a face and starts off again. Moving faster than human sight could perceive, Alex blocks her path and shoves her back.

"Don't touch me!" Stephanie's eyes glow fierce green.

"You gunna tell your daddy on me?!" Alex is consumed by rage; there is no way this will end pretty.

"You spoilt, elitist bitch. You call me or anyone here a freak again, you disrespect any of my soldiers, I'll kill you. You hear me?"

Stephanie snorts, strutting smugly off, "Whatever, freak." Alex pauses, allowing Stephanie and co. a spilt second of false victory then, possessed by her overwhelming rage, disgusted by the elitist Captain's superior attitude, Alex grabs Stephanie's long ponytail and drags her back.

The younger soldiers can't believe what they are seeing. They had heard Alex Valentine had a reputation for being volatile, but this was more than they expected – especially from a soldier of her rank. Stephanie attempts to shake Alex off but fails. Surrounding them Danielle, Elaina and Noelle square up to Stephanie's soldiers; however, none of them engage – they are too concerned with the primary conflict.

"I've had quite enough of your bullshit. I said, 'Do you hear me?'" Alex hisses in Stephanie's ear. Stephanie might be taller and more intimidating than

Alex in her superiority, but she is no match for Alex's strength and skill. She is no match for a Midnight Child. "Get off me you fucking psycho!" She exclaims.

Looking towards the Ankh, Alex takes a deep breath and hurls Stephanie towards it. Surprised by her own strength, she watches with a sense of minor dread as Stephanie's bones crack against the stone and blood spurts. A quick to action soldier manages to grab the wounded captain and haul her away as the blood-splattered Ankh sways forward, rocks for a moment, appears to steady then crashes to the gravel ground before cracking into three pieces.

The loud cracks echo throughout the courtyard. The entire audience is stunned. Dust filters through the air and glides to the ground. The courtyard falls silent as they stare at the broken relic.

An overwhelming sinking feeling rises in the Midnight Child's stomach. She knows she will pay the price for this, "Oh, fuck."

After a moment, the sound of doors being thrown open breaks the silence. Storming into the courtyard Lieutenant General Evelyn Delin appears flanked by two officers.

"What in the name of God happened here?!" she roars. Her eyes blaze as she stares in horror at the broken Ankh. Again the courtyard falls silent. Stephanie cries out in pain as Alex's comrades glance nervously to each other. Delin turns her fury towards the audience of soldiers

"All of you get back to your quarters!" the soldiers immediately obey and flee the courtyard.

Stephanie remains on the ground where her lackeys attend her. Without a shard of sympathy, Delin points a threatening finger in her direction, "Get her to the infirmary immediately." Her section obeys and helps Stephanie to her feet. As they carry her away quietly, Delin turns, looking past Trente, Ten, Elaina, Catherine, Danielle, Noelle and Holly. Her gaze locks on Alex, "My office, ten minutes, do not be late."

Delin storms off followed by the officers. With the courtyard now empty of observers Alex's squad stands sheepishly as their uncontrollable lieutenant watches her superiors enter the building. Once they are gone and all is silent, Alex turns back to look upon the broken Ankh. Deep down, she knows she has done it this time. This time she knows she has definitely gone too far.

Chapter 4

Alex slumps back in an oxblood leather chair in General Delin's secretary's luxurious office. The light outside the room casts a yellow glow over Alex as the secretary, Major Shanay types at his computer, every so often shooting a judgemental glare in Alex's direction.

Knowing she is in a world of shit but contemplating how much she actually gives a shit about it, the rebel soldier rests her head in her hand, staring out the window. A beaten hardback book on consequentialist ethics and philosophy rests on her crossed legs. She then leans back, flicking her long black hair from her face and scans the antiquely decorated room.

Checking her watch, she drums her fingers on the book then flicks the pages with disinterest. Easily distracted, she stares through the glass partition as Ira Tallon stops to speak with a comrade. Ira Tallon was renowned within Ar Novad's as the resident heartthrob. For the female soldiers, Ira was everything; he was strong, handsome, gently commanding, smart, humble – everything women wanted in a partner, and everything men wanted to be.

Shanay finally has enough of Alex's impatience. His Giovanni green vampire eyes are full of irritation, "Is there a problem, Lieutenant Valentine?"

Outside in the hallway, Ira Tallon, the shrewd, quiet mannered Captain catches sight of Alex with a glimmer in his pale blue ethereal eyes. He observes as the beautiful, but unruly soldier turns confrontationally to the Major.

The Major has stopped typing. Hands clenched tightly, he confronts the Midnight Child, "It's funny. One would think you would have learnt a thing or two from that book on your lap; consequences are harder to view in retrospect…" he trails off, prompting an exaggerated eye roll from Alex. He continues, "Here you are seemingly more interested in staring at a pane of glass than considering the consequences of your actions."

"Perhaps it's not the consequences of my actions I'm considering." The brazen Midnight Child retorts. Shanay glares at her but seeing Alex is not for backing down, the Major sighs with disgust and turns back to the computer. Alex glances down at her book where she has flicked to a section on 'the Greater Good'. Her eyes scan the page intently.

The arguments have sparked thoughts in her, stirred emotions she would prefer not to face. Ever since she set out on her journey, she had been faced with serious decisions to make and faced serious questions about her own morality. Alex had a reputation for being cold, unapproachable, but in reality, she was just hardened – she had to be. She had a job to do. Emotions – sadness, regret, guilt, these were for the weak, but Alex could not afford to be weak. Could she risk her life fighting for the greater good of the vampire clans, or, could she just work solely in her own interests? It was a dilemma she had faced from day one.

Tossing the book aside, Alex looks out the window once more and stands. Shanay stops typing, gritting his teeth in irritation.

"Nothing's ever simple, is it?" Alex starts. Her question throws Shanay off, and his anger quickly gives way to curiosity. "I'm to consider the consequences of my actions, and I'm to be punished for my actions yet my actions today are a direct result of the Authorities' actions when they chose to kill their creator and consequently create the Midnight Child. Therefore, my actions are excusable and justifiable by the fact that they are merely the consequences of the Authorities' actions so many years ago."

"Be careful, Valentine," Shanay warns.

"You're a psychologist," Alex smirks, using the term loosely for it was no secret that Major Shanay had been the Giovanni Authorities' most notorious interrogator.

"Isn't that called the Butterfly Effect?" with an air of knowing superiority she stares directly at the Major who again warns.

"Be careful whose toes your tread on." Smirking bitterly showing a little fang, she replies:

"Oh, I'm not worried about whose toes I tread on, Major, for they tread on my dreams." For the first time, Major Shanay's posture and expression softens seeing the light flicker in Alex. For the first time, he sees her as a creature not to be feared, revered or jealous of but see the flicker of fragility from the human that is dying in her.

Suddenly General Delin's office door is thrown open so hard it smacks the wall with a loud bang. Major Shanay half jumps out of his skin but quickly attempts to disguise this as a jump to attention. Delin's steely expression says it all, "Valentine. Get in here."

Flustered, Shanay observes Alex as she slides into her long black coat, grabs her bag and enters the office. Delin slams the door shut behind her. The loud bang of the door catches Ira and the other soldier's attention. Seeing Alex gone from the secretary's office, he eyes the General's office warily before parting ways with the soldier and continuing on his way.

Inside Delin's office, Alex remains standing, scanning the meticulously tidy room, noticing an old black and white photograph of the Ankh on the wall. She stares at the Ankh as Delin moves to sit behind her desk where she has organised a stack of paperwork to one side.

Evelyn Delin is a far cry from her usual appearance as an Authority within the Hall of Vampires. There is no room for expensive garments here. Remaining prim and proper in appearance and mannerism with her white hair and delicate silver glasses, she now wears a flawless skirted military uniform – it doesn't suit her. Delin is a tough woman, a powerful woman but a pawn nonetheless. Although heavily decorated in medals of honour, it is clear that these have been earned through acquiescence to Zanned's will and survival in a male-dominated world.

There is a calculating coldness in her as she ensures her desk is ordered to perfection before looking to Alex. "Sit," she commands. Reluctantly Alex obeys.

"I believe that blood inside you, Alex, is starting to boil your brain. You'll be lucky if you aren't court-martialled for attacking a superior officer."

"She's no superior officer." Alex snorts.

"Enough." Delin inspects the dried blood that remains on Alex's forehead, "I hear that you entered the Institute tonight bleeding. A previous fight perhaps?"

"Nothing I couldn't handle." Delin stares at her, frustrated. Usually, when she wants answers, she gets them without hesitation. However, the Midnight Child, unlike the other soldiers, is not afraid of her or her authority. "Don't lie to me." Delin threatens, "I've had a phone call from the police." Alex smirks cheekily.

"Uh, oh. What did you do this time?"

The General stares at her in silence for a moment, her eyes glaring. She finally breaks, "Your car was recovered from the Liffey! Tell me what it was, Alex." The reluctant soldier straightens in her chair, savouring the hold she has on her superior. Finally, she releases simply, "Renegades." The usually coldly composed General appears panicked.

Alex relaxes back in her chair, "So does that absolve my crimes against Mesmit?"

"I don't think so."

"Neither did I." Alex chuckles knowingly, inducing her Authority to lose her composure.

"Alex, this is no laughing matter! You're supposed to be using this time to learn discipline-control! Not to vent your frustration! Not prove to everyone what they already believe you to be!" Again Alex laughs.

"You think anything I do in here is going to earn me a shard of respect? You think obeying and bending to the regime is going to redeem me of centuries of hate? Of fear?" Delin knows the score. The Midnight Child will never be trusted. However, she has a mission to break the young vampire into submission.

"Use your head, Alex – learn restraint. You cannot just show off." Warns Delin.

"I wasn't showing off – I was angry!"

"Alex, that's no excuse. You need to calm down and learn to conduct yourself appropriately. Or you'll never get out of here."

"I was attacked! Every day I live to fight. I was attacked because you made me what I am!" They lock eyes. Alex is furious. Softening slightly, knowing not to escalate the situation Delin speaks calmly:

"That is your life, Alex. I can't do anything about that."

"Uh, huh, yeah sure." Alex grunts.

"Alex, you instigated a reckless brawl, you're drawing too much attention to yourself." warns the Authority, "This is a major Giovanni business, if we lose it, it would be devastating to our…" She trails off.

"Accounts?" Alex interrupts. Far from amused by Alex's smart-ass remark, Delin decides to take her down, "You broke the Ankh of the Dead." Alex pulls a face, playing with her rings. She notices a large silver ring on Delin's finger; it is the Seal of the Incumbents – Delin is much more than a Giovanni Authority. Delin was actually involved in the original plot that created the Midnight Children. Becoming suspicious, Alex decides to listen more intently.

"Alex, you're scaring me," The General confesses, "You've been placed here for observation, and God knows I'm trying to keep you from trouble. The Authorities will never let you go if they think you'll wreck havoc. If they think you're at all hostile…" she trails off as she observes a patronising smile creep across the rebellious Lieutenant's face. Delin frowns, "This is not amusing, Alex."

"Not at all, General Delin. I have done a very bad thing." The General seethes at Alex's sarcastic attitude.

A silence falls between the Authority/Incumbent and her rebellious soldier. A clock ticks. Neither of them will give in. Tick-tock-tick-tock-tick-tock-tick-tock. Delin glares at Alex. Finally she caves. She does not have time to waste on nonsense. "You know this cannot go unpunished," she declares at last, "I've tried to be civil. I've tried my best, but there is no getting through to you. What scale of punishment are you aiming for exactly?"

"You misinterpret me completely!" Alex gasps through a half laugh, "This isn't me aiming for a punishment. This is me knowing I'll be punished whether I co-operate or not. That's how you people work, right? The Authorities take me in, grill me spit me out and try to teach me how to grow. I have my own mind. I used to have my own life too, but you took that from me. What more do you want?"

Delin knows this argument is her Vietnam – unwinnable. There is no point in voicing her opinion – the opinion of an Authority. No matter what she says, she knows Alex will always play the card of the betrayed. Unhappily, she surrenders. "Go, Alex. I've had enough. I don't want to hear another word from or about you. I'll handle the police."

"You got the Giovanni boys in there too, huh?" Alex rises with a knowing smirk. The extent of the Giovanni's reach and power has been well speculated by all but the Midnight Child knows too much. And worse, she has no fear of being chastised for openly commentating on her Authorities' activities. Therefore, Delin ignores the statement. She continues, "In the meantime, I'll arrange a suitable punishment and Alex, tidy yourself up."

Alex checks her dishevelled and blood stained uniform but ignores the General, exiting the room where she addresses Shanay sarcastically, "Later, Major." Delin and Shanay watch her exit the office and disappear into the hallway.

Delin knew this mission would never be easy, but she has now begun to believe that this mission would never be accomplished. The Authorities had got to the Midnight Child too late. She knows too much. She cannot be programmed to accept the Giovanni power structure. She will never bow to them. She will never accept her fate. Delin has now begun to believe that a new tactic will have to be employed.

Chapter 5

In Ar Novad's Institute, it was compulsory for soldiers to take educational classes. Of course, military-based skill classes were compulsory, but soldiers were then given a choice of other classes of personal interest to take up while stationed in the barracks. When participating in such classes, soldiers were seen by the powers that be as being 'on duty' the idea being that education – Giovanni Authority approved education only aided their reputation as powerful in not only a physical but also mental sense. It may be, the oldest cliché – knowledge being power, yet not untrue and not to be forgotten in the Giovanni Authorities' eyes.

Ira sits at the back of the lecture theatre attending his class of choice – ancient history. His black trench coat sits folded neatly on the chair beside him along with his satchel. His black shirt is buttoned to the collar. His black-tie rests on his chest, precisely in place. He taps his pen on a leather-bound notepad as his pale blue eyes observe the lecture with the scepticism of a creature that knows that this is just the tip of the iceberg. Everything he will learn here will be nothing more than Giovanni propaganda – preapproved bullshit.

Two young cadets who appear to be in their early twenties sit in the middle row chatting as their stylish or what some would call 'metro-sexual' lecturer Ian Torvel turns on the screen. He is not dressed in military regalia but rather looks as if he'd just walked off the runway at Paris Fashion Week.

One of the cadets, Logan speaks up to question, "Sir, is it true about the Ankh? Is it really broken?" The lecturer turns to the class with a smirk, amused by being taken off the beaten track. Recent events have sparked a wide interest, not only for the social aspect – everyone likes a bit of gossip – but this was much more than gossip. This event could be the zeitgeist for possible predetermined events.

"You're referring to the legend?" Smirks, Ian, knowingly. Logan nods.

"Yes, sir. I hear there was supposed to be a curse or somethin'." Ira observes with interest, resting the tip of his pen on his notebook. The lecturer begins pacing as he begins his unofficial lecture. "Many of you who attend Ar Novad's will know that he is the patron saint of this institute and therefore, many of you will also know that he went on a missionary journey to Egypt hundreds of years ago." The student soldiers watch him interestedly, but Ira quickly loses interest and proceeds to doodle in his notepad. He has heard this story too many times before.

Excited that recent events have lined up so perfectly with the history he has taught for so long, Ian continues, "When Ar Novad returned back to Bodmin, he brought with him the Ankh of the Dead. When this institute was founded in his name, the Ankh was placed inside. The Ankh represents eternal life."

Logan is unsatisfied. The lecturer has not tread into the territory he was aiming for. He pushes, "Yes, sir, but what about the curse?"

Ira sets down his pen beside his drawing of the broken Ankh and looks up, awaiting a political answer. Ian stops pacing to take centre stage, "Yes, there is a curse associated with the Ankh – if you believe that sort of thing, of course." There is a glimmer in his ethereal eyes.

"So, what is it then?" The other cadet, Dylan pipes up with impatience. The lecturer obliges.

"As the Ankh represents eternal life, there was a legend that told that should the Ankh be destroyed so would the entire vampire nation. That's if you believe that sort of thing of course…" he trails off, leaving the soldiers to make up their own minds whether or not to adhere to superstition or to take the logical mindset of a trained soldier.

Ira smirks as he picks up his textbook on ancient history and flicks the page to reveal a spread titled 'Reform and Revolution'. Ira was not a born rebel. He was never confrontational or opinionated except at work which he took very seriously. However, he was ethical and just and he always knew the right time to step in. A pragmatic man, a righteous man, he knew when to stand up against injustice and when to fight for the right cause. Discipline and education were second nature to him, so the role of a Captain in the Giovanni army was an occupation he could carry out to perfection. During his time at Ar Novad's he has silently and easily climbed the ranks yet, Ira is a pacifist. Forcing weapons into his hands was a poor shove by the Giovanni Authorities. Ira's weapons of choice are facts and evidence, and this is exactly how he plans to take them down.

Chapter 6

Lost in thought, Ira strolls down the long white-walled corridor of the left-wing of Ar Novad's Institute. His past haunts him. Troubled thoughts stir in the maelstrom of his mind. He places his hand briefly on the hilt of his sword at his side as thoughts of inevitable violence torment him.

However, the sight of Alex approaching breaks his concentration and he quickens his pace to meet her. "Alex Valentine, right?" It wasn't really a question. While quite enjoying being approached by the handsome solider, Alex rolls her eyes involuntarily anticipating his reason for approach. "Ira Tallon," she addresses him. "I'm guessing this has something to do with the Ankh incident?" Ira confesses with a smile.

"Yes, and no. You've set a dangerous precedent."

"That was done long ago, Tallon," she interrupts and starts walking. Ira walks with her. "For more than one reason you've created some sort of social hysteria" he finishes.

"That's what I'm here for – showing my true colours. Demonstrating to the vampire community how awfully volatile and untrustworthy I really am. According to Delin of course. But I'm glad I could provide the latest gossip. You don't get much around here. So honoured to be the source of entertainment for the masses." They pass through a door, and she holds it open for him. Ira thanks her politely in a soft English accent..

However, he is unsatisfied. He hasn't made his point. He needs her to know that she is in like-minded company. "I just wanted to let you know; I admire what you did out there. I didn't see it, and you know how stories escalate. Chinese whispers. Even soldiers aren't exempt from exaggeration." They exit the building, crossing the courtyard and scene of the crime. The Ankh remains in pieces, cordoned off. Ira continues, "But I heard quickly from a trusted source. Mesmit had that coming. She's supposed to be a leader – a role model for the recruits and cadets and whatnot. Who wants to look up to an arrogant despot who relishes the opportunity to put her 'inferiors' in their place? Not many people have the guts to do what you did."

Alex stops dead mid-march, her boots crunching on the gravel ground. She sighs, "She had it coming. Bitches like her think they're on top of the power hierarchy and fall under some disillusion that they're untouchable hmm…" she trails off. Ira laughs slightly.

"Well, you're the first to commit treason against the Queen Bee, I'm impressed! I've been dying for someone to do that for a long time."

"Glad to know my efforts are appreciated, not many people have the guts to agree with me." Alex gazes at Ira curiously – borderline suspicious. Her first thought was that he was attracted to her – she contemplated the thought and while flattered by it, she rejected it. Alex was far too cynical for such ideas. Even though Ira Tallon was a handsome figure with his alluring accent, his pale blue eyes, pale sculpted features, undercut brown hair and gentlemanly gestures, she couldn't let that cloud her judgement. In her head, it was obvious – Tallon had an ulterior motive.

Her attention is diverted as she catches sight of Stephanie who appears to be milking sympathy for all it's worth, while walking from the bar with a group of friends. Alex scowls, "Let's see if I can lip sync this – 'Oh my God, well, I was on my cell and I thought I was walking into Gucci, but I walked into Louis Vuitton! Oh my God, how could I be so stupid?'" she rolls her eyes again, coming out of character. She mutters, "You'd be surprised, Mesmit."

Ira backs away slowly, his pale blue eyes shimmering in the spotlights of the courtyard. There is a cheeky glimmer about his features as he speaks, "Valentine, you should have hit her harder. No matter how hard they're hit, some people never learn their lesson." With a nod, he gestures 'goodbye' and starts off. Alex watches him walk away as the revered Ankh lays in pieces cordoned off on the ground behind him. It looks like a crime scene. Alex is surprised Delin doesn't have forensic teams and a tent set up. She knows the repercussions of this incident will be severe, but she can't help but smirk at the sight.

Chapter 7

Bursting through the doors of the bar like a gunslinger in a Wild West saloon Alex enters the barrack's bar. She is met immediately by multiple glances and whispers. She is the rebel – the outsider with her cocky attitude, beauty and dangerous presence. With the night well and truly down the toilet, she grabs a drink– a glass of black Absinthe. Vampires are hardened drinkers – that is, it takes a lot for alcohol to take effect. Absinthe is Alex's preferred beverage for an immediate buzz – it's the only thing that makes her still feel human.

Holly, Danielle, Noelle, Catherine and Elaina look up questioningly when they see her approach. They are off duty, so all uniforms sit in a state of dishevelment except for Holly's whose uniform remains meticulous. Danielle is the first to question her, "How did it go with Delin?" Alex pops down on a chair at the table as the girls huddle closer.

"We tried to wait around the corridor for you coming out, but Shanay chased us. I don't know what his problem is." Elaina cut in before Alex could speak.

"I'd like to thank you for your enthuse and extensive investigation into my disappearance, but I can handle Delin. She'll be fine. She'll calm down soon."

"What took you so long to get over here then?" Elaina questions. Alex smirks, teasing their interest, "Oh, you're going to love this."

Noelle's eyes light up, "What? What?"

"I was… conversing with Ira Tallon. Fancy that!" the girls, although all appearing to be in their early to late twenties become excited school girls at Alex's announcement.

"How did that happen?" Alex turns to the eternally inquisitive Elaina, the pretty young blonde baby of the group, "He just came up to me. I suppose all you have to do is commit basic manslaughter and butcher an ancient artefact to get a man's attention." The girls aren't surprised by Alex's sarcasm.

Noelle leans in cheekily, "Is he a good kisser?" Alex laughs, "Noelle, there wasn't exactly any opportunity for an investigation."

Holly snaps spitefully at Noelle, "Yeah, she's not you, Noelle." The group is taken aback by Holly's abrupt bitterness. Alex intervenes.

"Ooh, do I detect a certain hostility from the corner with the big black cloud?"

Noelle fights back, "Well, Holly, at least I could pull such a fast move. I don't see anyone moving too fast in your direction." Noelle and Holly eyeball each other for a few seconds.

Being the most maternal of the group, Catherine decides to change the subject to break the tension, "So what did Delin say to you?" without a moment's hesitation, Alex makes a Nazi salute.

"Heil Hitler!"

Catherine shakes her head, "You weren't listening, were you?"

"Selectively," Alex chirps in response as she takes a sip. Danielle speaks up:

"She called me as soon as you left. She wants us all to come back together before we go on duty. It can't be good."

"She called you?" Alex laughs, "What are you two on first name terms too?"

"She tried calling you when you left. She'd had an afterthought." Danielle informs then pauses for effect, "You have her number blocked." The group giggles. Alex sniggers into her drink.

"For obvious reasons."

Danielle rolls her eyes and continues, "Well, whatever she's got in mind it sounds like we're not getting out of this one easy."

"Well, thanks very fucking much, Alex," Holly grunts. The group is taken back by her scorn. However, Alex laughs with delight – she's managed to push Holly's buttons.

Holly wasn't made for this military world. She only volunteered to serve in Ar Novad's to win favour and climb the ranks. More accountant than solider – the Giovanni powers that be knew that and recognised that she was an asset for her bookish intelligence. However, the Giovanni Authorities would never allow those of impure blood to climb their ranks without proving they deserved it. Alex knew the Authorities were toying with Holly and not just Holly. She knew they were playing games with any Giovanni vampire in her position. Alex knew because she had met the Authorities and she knew that Holly did not have the strength to play their games. Eventually they would break her down, make her feel like she was worthless, make her feel that life had no meaning. So, Alex loved to push her – push anyone for that matter – to bring out the fight in everyone.

She scolds Holly playfully, "Language, Holly! No fuckin' need for that!"

The group giggles. Noelle, not content to let Holly's earlier jibe rest, decides to jump in, "Bold words. When did Saint Holly start swearing?"

"Let it go guys." Catherine intervenes, sensing Holly's anger. However, Holly has had it, "Do you not understand the severity of this? Do you not take anything seriously?" Exasperated, she shakes her head, "Look who I'm talking to – 'the Midnight Child'. Of course, you don't! Alex, I don't know what's wrong with Julius,"

"Holly, watch it!" Danielle snaps.

Holly doesn't stop, "But he seems indifferent to anything that you do. But, you wait until he hears about this! You are ruining his character, his reputation. You are determined to drag him down with you! Do you ever think about anyone else apart from yourself? Do you ever think of the consequences of your actions?"

Silence. The group waits for Alex to explode in a tirade. Surprisingly she remains calm and silent. She takes a drink then speaks softly, "You are so misguided, Holly and you know what? Say what you like, go on, say it 'cause I can take it."

Catherine interjects, "Alex leave it alone."

Alex ignores her, "Let it out because nothing you say means a thing. Nothing you could say would ever have an impact on my life."

"Alex, stop it," Catherine hisses more forcefully, seeing Holly recoil.

"No. No. No. Holly needs to hear this. I'm sorry if I disrupt your perfect world and your perfect illusion. You think if you play along you can pretend it's some kind of life – some sort of normality. Wake up. You are a pawn," Fear fills Holly's eyes. Alex has pierced the veil.

"I'm sorry if I'm the thorn in your huge sense of importance and value." Alex feigns empathy, "But you need to open your eyes. I play the bad guy; I don't mind. But you need to realise you're a sheep in a den of wolves. Your obedience, your weakness will be your undoing."

Holly remains silent for a moment. The group glances between them. Alex holds Holly's gaze until she breaks. "That's rich coming from you, Alex. Your name will be your undoing, Midnight Child. And it seems more and more to be your intention." Holly sounds just like everyone else – all of those that curse the idea of the Midnight Child. But she knows Alex. She's supposed to be her friend. Sickened by her deceit, Alex erupts.

"Who stood by you, you little weed? Who stood by you when Mesmit took you down? When she treated you like shit on her shoe? I took you in. I fought to get you assigned to me to get you away from her." Holly flinches at the fire in Alex's eyes. They have attracted the attention of other groups who have been eavesdropping.

Again, Catherine attempts to calm the situation, "Alex just drop it."

Again Alex ignores her, attention locked on Holly, "It's better when I'm on your side, isn't it? The difference between you and me is, I stand up for myself. It's a shame when people don't have the courage to protect their own dignity."

"Ah, you think you're such a rebel, Alex!" Holly jumps up from the table, "Sometimes it's braver to just sit down and shut up!"

"That's obviously working for you, right?" Holly is left speechless by Alex's sarcasm. Defeated, she grabs her bag and storms out. Alex holds her drink up to further her sarcasm. Noelle and Danielle clink glasses with their 'hero', Alex while Elaina attempts to hold back a giggle. Catherine eyeballs her lieutenant.

"Did you have to go that far?"

"She started it." Alex chirps childishly.

A news report comes on the TV in the background catching Alex's attention. The girls follow her gaze and listen as the footage reveals CCTV footage of a bright red sports car getting rammed into a river wall then cuts to the wrecked car getting hauled from the river as civilians, police, news crews and a fire engine fills the scene.

The girls glance to Alex knowingly. The reporter makes his piece to the camera, "The incident took place here. Rescue teams have managed to haul the vehicle from the river, but so far not much is known about the incident other than that this was a deliberate attack. Witnesses recall the victim of the attack, a soldier from Ar Novad's Institute, managed to escape from the vehicle before it plunged into the river. Rescue teams are scouring the river for traces of where the drivers of both vehicles could have gone. However, with Ar Novad's Institute refusing to give a statement, for the time being, the motive for the attack remains a mystery."

The group turns to Alex, who sinks her head into her drink. "You wouldn't happen to know anything about that now would you, Alex?" Catherine questions knowingly.

“That was your car…” Elaina states the obvious, “What the hell happened?” Alex lifts her head guiltily from her glass, not even attempting a proper lie.

“I had no tax?” The girls aren’t fooled. Alex caves, “OK.OK. Look it’s OK. It doesn’t concern you. They’re after me.”

“Renegades?” asks Elaina innocently; however, she is quickly ‘shushed’ by Catherine. Alex nods lightly.

“It’s nothing to worry about.” Again the girls are not fooled. Alex brushes it off, knocking back her drink. Catherine knows this is not a subject to be discussing beneath the gaze of prying eyes and greedy ears. She diverts the subject, “Come on. The sun will be coming up soon. I would suggest we head back to the dorm and get a good rest because God knows what Delin has in store for us tomorrow.” The group accepts Catherine’s suggestion and immediately finishes up their drinks before stacking them neatly on the table.

The crowd in the bar observes as the group make their exit. Being in association with the Midnight Child, they all got tarred with the same brush. Noelle and Danielle were rebellious in a somewhat teenage way, having coloured hair – Noelle with her dyed pink hair and piercings and Danielle with bright red hair. Delin had spoken to them about this on numerous occasions, but Delin knew all too well that when soldiers were a necessity, hair colour was the least of her worries.

Catherine and Elaina were not naturally rebellious. They would never go out of their way to provoke or cause protest. However, Catherine knew when to speak up when needed. Catherine was a great leader – a great soldier. Her maternal instinct drove her to protect her flock against injustice. Elaina, on the other hand, was just innocent. She was the youngest. She hadn’t been turned for very long before she was recruited. She just happened to be assigned to Alex’s unit and therefore she became guilty by association.

Noticed everywhere by image and reputation, the group thrived in it. It was a small sheltered world they lived in. None of them had seen any real action beyond the walls. None of them except for Alex had actually visited the Hall of Vampires – they had not proved their worth. They were being trained as the Giovanni Authorities’ foot soldiers and unfortunately for all within Ar Novad’s Institute none of them would ever see the hall as they were being prepared for a fight outside its privileged walls.

Chapter 8

Alex lies wide awake in her small bed in the dormitory she shares with Elaina, Noelle and Danielle. Agitated by her swirling thoughts she rolls from her side on to her back and stares up to the ceiling. Elaina lies on a bed next to her sleeping soundly. Noelle and Danielle are across the room, out for the count.

Alex might play the hardened warrior – like nothing worries her, but really she just buries it deep. She had heard the rumours regarding the Midnight Child and what that would mean for the Giovanni Clan – their downfall. The Giovanni Authorities have her on a short leash – trying to coerce her to conformity, but she is not biting.

Their downfall. She knows that is ultimately what she is fighting for, her ultimate goal. But how can she do it? How can she release their grip on her enough to strike a blow? And, above all, how can she do it without taking those she cares about down with her? That sort of thing happened before and deep within she knows her heart would break should it happen again.

She lingers for a moment on her back, listening to the cheery morning songs of birds outside. Sighing, she decides to have a peek behind the blackout shade over the windows. As she draws back the blackout, a sword of light plunges through the darkness of the room. The three sleeping vampires immediately panic. “Alex close the blackout!” Noelle cries.

“What are you doing?” Danielle hisses from beneath her blanket. Elaina cowers in the shadows as Alex quickly recovers the window, shielding them from the offending sun.

“Sorry, I forgot…” Alex apologises as she sinks back down into her bed. The girls grumble and go back to sleep.

Elaina crawls back into her bed and observes Alex for a moment as the raven-haired warrior once again lies wide awake in thought. “Alex.” Elaina whispers, “What’s wrong?”

"Nothing. It's fine. Go back to sleep." However, Elaina purses her lips in thought. "Alex." She starts, "Can I ask you something?" Alex rolls on her side, looking to the young soldier questioningly. "Have you ever been in love?" asks Elaina. Alex is thrown by the question. It is completely unexpected. It has come without context or explanation.

"Love is a difficult concept, Elaina, and one I'm not entirely comfortable with."

"You must have been once?"

"Where are you going with this? Wait. Back up. Where are you coming from with this?"

"I met someone," Elaina blushes.

"In here?"

"No," Elaina smiles like a teenager with a crush, "Last time I was on leave. I met him. I met him at a vampire club."

"And you're in love?" Alex can't control her cynicism.

"No," Elaina confesses, shifting closer to the edge of the bed, curled up in her blanket, "But I'd like to be. I've never really been in love. I had boyfriends, yeah, but I was turned before I could ever have something real. Then I was put here, and it's difficult to have any sort of relationship in this place."

Alex sighs. She is holding back. She wants to be honest with Elaina. She sees her innocence and naivety and wants to protect her. But, she knows they all deserve to have a life. They all still deserve, should they want them, to have those humanly privileges of feelings and emotions and a social life in some form. "Elaina, be careful. I'm not saying don't do it but be careful. It's not only Delin you have to worry about, but there are a lot of vampires out there hostile towards the Giovanni. You could get hurt." Alex warns, "I want you to be happy. You deserve it. Everyone here does. But these are very dangerous times."

Elaina appears downhearted. After a moment, Alex's acute eyesight catches Elaina wiping away tears in the darkness. "Elaina, don't cry."

"I'm just so stupid."

"You're not stupid. You're far from stupid."

"I just. I just…" Elaina finally breaks. Tears trickle down her cheeks as she edges closer again, speaking in whispers, "This isn't a life Alex. I didn't want this. I was just in the wrong place at the wrong time. I'll never meet someone, fall in love and get married and have children. That's all I wanted." Alex is lost for words. She can't empathise. Her life was never built on that dream, but then again, her dreams had come crashing around her. She can't offer Elaina any sympathetic words of comfort, but she can drop her guard. She can show Elaina a hint of her own vulnerability.

"I was in love once," Alex confesses. Elaina stops sniffling, taking interest in Alex's statement. "It didn't work out. But I believe we all deserve to find it, to feel it. The Giovanni Authorities think that when you're turned that all your humanity dies with you. It doesn't. And that's a good thing. It keeps us from becoming like them." Elaina takes no heed of the moral of Alex's statement. Instead, she focuses solely on her own interest. "Why didn't it work out?" Her questions, while innocent in nature, make Alex uncomfortable. These are thoughts and feelings she had long fought to suppress. "I'm a Midnight Child. My path was already paved, and it was in a different direction to his." Her disposition falls solemn in reflection, "That's why." Elaina is not satisfied, "Is he alive? Is he human?"

"I have no idea," Alex falls silent again. This time Elaina sees that she has provoked Alex to a state of melancholy.

"I'm sorry, Alex," she whispers.

"Don't be sorry," Alex advises her, "And don't be sorry for your own feelings. Do not let this place rule your life. Do not let it destroy you. Do not let them kill your will to fight. To live." Alex holds Elaina's gaze for a moment before turning away to face the wall. Elaina pauses in contemplation before relaxing back into bed herself.

"Sleep tight, Alex."

"Don't let the bed bugs bite," Alex whispers.

The conversation has stirred unsettling memories. Despite her words of wisdom to the younger vampire, Alex struggles to come to terms with her own philosophy at times. A tear trickles down her cheek to her pouted lips. She wipes it away, saddened by the memories of all that she has lost and maddened by the reality of everything she needs to fight for.

Chapter 9

Night has fallen. In full uniform, Alex's section assemble in Delin's office. The tension is obvious as the girls stand before the steely General to await their sentence. Every movement Delin makes is precise, almost predetermined. She sighs and removes her silver glasses.

"I've always believed in the need to have the punishment suit the crime. But there is no punishment suitable for this crime. That precious artefact was thousands of years old – priceless, one of a kind," Delin pauses for effect, "I had thought of expulsion, disqualification from promotions…" Holly's eyes widen with fear. Elaina and Catherine glace to each other worriedly. "But I do not have time for squabbling youngsters who cannot control themselves. Hopefully, you have learnt your lesson. Now, I don't care if Captain Mesmit slandered you or physically attacked you, you should not have retaliated." Delin states forcefully, pulling Alex's trigger.

"Bullshit!" she exclaims.

"Excuse me, Lieutenant Valentine?" Alex's fellow soldiers don't know where to look as Alex starts, "All we ever hear is 'Be the best!' 'Better yourself' 'Don't let anyone put you down!' So when assholes like Mesmit try it, you'd rather her walk all over us? You think that's just the way it happens around here?"

"You do not better yourselves by becoming involved in mindless, undignified brawling."

"But you cheat yourself if you don't make a stand! You sit by passively and let them walk all over you once, and they'll do it again and again."

"Alex Valentine you will treat your Superior Officer with respect!"

"Earn it!"

"I don't have time for this nonsense!" Delin slams her palms on her desk, causing her carefully ordered paperwork, pens, glasses case and Giovanni Crest plaque to shake. "You're lucky I'm letting you off as lightly as I am."

"I feel so privileged," Alex snorts. Everyone but Holly cringes. Holly shoots Alex a venomous glare.

Delin stands, crossing her arms, "Tomorrow night, you will report to M23 where you will spend the night organising the inventory."

"The weapons locker?" Catherine questions. Delin snaps her gaze around quickly to Catherine, who has made the mistake of not addressing her as 'General Delin'.

"Yes, the weapons locker. A thorough cleaning and organising are long overdue tasks." The entire group but Alex relaxes slightly, feeling that they had escaped lightly. "Following this you are suspended from duty for one week. This will go on your record. You will then be removed from your posts until further notice and will be designated a brigade of recruits to train. Prove yourselves to be worthy role models and may be returned to your active duties."

As trained soldiers who had proved their worth, this is a terrible blow to their reputations. They may be notorious for many reasons, but one reason was always that they were damn good at their jobs. Being a good soldier, rising through the ranks means that they had more chance at securing a normal kind of life. At a certain level, they could choose to remain in the Giovanni army or seek a form of freedom through various other occupations within Giovanni businesses. Too many bad marks meant more years in servitude. Their hearts sink. Alex rolls her eyes, "And what if we refuse?"

"Then, it is dismissal," Delin states simply. The soldiers' hearts sink further. Dismissal made it even harder to secure favour and a more privileged position within the Giovanni Empire.

"So dismiss me," Alex pushes. The girls glance warily between the General and her unruly lieutenant. Both were too stubborn. Alex is crucial to Delin's agenda and pushing Delin to release her is part of Alex's agenda – it is a stalemate.

"Get out," Delin orders, "Report to M23 tomorrow night at precisely 10 pm. You remain there until 6 am when I will inspect your work. Following this, you will leave the barracks for one week. You are dismissed." Delin sits back at her desk, eyes cold and calculating.

Catherine is the first to stand to attention, address her General and exit. Her fellow soldiers follow suit then file out. Alex lingers to make a point. Delin looks to her, expectantly as Alex pauses long enough to show Delin she won't even contemplate saluting her. She then marches from the room leaving the door wide open. That is exactly what Delin expected. The steely General then has to rise from her desk, cross the room and close the door herself. She bangs it closed. Her irritation has got the better of her. However, calming down, she kisses the Seal of the Incumbents ring on her finger, takes a deep breath and returns to her desk.

Chapter 10

Alex walks along the path to Julius' expansive sandstone mansion, San Lorenzo, on the outskirts of the city. It was an old Giovanni stronghold but for many years had been used only for meetings and celebrations. Rather than have it unused and fall to ruin it was gifted to Julius to live in as a custodian. The palatial building is somewhat superfluous for two to call home, but it does have a vast wealth of old Giovanni literature stored within its ancient walls – perfect for two scheming conspirators.

With the weight of the night upon her, Alex trudges to the building, stopping outside the brightly lit doorway. Quietly unlocking the heavy hand-carved door, she creeps down the dim hall towards Julius' study where he is busy transferring writing from ancient books to computer files. She lingers outside the door.

"I suppose you walked home?" Julius doesn't lift his head from his work.

"Well, I can't fly and I don't think I'm suited to public transport." Alex attempts humour to lighten the mood but ends up cringing at her uncontrollable sarcasm.

"Get in here," Julius commands her. There is a tense pause as she steps into the room and sits on a deep captain's chair across the desk from her guardian. He stops typing to look at her. "What happened?" He asks.

"Some Renegades tried to make a statement," she tries to brush it off.

"Where did they go?"

"Anywhere but home," Alex shrugs, "Delin's taking care of the car and the police."

"So I hear," Julius clasps his hands and softens his body language, "I haven't heard your side of the story, and I don't need to. I know it's hard to take the blame for something that's not your fault."

"I don't mind taking the blame, it's the punishment I object to!" Alex laughs.

"Unfortunately there's no way out of it. You're going to have to bow to Delin's orders on this one. This is no ordinary incident. This is the incident the

Authorities have been fearing. This is their sign that the war is imminent. They will fear you now more than ever. They're going to panic and attempt to find a solution to their problem. You will find soon, her grip will tighten," Julius warns, "And if Mesmit ever starts again, just walk away. As much as the thought of doing so pains you, just walk away. Her father is high up the Giovanni ranks. Or should I say, Giovanni banks… He's a Giovanni account."

"Well, you know what they say, the rich will always side with the rich. Money knows money." Alex's tone is permeated with derision.

She then revises the subject matter back to the matter of most offence, "And the Ankh?"

"It had it coming. Now we can only wait." Julius smiles, his eyes sparkling with an ethereal quality, "There's nothing I can do about Delin's punishment, we must oblige her on this one, but we can avail of the opportunity."

"Opportunity?" Alex questions. Julius picks up the Ankh shaped key and passes it to her. Alex studies the ancient object as it rests in the palm of her hand.

"You can get closer to the Ankh than I ever will, unguarded." Julius' eyes shimmer again. Alex continues to inspect the key. Her protective guardian reaches over and closes her fist around it, "Guard it with your life." Alex makes eye contact with him and nods before dropping her gaze back to the key. Satisfied that she understands him, Julius lets go of her hand.

"Now go get changed. We're going out." Beaming with delight, Alex makes no hesitation in exiting the room to do just what Julius has ordered. Julius logs off his computer and shuts the large leather-bound book.

Chapter 11

Like two flitting shadows, Alex and Julius pass down a long dark corridor in the city's main hospital. Moving so swiftly that they make no sound, they pass wards full of elderly sleeping patients. Through a large circular window, the bright light of the glowing full moon shines across the linoleum floor.

The only noise is the beeping of machines; the rest is silence. Julius taps Alex on the shoulder, gesturing that he is changing direction. Alex nods as he ascends a wide staircase. She and Julius often frequented the hospital when in need of blood. The Giovanni had sources – they had dealings for blood, and this is exactly what Julius is here to collect. Alex, on the other hand has a unique ability that other vampires do not. Alex has the ability to heal the sick and those with 'bad blood'. Prisons are another haunt of hers. Draining the 'bad blood' from the worst of society is something she very much enjoys. However Alex can only use her unique ability once in a while as it takes too much from her. It drains her. This is why she always tries to find someone in most need of her gift.

Vampires do not need blood in large quantities. They have a genetic mutation that means that they cannot absorb enough vitamins, iron especially, through any other means. It is supposed to be a necessity not pleasure. However, there are those that gorge on it. The energy contained within blood creates a rush – like nothing else. The Giovanni Authorities are guilty of such abuse. They have the money and the sources to purchase the best of the best. This disgusts the Midnight Child – one of the many issues she has with her superiors.

Turning the corridor, she pauses momentarily reading the sign for the children's ward. Despite having done this on several occasions, the thought of sick children – the thought of suffering children breaks her heart. Sombrely she proceeds into the ward where she inspects the beds of children sleeping soundly, unaware of the presence of the beautiful monster above them. Alex scans the toys, the teddy bears and small clothes by their beds as she flicks through the medical records, moving around the room one by one. She finally makes her choice – a young girl of seven with leukaemia. Alex snaps the chart shut and moves closer to the child.

She must work quickly. She covers the child's mouth as she sinks her fangs into the child's delicate neck. The young girl snaps awake, panicking. Her eyes bulge in her palc face. She is too weak to fight. Alex continues to drink, taking the child's sickness into herself. She fights through the pain as the energy transfers. The sound of the hospital machines rises to a screech in her head. She blinks away, glowing orbs of light as her head begins to spin. Her heart pounds. At the point of collapse, she releases the child from her grip, falling back against the wall. The child falls still on the bed. Alex struggles to steady her breathing and fights to stand watching as the healthy glow of life floods the child's features. She has not been drained. She has not been turned. She has been given a second chance.

As her new life rushes through her veins, the young girl sits up in bed. Her big eyes fix on the dark figure beside her. Shakily, Alex forces herself to stand. "How do you feel?" she asks. The young girl is confused by the feeling in her body, her new strength. She smiles and nods.

"Good," Alex starts away. The young girl shuffles to the end of the bed, "Are you an angel?" Alex is emotionally winded by the innocence of childhood.

"A fallen one," she whispers, "Go back to sleep." The young girl watches as the dark angel slips silently from the ward then clutches a soft toy unicorn to her chest and curls back into bed to return to her dreams.

Weakened, Alex hurries for a staircase as fast as she can – she needs air. The bad blood rushes through her body, polluting it, wounding it. She is burning up. Using the railing to pull herself up the steps, she rushes to an emergency exit and plunges through the dark void into the cool, crisp night air where Julius awaits. She collapses to her knees beside her guardian, who manages to grab her arm, lessening her fall. She leans on the small wall on the roof, taking deep breaths. "You take too much out of yourself, Alex. Or rather too much in."

"If it's the only good thing I can do in this life, it's worth it."

Silhouetted by the moonlight, Julius crouches down beside his prodigy. Alex wipes blood from her mouth as the pain dissipates and her strength slowly returns. There is a silence as they gaze across the twinkling city lights. After a minute, Julius turns his back on the city to face her.

"Alex, you were born to do good for this world. Despite what had been said about you and despite what the Authorities believe, you will do good for this world," he encourages her.

"You risked everything for me, Julius. You're the only one who believes in me." Alex sighs, "They'll never release me, will they?"

"We'll figure something out. This was the terms of the agreement. If we run, they'll hunt us. Would you prefer a prison?" Alex turns to Julius, pulling a face.

"Isn't it a prison?" Julius shrugs – she has a point.

Rolling around on the balls of her feet, Alex slumps back against the wall in frustration. "I'm fed up with being watched like some fuckin' animal in the zoo. It's in my nature to challenge the system. It's frustrating when the system just won't give… I thought if I pushed their buttons, they'd let go. Why are they taking it from me? I keep pushing and pushing my luck and nothing. If anything, it just makes her grip on me tighter, and so I try harder." Julius leans in closer to her.

"Alex, it's because of what you are. You are precious. You are a threat. They have to keep you close. They have to study you. The Giovanni Authorities will never trust something more powerful than themselves. But, you're more dangerous to them as enemies, not allies. That's why they know they must keep the Midnight Children close."

His words have struck a chord in her. She eyes him suspiciously bordering on gravely. If she has heard him right, his words have just changed everything. "The Midnight Children? Children?" Julius nods, a gesture that leaves Alex completely astounded. Her mind rushes. A hot prickling sensation crawls up the back of her neck.

"Delin is anxious, as are all the Giovanni Authorities – not anxious fearful. You see, the prophecy foretold of the Midnight Children's arrival. I must apologise. I concealed that information from you. I didn't want you distracted from your training. But you need to know now." Julius' dark eyes are penetrated with fear, causing Alex concern.

"Why now? What's coming?" she questions. She had always been aware of the burden on her shoulders. She had always known they were working towards an eventual goal, but Julius' statement startled her to the core. The reality of a war that had been long spoken of in worried whispers now washed over her. She had lived in the belief since she had first met Julius that she was in this alone as the Midnight Child and Julius was her one and only ally, the only person she could trust. Her mind races – Midnight Children – but how many? Could she trust them?

"The prophecy was consolidated when the Ankh was broken by you – a Midnight Child. A chain of events has begun – the butterfly effect – one small change could change everything and the Authorities smell disaster…" Julius rises to his feet as Alex fights to organise her thoughts. She looks up to her guardian, her teacher, her protector – the man who had turned her. "Midnight Children. Julius, how many? Can we trust them?"

"Three." He has his back to her, speaking in a tone attempting to sound matter of fact but his voice trembles. Alex hesitates.

"Who?" for a moment, Julius stands in silence, the cold light of the moon illuminating the edges of his green velvet coat and profile. At last, he speaks, "Ira Tallon." Alex falls apart inside. She can't believe it. She should have known. She reflects on their conversation – his empathy, his intrigue and his overall demeanour – silent, brooding, plotting?

Alex rises to her feet, pulling out a packet of cigarettes and lighting up. Inhaling the smoke, she paces a few steps, her mind saturated. It all makes complete sense and none. She takes another drag then watches the swirling smoke as she exhales slowly. A sudden thought stops her in her tracks. She turns to Julius, "Did you turn him?" sighing Julius admits, "Alex, I do not want to tell you too much right now. You must not be distracted. I just needed you to be aware. But do not lose your focus."

"But–But. Are we all being watched? Who's the third? Julius? Are they in Ar Novad's?" A sickening thought dawns on her, "Please–Please tell me, it's not Mesmit? Please. It's not Mesmit…" Julius moves closer to her, the purpose to comfort her with his proximity, "Think not of it, Alex."

"Julius, it can't be her. It just can't be. I'll kill her. I swear." She vows. Julius shakes his head. Alex senses her guardian growing sombre. "Alex, I need to ask you something."

"Uh, huh?"

"You know what you have been trained for. You know the Prophecy. This is no joke. I need to know if you are truly prepared for what you have to do to save insurmountable bloodshed."

"Insurmountable?"

"The third Midnight Child will bring devastation to the vampire nation if they are not stopped."

"Yeah, that sounds like Mesmit all right," Alex snorts, rolling her eyes.

"Alex." Julius' tone is stern.

"Yes, Julius. Yes, I am ready to kill – not because I have any love for the vampire nation and not because I need to fulfil some Prophecy. I will kill because I have nothing left to lose. Fuck it."

Julius remains unconvinced; however, he does not want to press her. After everything that has happened in the last twenty-four hours, he decides she needs to settle her thoughts. Using humour to relieve her tension, he says, "Put that out." He takes the cigarette from her blood-red lips.

"Oi!" Alex snaps, hurrying after him as he crosses the rooftop taking a long drag. Catching up, Alex reclaims her cigarette, which Julius relinquishes willingly.

"You shouldn't be smoking," he chastises.

"What? It's not like it's going to kill me!" Alex finishes it off before flicking it away.

The two preternatural creatures drop from the rooftop into the darkness of the back city streets while the glowing embers of the cigarette burn out on the cold opaque ground.

Chapter 12

Sleep eluded Alex. Too restless to retire, she had parted ways with Julius as the sun arose above the waking city, and she wandered through the desolate streets, her mind spinning. Through the grey, drizzling sky, the sun seeped through the cracks of ghostly clouds. She had walked for so long, wandering aimlessly that the light rain had saturated her. Now, she finally comes to a stop in the middle of College Green, scanning the rooftops as rain trickles down the gutters. The morning traffic slowly builds as shop shutters are racked up with dull screeches.

Crossing the wide street from the old Parliament and bank building she moves past historic Trinity College university. Even from afar, Alex can spot the Giovanni Crest upon the old Palriament/bank's sign. Her gaze hovers on the Crest momentarily before she quickens her pace. As groups of students arrive off buses en route to the university, eyeing the drenched gothic beauty as if she were doing the 'walk of shame', Alex decides to head southwards towards Grafton Street.

The famous and usually crowded Grafton Street is in almost complete silence as the shops begin to prepare for the days' undertakings. Traders from a local flower stall chat and smoke as they arrange their displays. Coffee shop owners feeling optimistic that the rain will die, set up outside chairs and tables. Despite it being the quiet birth of the day, Alex is overwhelmed. She feels constricted, like she is stuck in Limbo. The normality of human city life is building, and she needs out. As she emerges from the south end of Grafton Street, she sets her sights on the entrance to St. Stephen's Green so hurries towards it.

The sound of growing traffic, shop shutters, conversations and general city ambience fades out as she moves deeper into the park. She knows where she is going. Back in her 'human' days, she would visit this park almost daily. There was something so enchanting about it. In the middle of the crowded city it had always been somewhere she could go and clear her head. She passes by the

Fountain of the Three Fates, with only a side-eyed glance. Its name is far too on-the-nose for her to deal with at this point in time.

She reaches her stop and takes a deep breath. There in the middle of the historic park, she stands in reverent affection before the bust of the heroine Constance Gore-Booth more commonly known as Countess Markievicz, the female face of the 1916 Rebellion. Alex had always admired her. She had always wanted to follow in her footsteps. Her unflinching devotion to her cause, her selfless commitment to lay down her life for the rights of those with nothing, her fearlessness to give up her wealth, put on a man's uniform and take up a gun to fight an oppressive empire were only a few reasons why Alex was so inspired by this woman.

When she has finished paying her respects, Alex continues on to find somewhere quiet where she can just gather her thoughts without distraction. Crossing a small, sheltered bridge over a large duck pond, she stops to listen to the rain tickling the leaves and rippling the water. The trickling rain is a welcome, almost meditative sound. Soothed by the pitter-patter she goes to sit at a bench where the trees have created a natural shelter. She slumps down, exhaling loudly. No longer able to cope with the normality of humanity she needs to sit to collect her thoughts. Her eyes had been opened. Humanity lives in blissful ignorance. Many vampires such as Elaina craved this. All they want is to go backwards, wishing their turning had never happened.

Alex wished a lot of things hadn't happened but it was not worth thinking about. There was no going back. She was born to fulfil a forward-facing prophecy – forward was the only direction. Having a goal kept her from reflecting on the past. However, recent events and Julius' words had jolted her mind. Deep down, she had known it was only a matter of time before she had to face her past. She knows she must accept now that it is all coming together but the weight crushes down upon her shoulders. She needs revenge for what was taken from her and for this she needs to regain her tunnel vision for she is all too aware that when love is lost, and trust betrayed, looking back only leads to regret and madness.

For almost an hour Alex sits alone in the rain, drenched but oblivious to her appearance. It is only when she manages to find some clarity that she looks up and notices people glancing at her as they pass – those glances that people give homeless people at the side of the street hoping they don't ask for anything. But,

Alex doesn't actually give two shits what people make of her. What does it matter? It is of no consequence. She has more important things to worry about.

Dog walkers, couples, students, businessmen and politicians, parents cutting through the park to take their children to school all pass Alex eyeing her curiously. Lighting a cigarette, she simply observes the early morning rush of traffic through the high iron fence. People push past each other on their way to work and otherwise. Tourists assemble at bus stops and tourist spots. Taxis and buses beep their horns. A woman fights with a broken umbrella but gives up and throws it in the bin.

In the children's play area of the park, Alex watches the gentle wind pushing the swings like ghostly hands. In her mind, she hears Julius' words echoing over and over, "The Giovanni Authorities will never trust something more powerful than themselves. But, you're more dangerous to them as enemies, not allies. That's why they know they must keep the Midnight Children close." The Midnight Children. She can't believe it. For the last four years, she had lived in the belief that she was alone. How had this been hidden from her?

The loud 'donging' of a chapel bell takes her attention. She frowns in thought and looks in the direction of the chapel to watch as the laypeople people filter in. People have passed her by all morning, and she, for the most part had casually ignored their presence. She was minding her own business and had sat under the philosophy that, despite their judging glances they would also mind their own business and leave her alone. However, one passerby takes her attention.

A tall, handsome man in his late twenties/early thirties with pale skin and dark sapphire blue eyes, wearing a long black overcoat passes by her. From the corner of her eye, she catches his gaze; however, it is only for an instant. She is intrigued. She turns her head to watch as he continues on towards the gates. Having only seen him at a glance she is curious of his presence. There was something in that gaze – something familiar she just can't quite put her finger on. Something is drawing her to him.

Easily tempted and naturally curious, Alex pursues the man towards the Grafton Street side entrance/exit, and through the great, granite structure of Fusilier's Arch. She quickens her pace, emerging from the park close after him, but he is nowhere to be seen. She stands, confused. She has been only seconds behind him, where could he have gone? The city streets, now packed with people are impenetrable to her sight.

She scans the crowds, past the locals going about their business; tourists taking photos; young couples shopping; friends chatting in coffee shops; a man at a stall buying flowers for his wife. She stops scanning. She has lost him. Something in her gut tells her something is wrong. Her hand hovers over her gun as her gaze lingers on a man picking out roses at the flower stall.

The rain has stopped, and shards of light pierce through the clouds. As Alex observes the flowers being wrapped, passers-by observe her. They see her black leather military regalia, her labradorite eyes and her hand on what they know is a gun. They eye the Giovanni Crest on her left arm with unease. Ar Novad's Institute had always been a bone of contention with the locals. For the locals, the presence of a military Institute in their city that they knew nothing about had always caused concern. Alex knew all about it. She had lived in this city as a 'human'. She had walked these streets as a civilian, and she too had always viewed Ar Novad's Institute with similar suspicion. Never did she suspect that she would ever be walking through those gates as one of them.

Figuring it was probably best that she got out of the way she begins to pace along the path outside the park. She gazes at the incredibly grand and aristocratic Shelbourne Hotel complete with a doorman with a top hat out front. She rolls her eyes, thinking about the politicians and upper-class clientele dishing anything up to a few thousand euro a night for a hotel room and necking expensive alcohol back in the restaurant. Sure, why not? They weren't paying for it.

"You got the time?" Alex's train of thought is broken. She snaps her head around, coming face to face with the man she had pursued. Their eyes connect. Something about this person's presence disturbs and intrigues her. Reluctantly she removes her hand from her gun.

"I'm sorry, what did you ask?" she questions.

"Do you have the time?" his accent is mixed – something she struggles to place. Although his head is closely shaved, Alex can tell his hair could be dark, almost black. From his sapphire eyes to his pointed cheekbones, she follows his strong jawline down to his full lips. Protruding from his collar, heavy tattooing is visible. This is one seriously attractive man, Alex notes. But, despite her attraction to the man there is something in the back of her mind – something familiar about his face. Some distant irretrievable memory tortures her. Some association she just can't quite clasp. She checks her watch. "It's ten fifteen – ish."

“Thank you.” Instead of moving on, the man’s gaze lingers on the Giovanni Crest on Alex’s arm.

“You’re one of those soldiers?”

“I am.” Alex was always wary of discussing Ar Novad’s for various reasons.

“I’ve heard a lot of stories about that Institute.”

“Nothing good, I suppose.”

The man laughs lightly, “Which direction is it?” Alex’s suspicion strengthens.

“You’re not from around here.”

“No. And I can tell you aren’t either. I’m from here and there. I’ve been around. Thinking of settling down, though. Just have some things to take care of first.” His statement gives Alex chills, and reluctantly she provides the directions, “Ar Novad’s Institute is that way, on the other side of the bridge. Just keep walking until you come to a sign for it. It’s a thirty-minute walk.”

“That’s no problem.” The man smiles up to the sky, his pale skin illuminated by the light. He smiles to her, “Sun’s coming out.”

Alex hesitates. There’s something vampiric about this man’s aura, but it is dark. Could he possibly be the other Midnight Child? Or could he be something else? Something from another clan also immune to the sun?

“Why do you want to go to Ar Novad’s?” she questions.

“I’ve heard it’s quite beautiful. I’d like to take pictures.” The man reveals a camera from his bag.

“Just warning you, you’ll have to get permission to do that.” The man shrugs, “I’m a photojournalist. I’ll explain myself.” Alex watches him return the camera to his bag. She is captivated by this man. She feels an inclination towards him. An immediate attraction. However, there is something unnerving in this. She doesn’t believe his story. Not for a second. But she is not in the mood. If he was up to no good, the Institute was full of soldiers trained to handle it. Plus, she is suspended, technically – it isn’t her problem.

“Look, Ar Novad’s is that way – if you follow the signs, you’ll find it,” she states. The man nods and moves to head onwards then hesitates.

“Can I ask you something? Why did you join the army?” Bad question. He’s pushed Alex’s buttons.

“Because I didn’t have a choice,” she snaps. Hearing the contempt in her tone, the man thanks her and starts off. She watches him walk away before starting across the road towards a newsagent. Before entering the shop, she turns to find no sign of the man. He moved fast. Again just the usual crowds fill the street. Frowning with suspicion, she turns away and notices the front page of a newspaper on a stand in the doorway of a small convenience store.

Picking up the paper, her eyes scan the front page, the cover story of which being the incident involving her car and the Liffey.

"Strange one that, isn't it?" Alex turns to the find the source of the voice. She looks at the elderly shop owner, realising that being in her military uniform, the question is more of a 'you must know something' type of accusation. "Yeah. Strange one." She replies plainly. Remaining suspicious as this sighting of an Ar Novad's soldier in daylight is an odd occurrence, the shop owner asks, "Can I help you with anything?"

"Yes." Alex sets the paper down and asks for a packet of cigarettes. As the shop owner obliges, Alex notices a modest silver crucifix hanging around the woman's neck. She can't help but think how foolish the woman is to believe in such forces. She herself, had never believed in such a thing but then again… She is a preternatural creature and little does this elderly Christian woman know she is serving cigarettes to it. In all her lifetime and all the creatures she has encountered, Alex has never found any evidence of 'God.'

From the corner of her eye she catches a dark figure and turns to see a police officer approach the door. Her blood runs cold(er). She really doesn't need this right now. "Is that everything?" The shop owner asks. "Yes that's it, thanks." Alex pays quickly and hurries towards the door as the officer enters. "Good morning." He greets her, slowing his pace to a stop. "Good morning." She replies and exits. Having expected her to stop as he did, he pauses before going after her. Emerging from the shop he expects to see the soldier and call her back but she is nowhere to be seen.

Alex has taken to the side streets at a determinate but careful pace – careful not to draw too much attention. She is not in the mood to be pursued when she is also pursuing. Despite not wanting to get involved, the conversation with the man has thrown her – she needs to get back to Ar Novad's regardless whether she is welcome or not.

Chapter 13

The sun beats down on the back streets of the city as Alex hurries towards Ar Novad's Institute, hand on her gun. She checks the streets – no sign of any man taking photographs. There is a new guard on the gate. Despite the fact that Alex red flags on the system, she outranks the newbie and is a Midnight Child and is pretty adamant she needs to speak to Delin so the newbie panics and permits her access. Slipping through the gate, she rushes through the portico, past the empty space where the Ankh previously stood and across the courtyard towards the General's quarters. The place is in lockdown. The deadly sun has forced the inhuman soldiers inside.

Two guards block the Midnight Child's entry as she approaches General Delin's luxurious domicile. "Look I need to speak with Delin immediately." The guards hear the urgency in Alex's voice and glance to each other for support. One takes the lead.

"Sorry. You know the rules."

"Fuck the rules! This is important." She tosses the guards aside with ease before barging through Delin's door.

The slumbering Authority is completely caught off guard. Seeing the light she shrieks and darts for cover. Alex slams the door closed, sending the room back into complete darkness. She has broken the lock. Delin emerges in her nightwear; gun pointed to her assailant. Suddenly she realises it is Alex. "Alex Valentine! What is the meaning of this?"

"I have reason to believe that the Institute might be under threat." Delin can tell that for once, Alex is being serious. Clearly Alex hasn't slept for quite a while and her uncharacteristic shaken disposition tells the General she needs to listen. Setting down her gun she lets down her guard but remains hostile. "It better be a good reason." Delin sits down on her bed.

"I had an encounter with someone. I have reason to believe that he may be something, something like me. But not a Giovanni. I don't know. He's not a Renegade – he didn't have red eyes. He was walking in daylight."

Delin's concern is obvious in her expression. Her green eyes glow ever so slightly. However, she remains composed. She does not want to reward the Midnight Child by revealing her fear. "And what brought you to the conclusion that this single entity poses a threat to this Institute?"

"A feeling."

"A feeling?" the sarcasm in the General's voice is tangible. "Get out," she orders.

"But, Delin. Something's not right." Rising to her feet, Delin crosses her arms. "Valentine, first of all, you will address me as General. Secondly, there are two thousand soldiers stationed here. I think we can take care of one man." She points to the door meaning 'get out' in no uncertain fashion. Alex pauses. Delin has brushed her off, and she is not a bit impressed. She knows Delin knows more than she is revealing and she knows Delin has more fear than she is revealing. Reluctantly Alex opens the door, letting it slam shut behind her. The Giovanni General, Giovanni Authority and Incumbent trembles as she steps back into the shadows.

Delin's knees buckle. She drops to the floor. The three Midnight Children are too close. As far as Delin is aware, Alex has no idea that Ira Tallon also shares her blood. However, this third Midnight Child, if this was in fact who Alex had encountered, is not a good omen. In fact, if the prophecy is to be believed, then this Midnight Child will make Alex look like a saint.

Chapter 14

The sun has sunk into the darkness of night. Ar Novad's has come to life beneath the pale moonlight. Under the cold light of the moon, Alex stands on a balcony above the portico that surrounds the courtyard. Drinking from a hip flask, she stares down at the empty space where the Ankh has been removed. Inhaling shakily she fights her discontent. Everything is too silent – too calm. Eerily quiet. Nothing stirs. The soldiers move about their business in a strange veil of normality. A soft wind blows strands of black hair across her pale face. Something is coming. Alex knows it.

"Alex." Catherine's voice comes from the doorway behind her. Alex turns. "We need to go," Catherine states. Alex nods, overwhelmed by her sense of impending tragedy. Astute, Catherine becomes instantly afflicted with the same weariness, feeling it emanating from her commander. "What's wrong?" she asks as Alex moves into the corridor and starts onwards towards the dorms. "We need to be on our guard," Alex warns. Catherine halts outside Alex's dorm, banging the door. "Elaina, Danielle, Noelle. Hurry up!" she commands before turning back to Alex. "Be on our guard for what?"

"I can't explain." Catherine is unused to seeing Alex so troubled. She can see her fellow soldier is trying to act cool, but below the surface, something is simmering.

The other soldiers emerge from the dorm-like delinquents. Ten and Trente, failing to hide their apathy take up the rear of the section while Catherine urges Noelle and Danielle onwards as they straighten their uniforms. Seeing Elaina appearing glum, Alex hangs back with her. "Well, I know why I'm unhappy. That's why I have this involved." Alex raises the hip flask, "But what apart from the obvious has got you so blue?"

"I was supposed to have a date," Elaina grumbles. "That guy I was talking about, he texted to see if I was free. But, I had to tell him what happened and what I was doing. Told him I'm free the rest of the week though. I'd just like to have seen him tonight."

"Hmmm, booty call?" Although Alex is wary of Elaina's crush, she decides against giving Elaina a warning. She didn't want to sound paranoid, stuffy or worst of all, jealous, so she opted for humour. "No, no, no." Elaina laughs, "He's barely touched me. He's a gentleman."

"Oh come on, give me some dirt." Alex snorts.

"We kissed."

"Wow. Saucy." Alex stops as the corridor splits, "Come on, life is dull. Give me some dirt!" Elaina's eyes look past Alex, who is on a roll and doesn't realise that Ira is descending the staircase behind her. "Come on, Elaina, details. Next time you see him, I want detaaaails. Make me prrrroud." Elaina cringes inciting Alex to dig deeper. "I want to hear that he needs psychiatric help for PTED, Post Traumatic Elaina Disorder. I'll tell all when I finally get my claws into Tallon." Cringing harder, Elaina glances behind to see Ira half blush but not out of embarrassment for himself. He coughs lightly to signal his presence but Alex, on a roll, does not listen. "Although I don't know what he's in to." Alex muses, "Girls? Guys? Neither? Both? Could go either way I suppose?"

Ira reaches the bottom of the stairs and coughs louder. Elaina giggles. This time Alex does hear the cough and knows immediately that she has been caught. Rolling her eyes, she turns to face the embarrassment head-on. "Hello, Tallon." Ira brushes a lock of shaggy hazel hair out of his eyes as he stifles a laugh, "Elaina. Alex…" he smiles and nods before continuing on his way. Alex swerves back around to face Elaina who bursts out laughing.

"I deserved that didn't I?" Again, Alex rolls her eyes, this time at herself. "Smooth, Alex." Elaina squeaks. Alex watches as Delin emerges behind Elaina, appearing appropriately unimpressed. "Corporal Hart. Lieutenant Valentine." Caught off guard, Elaina jumps, spins and squeals in Delin's face. Delin's anchor of anger hits the ocean floor. "Should an assailant approach unexpectedly, of course, that's exactly how you should react. I see your training here has served you well."

"I'm sorry, General." Elaina cringes.

"Perhaps it's in my best interests to extend the suspension."

"That's unnecessary, General." Delin looks to Elaina who visibly cringes as she attempts to compose herself. Delin then turns to the sniggering Midnight Child. "Wipe that smirk off your face, Valentine." She storms away, "Follow me." The two soldiers follow the leader. Nudging Elaina, Alex teases, "Smooth Elaina. Smooth."

"Shuuut up." Elaina is still cringing as she and Alex quicken their pace.

Alex's accomplices are waiting tensely in the weapons locker as Delin opens the door, gesturing for Alex and Elaina to pass through as she remains in the doorway. "Now, I have business to attend to so under no circumstances are you to leave the room – is that clear? Valentine," singled out, Alex perks up, "That goes for you also." Alex pulls a face. "I'm warning you." Delin's expression is fierce. She has already had enough of Alex for one day. With that said, she fixes her glasses and shuts the door leaving the group to get to work.

Chapter 15

Barely an hour since General Delin shut them in, Alex has already given up. Ten is playing music on his phone while he and Trente team up to clean guns. However, choosing songs has hindered their productivity somewhat. Bored, Alex sits on a filing cabinet where she pulls a bottle of Absinthe from inside her coat. Having taken up different stations, the group chat while cleaning, assembling and tidying the weapons. Holly works away with her back to them. Taking a swig of the bottle Alex starts to rummage through the filing cabinet, flicking through old documents until she comes to a folder reading 'The moral codes of crime and punishment' which induces the usual response from her – she rolls her eyes, takes another swig then bangs the cabinet shut causing her squad to jump.

Copying her Lieutenant, Elaina abandons her station and takes a seat. "Break time." She declares. Alex raises her drink in support. Pulling a face, Catherine points to the clock, "Guys, really? It's been like forty-five minutes."

"Some leader you are." Holly mutters below her breath to which Alex shoots her a look but before she can reply with a statement of equal snarkiness she is distracted by Elaina's activity. She observes as Elaina sends a text however she is not an angle that permits overlooking the message. Setting her phone aside, Elaina pulls a book out of her bag, finds her page and begins to read. "What are you reading?" Alex enquires.

"The Three Musketeers." Elaina flashes Alex a look at the cover.

"Any good?"

"It's a classic. Of course, it's no Wurthering Heights, but I love it. You should read it sometime."

"I'm more of a non-fiction type of gal," Winks Alex, "I enjoy the investigatory, sort of detective genre."

"Don't you start. I know where you're going with that." Catherine looks up from her station, knowing Alex all too well. Alex holds her hands up as ‘innocent’ then takes another swig as the room falls silent. Riddled with impatience she drums her fingers on the filing cabinet, causing Holly to seethe with irritation.

Eventually, Alex breaks. She has waited long enough as far as she is concerned. “Right, I’m bored.”

“You’re bored! You’re bored? You’re the reason we’re here!” Holly snaps.

“Touché,” Alex snorts, pacing the room. She has pushed Holly’s buttons, and she doesn’t give a solitary shit. Seeing that Alex has no remorse, Holly’s disgust heightens, “Honestly, do you ever consider the consequences of your actions? Do you ever think before you act? Do you ever think of what you could be doing to those around you? What effect it will have on them?” Round two. The rest of Alex’s entourage crumble in despair, feeling another clash of personalities about to start. Holly has hit a nerve with this one, and she knows it. Alex steps towards her. “Haven’t we already been over this?” Alex sighs before continuing, “At least I act,” she spits, “At least I take action.” She raises the bottle, “Slainte.” She takes a swig in Holly’s face and walks away. Not content that Alex has remained somewhat aloof, Holly bites again.

“You shouldn’t even be drinking. You’re so irresponsible.”

“Here, we go again.” Alex is nonchalant. Her attention is barely on Holly; she continues to pace the room as if looking for something.

“Holly, drop it.” Catherine shoots her a death glare but provoked by Alex’s apathy she rubs salt in the wound. “Just you sit on your high horse, Alex. It’s OK. You’re the Midnight Child. You’re so untouchable.”

“Holly, get fucked.” Alex stops. Trente and Ten explode with laughter which after a look that could kill from Holly, stifles to a snigger.

Awkward silence. Moodily, Holly continues to organise the weaponry, slamming and banging items away. Catherine pulls a face in Alex’s direction. “Can I get a hit off that?” Danielle stops working, gesturing to the Absinthe. “Ah ha! Partner in crime!” Alex outstretches her arm as Danielle approaches to take the bottle. As Danielle takes a drink, Alex draws the Ankh shaped Seal of the Incumbents key before looking up to her audience with a mischievous grin. “Are you guys aware that there is a network of tunnels under this building?”

“Of course,” Catherine answers, “Escape routes.”

“Yes. But were you all aware that these are not simply tunnels? They’re vaults, well catacombs.” The soldiers appear surprised but wary – where is she going with this? “Not only are these tunnels built out of catacombs but the catacombs were built on the site of an ancient burial pit. Hence where Ar Novad's got its reputation for being cursed." Alex beams. Catherine folds her arms. The squad know this isn't going to end well.

From inside her coat, Alex produces blueprints of Ar Novad's and the network of underground tunnels. "Who wants to go for a little adventure?" the girls shake their heads.

"Alex, aren't we in enough trouble as it is?" Catherine reminds her. Holly takes the opportunity to step in.

"My point proven," she mutters. Alex pulls a face at her.

"Fine. Stay." Alex, the Unit's Commanding Officer, proceeds to slide the heavy filing cabinet away from the wall with ease to reveal a dark chamber. The group move closer as the cold wind emerges from the darkness like a dying breath. Alex turns as Noelle gasps.

"Holy fuck!"

"Alex, for fuck sake! We're in enough trouble! Put it back!" Catherine knows that Alex is pushing her luck. If Delin finds out about this, she has just added insult to injury. They could all get permanently demoted. Worse, they could get sent to military prison, and they'd heard too many stories about the Bodmin prison. Holly completely freaks out. "I'm not part of this! I'm not part of this!" she exclaims, "If Delin walks in now you're on your own!" Alex Valentine, master of the side-eye throws some serious shade in Holly's direction.

"Some things don't change."

She steps into the black void ignoring the protests of the girls as she disappears into the darkness. "Alex, come back!" Elaina panics. Ten and Trente immediately dash for adventure after Alex. Elaina hesitates. Terrified but curious, she plunges into the darkness in pursuit. Catherine sighs, cursing under her breath. Noelle and Danielle shrug and follow suit. "Have you all lost your minds?" Catherine shouts after them, her voice echoing throughout the tunnel. She turns to Holly, pointing at the door to the weapons' locker. "Do not let anyone into this room. Do you hear me?" Holly will not mess with Catherine. She knows how serious it is for no one to discover what they have done. The tunnels had always been off-limits. Nobody knew what was down there. However, it seems like Alex has a good idea.

Chapter 16

Elaina hurries through the darkness to catch up with Alex. There is no need for illumination. Their vampire eyes easily adjust to see through the dark. Skidding to a stop, the young soldier reaches Alex, who has stopped in the main tunnel. Elaina scans around as Alex reads the blueprints. The catacombs are more like ancient cells. The skull and bone lined walls are divided either into more tunnels or sealed vaults. Elaina shivers at the macabre spectacle. "Alex, what are you looking for? What's down here?" Her voice shakes. The sound of hurried footsteps prompts them turn to find Noelle, Danielle and Catherine emerge into the tunnel. The expression on Catherine's face says it all. She glowers warningly at her irresponsible superior.

"I know. I know." Alex rhymes upon catching her eye.

"You know what I'm going to say. Let's get out of here now." Catherine urges as Alex moves to wipe the dust and cobwebs off a vault revealing a door number written in roman numerals, III.

"Well, I didn't drag you down here, now did I?" Alex cuts Catherine off.

As Alex turns back to the blueprints, the squad inspect the eerie subterranean warren. In an area where newer vaults have been built which require a code and fingerprint recognition to access, Danielle peers through the bulletproof glass window to find the broken Ankh. Behind her Noelle inspects the ancient skulls and bones, tracing the cracked cranium of someone obvious murdered by some blunt force. Pulling a face she mutters half to herself, "Who are these?"

"Purebloods." Alex answers, the revelation startling the group. "What?" Danielle turns, her expression full of confusion. "Don't purebloods get buried in Moor Falls?" She asks but follows with, "That's what I heard."

"I didn't say they were Giovanni." Alex replies and says no more leaving Noelle and Danielle full of questions but fearful of their answers.

Catherine and Elaina sniff the bitter earthy smell of the dirt floor and the cold walls. The sound of a small trickling of water drips and echoes down the chamber. As the girls begin to draw back together as a group, Alex starts off. "Alex!" Hisses Catherine. Alex's mind is set. She shoots off like a dart in the darkness. The soldiers struggle to keep up with her as she twists and turns through the warren disturbing decades of dust.

Suddenly Alex slams to a stop. The girls catch up as the Midnight Child stares at the vault. It looks just like all the rest. "What's wrong?" Elaina edges closer.

"Look around you," Alex tells them, "Look at the other vaults." Elaina, Catherine, Noelle and Danielle do as commanded before turning back to Alex questioningly. Sighing Alex crosses the tunnel, running her finger along the door and handle of the opposite vault before gesturing to the dust. She crosses back to the vault of interest and does the same – no dust.

"What's in this room, Alex?" Catherine's voice trembles slightly. Alex inserts the Seal of the Incumbents Key and turns. A dull, mechanical clicking tells them it has worked. When the tunnels once again fall silent, Alex replaces the blueprints within her coat and forces the heavy doors open.

Entering the room with careful steps, the group follow Alex inside, guns drawn. The entire vault is a safe. Alex flicks the lights on, illuminating the vast wealth packed into the arched vault. Weapons of every description; tapestries; paintings; precious gems, diamonds and jewellery; furnishings of the purest gold and gold bars; shelves and shelves of books and documents. The squad stare in awe, all lost for words. Eventually, Danielle utters, "Holy shit." However, movement in the doorway behind them forces them to jolt into defence mode, guns aimed at the intruders. "Fuck sake." Danielle lowers her gun and the rest do likewise upon seeing Ten and Trente enter. "Don't do that." Catherine hisses. "What the fuck?" Ten gasps, ignoring Catherine. Overawed, his eyes scan the treasures around him. Trente attempts to break his comrade's gaze by waving his hand over Ten's eyes but Ten is transfixed. "So Alex, Ten wants to know how this heist is going down." Trente jokes.

"There is no heist." Catherine warns.

"Technically," Danielle interjects, "We don't know that yet." As Ten reaches to touch a gold bar, Catherine slaps his hand away. "Don't. Touch. Anything." She scolds and Ten replies by pulling a face at her.

As the soldiers move to inspect the room, absolutely overwhelmed, Catherine turns to Alex who has made a beeline for a large engraved Giovanni Crest on the wall. "How did you know about this?" she questions, "Why are we here? Alex, we will get in serious shit… If we're caught here, we could be accused of so many things. I can't even bear to think, let's just go."

"Not until I've got what I came for." Her mind set to mission mode, Alex pushes down on the crest and turns clockwise until it is upside down. It pops open. Catherine can't believe what she is seeing. She had always known Alex had a mission as a Midnight Child, but this was going too far. She felt like they were in this too deep with her now. Alex had never been vocal about what her and Julius' mission was but Catherine's suspicion – her fear – has just skyrocketed.

Alex uses the Seal of the Incumbents key to open a safe and pulls out a large wooden case with the symbol of the triquetra etched on top. Bringing it towards a desk, she wastes no time picking the lock where she finds a large, leather-bound book. Unlike every other object in the room, this treasure has been long neglected as Alex wipes away a fine layer of dust from the book revealing the triquetra symbol also pressed into the book's leather face.

The group gathers around to inspect what Alex is up to as Alex flicks through the book. Within its yellowing pages are Latin inscriptions and drawings. It is like a Giovanni Gospel. "What is that?" Elaina questions. Excited by her plunder, Alex rises, shooing the group so that she can get back at the safe from which she grabs a handful of scrolls and documents. Elaina panics, "Alex, I think we should go. I think Catherine's right. I think you should leave it." Alex ignores them, placing the old scrolls on an old table, spreading her palms across to reveal their contents in amazement. Outstretching one dusty scroll, Alex sees that it is a long poem. Shuddering as she reads, as if the sight of this is her death knell, she realises that this is the prophecy. However, she has no time to dwell on it, so she keeps it to one side. She then spreads her hand across the execution order for Gordin Veritas of the Teva Clan and another execution order for Alistair Aurelius of the Lanuonin signed by Zanned and Caros. "Holy shit," Alex gasps.

Catherine's nerves overcome her, "This is not a good idea – that's private – put it back!"

"Alex, listen, it's not worth it." Noelle urges her stepping back. Alex is not for budging – she has struck gold. She quickly folds the orders up and conceals them within her coat.

"Fucking hell, Alex, we are going to get busted. You're stealing from the Authorities!" Catherine hisses.

"They stole from me!" Alex hisses back, "Go if you want!"

Catherine is lost for a direction. She feels that they're already incriminated by association. Elaina paces the room horrified. Catherine looks to the other soldiers who are visibly uncomfortable. A bit of casual mischievousness was fun, but this was past mischief. It is obvious to them at this point that Alex is looking for serious trouble. If they are caught snooping in their Authorities' affairs, this would be more than a week's suspension and threat of demotion. This would be definite imprisonment. Catherine loses her patience, "Goddammit, Alex, put it back! What are you looking for?"

"The truth!" Alex takes out the Absinthe and drinks while she scans the pages, taking photographs on her phone. There were too many to steal, so she would have to be selective.

"The truth of what?" shouts Catherine. Alex ignores her. Having stayed silent, taking in the information on the table and trying to process it, Danielle lifts pages, and her hands begin to shake. "These are execution warrants for the leaders of the other Clans. Signed and dated following the Giovanni takeover of Bodmin. These are open execution orders. This could start a war. This is the motivation the Teva and Lanuonin need to fight." Alex is faced by a wall of accusatory expressions. "You're trying to start a war," Catherine concludes. It suddenly dawns on Alex how bad this looks.

"I'm not trying to start a war," Alex confesses seriously. "But war is coming." The soldiers share worried glances. They hadn't expected Alex to be so simple, so matter-of-fact.

"I believe the curse now," Elaina whispers.

Alex flicks to a page within the leather-bound book. It's some sort of census – some sort of Doomsday Book. Rank and status, age and all important information has been noted. Everyone is detailed, including members of all the other clans and their wealth. Authorities' status is marked against their names. Incumbents have the Seal of the Incumbents marked against their names. There are pages of accounts and columns with births and deaths written against a column of names. Zanned and Caros are documented as dead. Alex's eyes fix on this. It becomes clear to her that Zanned and Caros have been warmongering and as a survival tactic have faked their own deaths to protect themselves. If only the Teva and Lanuonin knew that these two cretins were hauled up safe and sound within the opulent Hall of Vampires that they cast the other clans from. Alex rips the page out and keeps it, a move that causes Catherine to hold her head in her hands in despair.

Alex then flicks to find a map and co-ordinates to a location in Egypt. She studies the co-ordinates carefully then slips it inside her jacket also. Behind her, Danielle has lifted a handful of certificates that cause concern to spread across her features. Catherine senses Danielle's unease first. "Er, Alex, don't know any other way to say this but er…" Danielle trails off, confused. She holds up a death certificate, "But you're am… dead." The group looks to Alex for an explanation.

"Well, that's not surprising," Alex responds.

"Are you fuckin' kidding me?" Catherine gasps. "Alex, you owe us the truth." She continues. Ignoring her, Alex mutters to herself:

"They're hiding us from the other clans."

"Us?" Catherine questions, exasperated.

Danielle turns the certificates round for the group to view, "There's one for Ira as well." All eyes look to Alex who snatches the certificates from Danielle. She looks at Ira's then her own. He eyes linger over her death certificate. Her cause of death is listed as blood loss as the result of an attack. She takes a deep breath. However, her breath catches in her throat as she looks to the next document. She chokes. It is another death certificate – a name she did not want to see. Quickly she folds up the certificates and stashes them within her coat. "What was it?" Elaina's face is awash with fear and confusion. "Time to go." Despite having Alex to utter those words, the girls are stumped. Something had induced this sudden change in Alex and whatever it was couldn't be good.

"Come on!" Catherine urges the group to the door as Alex tosses the triquetra book and box back into the safe along with the scrolls before slamming it shut. Rushing out from the vault, she slams it shut behind her with such force that the skulls on the walls tremble.

"Shit, which way do we go?" Noelle looks right and left. As they stand in the darkness, the sound of footsteps quickly grabs their attention. The footsteps are moving towards them – several pairs of booted footsteps echoing throughout the black tunnels.

"Oh my God someone's here," Elaina states the obvious. Alex draws her gun. Catherine steps forward to lower it. She whispers, "We're not shooting our own even if we're caught red-handed. Let's go this way. Get us out of here." She draws Alex in the opposite direction. Reluctantly Alex returns her gun to her holster as the footsteps move closer and closer. "Come on, Alex, please. If we get caught, we're in enough trouble as it is." Elaina begs.

"OK, come on." Alex spares one last glance down the tunnel before she leads the way legging it through the pitch-black darkness.

The pursuing footsteps continue behind them. The soldiers and their pursuers sprint through the catacombs. Suddenly Alex slams to a stop. They have reached a wall. Had they taken a wrong turn? No, couldn't have. She had studied the blueprints. Had her discovery thrown her that much? "Shit. Shit. Shit." Catherine swears, looking backwards. "Did we take a wrong turn?" Elaina questions as Alex attempts to think. No. They did not take a wrong turn. This was it. Suddenly the footsteps stop. Everything goes silent. It is only them and the black abyss. On Alex's orders, the section falls into formation, guns drawn just in case. The footsteps start again, closer.

"Come on, Alex." Catherine urges. Luckily Alex notices the wall is different than the rest – it's a fake. The wall is a concealed exit. A clever trick of its positioning makes it look like a dead-end, but it's just the shadow. Alex slips through first – there is only enough room for one. The footsteps grow louder. The girls have just witnessed Alex disappear into the void. They don't understand, but they know they need to get out. Suddenly Alex's hand appears from the darkness and pulls Elaina through.

"Hurry the fuck up!" They hear Alex's voice. With no time to waste, they squeeze through the crack in the wall into a claustrophobic chamber. They rush as fast as possible to end where Alex is the first to break out into the deserted corridor. Once they have all emerged to relative safety Alex closes the secret entrance to the catacombs – a life-sized painting of Lucifer's banishment from Heaven. For a moment, they stand in silence, processing what has just happened. Alex slumps back against the painting, her right hand resting above the documents she has concealed. Finally, Elaina breaks the silence:

"Who do you think was down there?" The group shrugs collectively. "Delin's probably got guards on patrol." Alex brushes it off.

"Well, you know what?" Catherine straightens, "I'm going back to the weapons locker, and I'm finishing this before Delin realises that we've been gone."

"What if she already has?" Catherine turns to Elaina, "Then in all likelihood, we're going to get our asses handed to us." She looks to Alex, "Are you coming with us?" Alex looks to her with a side-eye.

"No. Go on." Catherine raises her hands in defeat.

"Well, it's your choice. Enjoy scrubbing Mesmit's toilet." Alex pulls a face – like that would ever happen. Catherine starts off with Elaina and Noelle following. Danielle lingers with Alex. Noelle looks back to her.

"Go on ahead. I'll be a few minutes. I'm gunna take Alex to get some air." Noelle nods to Danielle then follows the others.

Danielle turns to Alex, concerned. "What's going on? What happened down there?" she asks. Alex takes a deep breath and bangs her head lightly on the wall.

"I need to get out of here."

"Come on then, let's get some air." Danielle pulls Alex away from the wall and towards the doors to the courtyard. They move down the long dimly lit corridor of the right-wing of the Institute. The building is silent. "It's strange being in here when the place is so empty…" Danielle comments.

"A lot of the recruits are away on training this week," Alex informs. Danielle notices Alex's gaze is locked on the light at the end of the hallway. General Delin's office is illuminated. Two armed guards stand outside the door. "Fuck. The big wigs must be having their meeting," Danielle observes, "Do you suppose they know that we aren't supposed to be here?"

"Lieutenant Valentine!" One of the guards calls, "You've strayed somewhat from your post!"

"So that's a 'yes'." Danielle mutters and curses again under her breath.

A shadow slips swiftly from the darkness. Alex and Danielle stop in their tracks, interrupted by its sudden appearance. Startled by this spectre, the guards break their form. There is no time to save themselves. Silhouetted by the lights of the General's office, Alex and Danielle witness in horror as the spectre slits the first guard's throat then stabs the other through the chest. They didn't stand a chance. This creature is swifter than any normal vampire and stronger. Alex immediately leaps forward to action, drawing her gun. The spectre narrowly avoids a bullet as Alex opens fire. She and Danielle then pursue as this shadowy form slips back into the darkness.

They chase the figure through the hallway. Alex is faster than Danielle, so races on up the stairs, closing in on the figure until it is only a couple of metres away. Alex shoots. The bullet hits the target between its shoulder blades yet fails to stop the fleeing figure. Danielle reaches the top of the stairs and seeing the direction Alex and the mysterious assailant are moving in she rushes back down the stairs and doubles back on herself, hoping to cut him off. Alex is almost upon him when he returns fire. She ducks for cover, and as she emerges to fight again, the figure dives over the balcony on to the portico and into the courtyard. Immediately Alex dives through the window to the ground below just in time to glimpse the figure re-enter the building. Again she pursues, bursting in through the swinging doors so fast she breaks them from their hinges.

The figure has vanished. Alex replaces her gun in the holster and instead draws her sword. Once she is content that the area is safe, she hurries back towards Delin's office where Delin, Shanay and two other high-ranking soldiers have emerged, having heard the commotion. They stare in horror at the two murdered guards. Seeing Alex approach Delin shoots her an accusatory glare. Danielle remains on guard. Delin turns to her majors, "Organise an entire sweep of the area. Make sure everyone is accounted for." The majors accept their orders and exit. Delin storms to Alex, "Might I enquire as to why you barged into my chamber this morning to inform me of a threat to the Institute, only for me now to find you in the middle of a crime scene when you were under strict instruction to remain in the weapons locker?" for once, Alex is lost for words. She knows how bad it looks. Delin turns her accusatory glare to Danielle, who is also speechless.

The figure appears behind Danielle. "Dani!" Alex roars. The figure tosses the young soldier aside as if she were nothing. Danielle's skull smacks off the wall, rendering her unconscious. The figure then lunges at Delin, so fast Alex does not see his features but she is certain she knows this man. She is certain this is the man from the park. As he lunges at Delin, the General narrowly avoids the blade of his sword. The next blow makes an impact, slicing her across the back as she attempts to escape. Alex intervenes. The attacker blocks. She manages to knock him off course, and jumps in to block his path to the wounded Giovanni Authority. Alex and the man clash swords in an 'x' shape. She now comes face to face with him. Yes, it is the man she encountered outside the park. She knew she would encounter him again. Blade against blade she gets but a second to look into his dark eyes. Who are you? I know you…

He breaks away. Alex fixes her footing and meets his attack with equal venom. The pair lock in conflict, each putting every fibre of strength behind their steel. The connection between them is electric. Their eyes again connect. Alex stares right through this man – right through his dark blue eyes to the fire of hate burning in his soul. She feels the connection as if his dark aura has engulfed her own or perhaps merged with it. They might currently be locked in opposition but something about him is luring Alex in. A memory is taking hold. As he swipes at her, his scent is so familiar. His eyes… It feels like home. Fearing this memory will weaken her, she forces it from her mind and then with every muscle in her body, knocks him backwards.

"What's wrong, Valentine?" He asks playfully, correctly reading her expression to conclude that Alex is struggling to associate him. "Don't you recognise me?" There is a glimmer in the man's eyes as he toys with her. Behind Alex, Delin groans, struggling to her knees. It wasn't unusual for a stranger to know the Midnight Child by name, but there was something worryingly familiar about this man's voice – something charming, endearing almost. "Who are you?" her question brings him to laughter. He directs his sword towards her in a gesture of judgement, "Perhaps they managed to brainwash you, after all, Valentine."

He lurches forward. As they take a few jabs at each other, Alex slashes him across the chest spilling blood. The man halts. Alex raises her sword defensively watching as the man presses his hand to the blood before extending it for her to view. She catches the scent of the warm red blood. Its fragrance brings her back – memories of home possess her. The sweet smell washes through her, flooding her mind with soothing sensations of love and safety. But, as suddenly, as it had washed over her, it recedes as the man steps closer towards her. The scent becomes bitter – an acrid smell of death. She gasps, taking a step back. "Look at me, Valentine. Tell me; you don't recognise me." His voice is low and alluring. She is completely thrown. It can't be. It can't be. The words circle in her mind. She refuses to face the truth – it makes her nauseous.

The man sweeps his sword in a swift arc. Alex manages to avoid a severe blow but is caught by the blade. She cries out, falling to her knees as blood pours down her face. Managing to retain her sword, she looks up to see him standing back, smiling proudly at his work – the Midnight Child has been scarred. His sword has left a long slash down the right side of her face narrowly avoiding her eye. He has left his mark. His work here is done for the night. Enraged, Alex jumps to her feet and lands in a fighting stance. The man laughs at her, "OK, Valentine, come on, then let's play."

Before she can engage him again, someone grabs her from behind, heaving her back. Alex struggles against her captor as she is dragged backwards. Just as she manages to break free her captor grabs her by the back of her coat and hurls her into General Delin's office. Using this as an opportunity to flee, the murderous assailant shoots at the glass doors, causing them to explode and shatter. As the shards of glass cascade on to the ground, his black clothed figure disappears back into the night.

Inside the General's office Alex struggles against her captor. Her feet hit the wall. She kicks back. Her captor smashes back against the wall with a grunt releasing his grip. Alex's feet hit the ground, and she breaks free. She falls to the floor and scrambles for her sword. Shooting quickly to her feet, she spins around to discover her captor's identity. "Julius?" she gasps.

Her guardian raises his hands in surrender; however, Alex remains on guard. She does not lower her sword – she cannot. She cannot trust anyone, not after tonight. "Alex, do you have any idea who that was?" Julius speaks softly. He knows he is walking through fire.

"Alex, lower your sword. I'm not trying to hurt you, why would I? I love you. I'm trying to protect you. I'm trying to save you." He pauses. His fear is tangible. "Everything we feared is now becoming a reality." He warns.

"Danielle!" she gasps through her shock and darts to the door. Julius slams his hand against the door, halting her.

"Alex. Danielle is fine. She's dazed, but she's awake. She's fine. You need to accept what just happened."

He watches as Alex's posture crumbles. She drops her sword. The proud warrior has been defeated. "Argon…" she whispers. Julius nods sadly. "Julius it can't be. It can't be him. Of all people why?"

"Fate."

"But he's dead. Argon died."

"Your Argon died, Alex. Their Argon," Julius gestures to a large painting of the Seal of the Incumbents on Delin's office wall, "Their Argon lives. The one that they created…" tears well in Alex's eyes. Her legs buckle, and she falls back on to Delin's desk. Julius may as well have stabbed her. "He's the third Midnight Child, Alex."

Alex is overcome. Lost for words, she struggles to process her thoughts. This is a man that she had loved. This was her oldest friend and she didn't even recognise him – what had they done to him? Finally, she finds the strength to speak. "Julius, why? Just why? Is our fate simply a self-fulfilling prophecy or is the prophecy true? How can this be? I never wanted to be a puppet." Julius moves closer, sinking into Delin's luxurious throne. Julius' chestnut eyes are filled with a sadness Alex has not seen before. A deep sense of guilt permeates his soul. "We are manifestations of corruption, Alex." He starts, "Like Lucifer himself, the Angel, the First was cast out of Heaven. The First misunderstood the world. He saw the corruption. He saw the world as a manifestation of God's corruption. He witnessed the cruelty and the greed of man. He saw God's creation raped and plundered by humanity."

"I don't believe in God." Alex snorts, "We're mutations. It's just evolution. Vampirism is a carcinogenic gene, a cell that mutates and corrupts. It kills everything that's good and pure inside you." Julius ignores her and continues:

"And so, the First rebelled against God. He couldn't understand why God would sit back and watch as all beauty and innocence was destroyed. He was banished from Paradise to learn a lesson, but he only learned hate. In his bitterness, he set on a quest to spite the God who had punished him – who had abandoned him. So he corrupted God's creation by turning the humans. He corrupted the life that God had given them – the blood flowing in their veins."

For a few seconds, Julius falls silent in thought. He purses his hands together as if in prayer. Alex attempts to hide the tears trickling down her face. Julius continues with a sigh. "You know how this story ends. Power corrupts. Those who had been turned, the vampires, began to form clans. Each clan fought for power. The First watched them with disgust. Just as God's humans had soiled what God had made sacred so too had the First's vampires. In his eyes he saw that they were monsters – abominations."

"And he was right," Alex interjects with a statement that sends shivers through Julius' ancient bones. "He set out to destroy them. A move the Incumbents of the Clans had seen coming. So they took matters into their own hands." The teacher and his pupil's gaze connects knowingly. "So what does that make us then, Midnight Children? What does that make us? Original monsters?" Alex's tone is steeped in animosity.

"It makes you pure. Your blood has not been tainted by humanity," Julius teaches.

"I was human!" Alex snaps. Julius shakes his head solemnly.

"I'm sorry, Alex, you never were. You were created by the Incumbents from the First. The three Midnight Children are one. That was never mortal blood in your veins. You just needed to be awakened."

The Midnight Child hangs her head in silence. She had heard bits and pieces of her creation before but never with such sincerity from her guardian angel. She knows that in telling her the truth, Julius too feels pain. "And so, what of this 'prophecy'?" Alex uses the word loosely, rising to go inspect her wound in the mirror. It is healing but slowly, too slowly... Concerned, Julius moves to Delin's safe where he inputs the code. Alex watches him in the mirror as he removes a bag of blood.

"The prophecy is this." He carries the bag of blood to her, making an incision. "The Prophet foretold that in destroying their creator, the Incumbents would secure their own demise. The Prophet saw that this soul, split into three, would manifest in three creatures who would seal the fate of the Incumbents and Authorities' in particular, the Giovanni. The First's life force would not be destroyed – that energy and consciousness would live on. The beings created from it, their blood and spirit would be stronger, faster – have far superior capabilities." He passes the blood to Alex to drink. She accepts uneasily.

Julius returns to his seat as Alex drinks. "It was prophesised that these beings would be the scourge of the Giovanni Clan. That being said the Giovanni took no heed. All they were concerned with was power. They were the driving force, and their arrogance forced the other clans to war and to exile. The Clans were done with the Giovanni's insatiable bloodlust for power. And, seeing as the war continued with no end in sight, the Teva and Lanuonin decided to go underground and abandon Bodmin. They decided to let the Prophecy play out. They were afraid that if they remained in Bodmin, they would soon be wiped out or worse, become the Giovanni's slaves. They saw it as better to abandon Bodmin, their home than take on the Giovanni who had grown too strong. The Midnight Children would be the Giovanni's curse." Alex finishes the blood and turns to the mirror. The wound is still not healing. Something is not right.

"The Giovanni Authorities would never trust anything more powerful than themselves, not when the spirit within the Midnight Children – a termed coined from the hour of the First's destruction."

"You mean murder. Patricide." Alex interrupts. Julius nods in agreement, always one to consider his words carefully.

"Not when the spirit, the soul inside the Midnight Children was a soul who sought their destruction."

"Why not just kill us then?" Asks Alex, tossing the empty bag in the bin, "Why waste their time on this delusional enterprise?"

"For the same reason as they could not kill the First. The Incumbents couldn't destroy the Angel. The Incumbents plotted with the Alchemists who advised that only by performing a certain ritual and incantation would they succeed. They forged a dagger and used an incantation to imbue it with the power to kill the

Angel or so they thought. They arranged a meeting of the Incumbents and began to perform the ritual. Balthazar was the one to stab the Angel in the back – literally. Only they didn't kill him. They only killed his body. His soul survived and what it materialised in were three preternatural embryos that could not be destroyed – the Midnight Children. But, like the Ankh of the Dead that now lies in three pieces, the soul may have been split but it was made to be one. You are one-third of a complete soul, and that soul wants to be whole again."

Alex feels like she has just been stabbed. Her chest tightens, and her breath shortens as she considers Julius' words. Seeing Alex's distress, Julius rises again and begins to pace the room. He swipes a tissue from a box on Delin's desk and hands it to Alex to clean her face. "So how did or how do you know the Prophecy's true? As I said, this could all have been some mass hysteria all a series events created by the butterfly effect of the First's death coupled by paranoia." Alex suggests, her mind beginning to open up after the initial shock. Julius stops pacing.

"Because I watched it happen. I watched as they grew fearful, threatened – what if they could not control you? What if the Angel within you held memories of his execution? If you fear something, you keep it close. You keep it guarded." Alex considers Julius' words tensely. "Worst still for the Giovanni Authorities, The Midnight Children are the purest bloodline in the Vampire line. The Midnight Children are the rightful rulers of the Vampire nation. The Giovanni know that if the Teva and Lanuonin discovered you were alive that you should be put on the throne, not the Giovanni Authorities. With the Giovanni Authorities in a subservient position, it would give the other Clans the opportunity to reform the true Vampire Court not the dictatorship of the Giovanni as it stands today."

Putting two and two together, Alex reaches inside her coat and pulls out the documents she stole from the vault. She flicks through them and tosses Ira, Argon and her own death certificates out for Julius to view. Picking them up and studying them Julius' demeanour changes. He appears morose, regretful even. "Unfortunately Belial knows of your existence. Unlike the Teva and Lanuonin Belial saw the Midnight Children as the opportunity to destroy the Giovanni and instate the Ronakites as rulers of Bodmin."

Alex falls silent for a moment, her mind drifting back to the fight with Argon and then back again, just over two years ago to the fateful night when she was left in the belief that she would never see him again. "I know what I did but if he is what I am, why is Argon trying to kill me? We're the same."

"Belial." The name is acid on Julius' tongue. "He was a Ronakite. He wanted to claim the Midnight Children. He was supposed to protect you, and he betrayed you." Alex screws up her face disgustedly as he stops by the small replica Ankh on the wall.

"We were the Guardians of the Midnight Children. We vowed to protect you from the Authorities and Incumbents who were continuing to pursue a way to destroy you. When war broke out between the Ronakites and Giovanni, Belial changed. Belial wanted to get his revenge on the Giovanni for the near genocide of the Ronakites. He wanted to use the Midnight Children. I had no other choice than to advise the Authorities of Belial's plan and with help I stole the three of you and smuggled you out of Bodmin where I thought you could be safe. Only I would know the location of the Midnight Children. Back in Bodmin, many of the Ronakites were tortured and executed. Belial and a handful managed to escape and were run into exile. He formed the Renegades and went on a mission to find the Midnight Children." Julius pauses reflectively, "I didn't want your lives to be like this. I clung on to hope that I would never have to interrupt your lives, but I had to in order to protect you. Belial was closing in."

Alex knows that Julius is truly mournful of his decision; however, the lance of regret has pierced her side. Not that she wants to turn the pain on the man who had sought to protect her, but she can't hold back her hurting. "For four years… for four years, Julius, you knew that he lived. We could have saved him!" Julius shakes his head sadly – he knew how bad this looked.

"Alex, I had many reasons to conceal the truth from you. Had I believed that Argon could have been saved at any point then and for the last four years, I would have taken action. The prophecy foretold in no uncertain fashion that one of the Midnight Children would be engulfed in darkness. The prophecy."

"Fuck the prophecy!"

"Alex!" for a split second Julius' regret suddenly turns to rage. "Belial has sunk his claws into Argon. His blood, his mind has been tainted. Belial has the Renegades, and we do not know at this stage the extent of his army. What army do we have? You and I are all alone."

"Ira Tallon," Alex snaps. "Make Tallon fight. Why has he been so sheltered? For the last four years, he's been the Prince of Privilege."

"He'll fight soon enough," Julius vows.

"What in the name of every God was that?" Alex and Julius snap to attention as the door is flung open by a blood-stained General Delin. She has healed, but the residue of the wound remains on her usually immaculate uniform. "I think what you meant to say is 'thanks for saving my ass, Lieutenant Valentine'." The General glares at the scarred Lieutenant, "Shut up, Valentine." She turns her attention on Julius, "What happened here tonight?"

"You had an encounter with the third Midnight Child." Julius is a matter of fact; however, the words make Delin's blood run cold. Taking the political road, Delin decides to distract from her own insecurities by turning the conversation on Alex and Julius. "And he got away?" she snaps. Alex rolls her eyes, "Typical." She marches towards Delin to exit the room, but the General does not move from the doorway. "Let me out."

"I am not moving until I get answers. What were you doing out of the weapons locker? A Midnight Child breaks into the Institute and attempts to kill me, and you have disobeyed my orders." Delin's forehead creases in fury, yet this quickly changes as a worrying thought arises. "Or perhaps you let him in…" Alex snaps.

"Does it look like I fucking let him in?" she points to the wound on her face, "Get out of my way!"

"I want answers."

"Get out of my way."

"Lieutenant!"

"Move!" In a fit of rage, Alex shoves her superior back through the door back into the scene of the crime.

Soldiers have gathered at the scene to ogle and await orders. The last couple of days had been nothing but drama. It was morbid entertainment. "This! All of this is your fucking fault!" Alex has tunnel vision, despite the onlookers she continues directing her hatred at Delin – she had it coming. "Alex!" Julius rushes after her. "The Midnight Children you so fear and despise – this was your choice! We are your mistake! I am in a world of shit because of the mess that you made!" Delin is speechless. Julius cringes. Aware of the prying eyes and ears around them, Delin knows to keep her mouth shut. They already know too much. Alex's use of the word 'children' has caused a ripple through the pond. The soldiers observe the fight with interest. "You think I let someone in to kill you? Please. If I wanted to kill you, I'd do it myself. I warned you yesterday! I fucking warned you! I knew something wasn't right and you didn't listen!"

“Lieutenant Valentine!” The General steps in – she has to. Alex has made her look bad-worse – she’s made her look like a fool. Delin had a reputation to keep. “That’s enough!”

As the scene falls, silent Alex looks to the observers so appear awkward but curious – eager for knowledge. At the edge of the crowd Alex clocks Ira Tallon. Their eyes meet. Ira knows Alex has learnt who is his. What he is. She grits her teeth. “You.” She turns her attention on him, storming towards him. The observing soldiers are fascinated. None of them knows what’s going on, but everything was kicking off, and it was the first thought within all their minds that Alex Valentine, the Midnight Child had snapped. That she had dug her own grave this time. Tallon is completely taken by surprise when Alex makes a quick fist and swiftly cracks him across the jaw. He goes down in a heap. The onlookers are equally gobsmacked. Delin and Julius’ jaws drop in horror.

“You fucking prick!” Alex hisses at Tallon as he pulls himself back to his feet, wiping away blood on his lip. “For the last four years, I have taken everything. I have taken all this shit while you sat back and let me take the fall.” As Alex scowls at her fellow Midnight Child, she is unaware that behind her Delin has ordered two soldiers to restrain her. She is suddenly grabbed from behind and pulled away before she can reveal anything else that Delin would prefer to keep hidden. Alex could easily break free of her captors, but as they pull her towards Delin she glances to Julius and witnesses the unease in his features that she reads as disappointment. She surrenders and stands restrained before the General. Alex has never seen Delin filled with so much spite. “Alex Valentine you are suspended until further notice.” Delin strips Alex of her gun, an action that brings Alex’s bitterness to boiling point. However, she smiles as her gun is taken from her. She has been humiliated by her superior, but she has gotten what she wanted – she has pushed the Authority’s buttons. She has caused her anger. She has caused her fear.

Disgusted by Alex’s smirk, Delin turns to Julius, who has gone to Ira to ask if he is OK. “Julius.” Julius immediately turns to her. “Get Valentine out of my sight.” Julius nods and promptly moves to unhand his rebellious apprentice from the soldiers. Alex continues to smirk at Delin as Julius swiftly and silently escorts her from the building. The war was on. As they exit the building and enter the dark city streets, Julius releases Alex’s arm. He stops with a sigh. “Julius.” He turns tiredly to see Alex pulling documents from beneath her coat. He sees the documents and letters relating the execution of Alistair Aurelius and Gordon

Veritas. She smirks. Julius gasps, reaching for the papers and scans them rapidly. His eyes illuminate with a smile. At least this night was not a complete disaster.

Chapter 17

The darkness of night has descended on the city. Within Julius' beautiful sandstone mansion, he makes his way down the long undecorated hallway to the expertly crafted stone staircase and descends to the training room. Although having no affairs to attend to he remains dressed to perfection in black trousers and a white shirt and waistcoat. The outside sconces and moonlight streams in on to the pale stone walls.

Inside the training, room rounds blast the body of a target as Alex lets off steam. A bottle of Absinthe and a half-drunk glass sit on the counter while heavy metal music blasts through speakers around the room. On the targets, she has stuck images of the Authorities. She shoots 'Delin' in the forehead. With her long hair tied back and tight black training gear on, she means business. As more targets appear, Alex pounds their bodies repeatedly until she runs out of bullets then hurls the gun at a target. Storming to the weapons locker, she grabs a shotgun and opens fire on the targets. As the targets are pounded, they begin to fall apart as the bullets blast chunks from them. The 'Authorities' are blown away. Alex keeps shooting as Julius enters the training room behind her, wincing at the deafening noise.

The deafening music cuts out. As the shots pound the walls, it takes Alex a moment to realise before turning to figure out why the music has stopped. Case closed – Julius is standing there. He exhales calmly, "Hmmmm silence." Julius points to the destruction. "Enjoying yourself?" Alex stares at the damage catching her breath as Julius then moves to the counter, picking up the bottle of Absinthe.

"I think you'd need to drink something other than alcohol," He advises. "You need to relax." Alex dumps the gun on the counter and picks up the glass to drink.

"I am relaxing."

"By relaxing, I'm suggesting perhaps you go take a bath, curl up beside the fire with a book." Alex pulls a face at him.

"That's your idea of relaxing not mine."

"Wouldn't hurt you."

"How can I relax when I'm losing count of how many people want me dead? Belial, the Authorities, Argon all want me dead. And who's to say Ira Tallon hasn't been swayed to their side?"

"I assure you he hasn't. Ira doesn't even want to take sides."

"Clearly," Alex snorts. "He's a fucking sissy. What's his deal?" Julius sighs, folding his arms.

"Ira didn't want any of this. He refused to accept it."

"Because it's so easy to opt-out of. You covered for him?" Again Julius sighs, he understands how this must look to Alex. "Ira would not agree to fight. He ran away from me when I found him and he learnt the truth. I had to hunt him down again. We came to this agreement so that he would come to the Institute. I was afraid if I pushed him too much he would run away again and I was afraid that if he did, Belial would get to him or Argon would get to him."

Julius' logic rests in Alex's mind – he has a point. She drops her guard. "I'm not mad at you for this. You did what you thought was right. But I'll never understand why we couldn't save him. Tallon, on the other hand did nothing. And when I get my hands on him."

"You've done enough." Julius raises his eyebrows. "I'm sorry you had to bear the weight alone, but you've done an incredible job so far. And you did an incredible job last night. I'm sure the Teva and Lanuonin will be quite interested in our operation." Alex attempts to hold back a proud smile, so nods to acknowledge his statement. Luckily her phone beeps as a text is received. She breaks away from Julius to read it. It is a message from Danielle simply reading 'pub?' Alex smiles and turns back to Julius. "You know what? Maybe I will relax."

"You're going to the pub, aren't you?" Julius pulls a knowing look.

"Indeed, I am!" Alex beams, her mood miraculously lifted by Julius' praise and Danielle's text. However little did she know that an innocent night at the pub would turn into one of the worst nights of her crazy life.

Chapter 18

The city buzzes with nightlife. The lights of taxis, advertisements, shops and streetlights sparkle on the flowing river. Music emanates from bars and buskers. Dressed to kill Alex and Danielle stand having a smoke at the entrance to a narrow alleyway below a train station. They chat in the darkness as groups of friends and couples out for the night pass by on the street.

Out of uniform, the preternatural soldiers appear just as goth girls with coloured contacts in their eyes. A group of drunk raucous young men passing by see the girls and wolf whistle. The sight of Alex in a tight black leather dress ripped tights and black thigh-high boots with her smoky eyes and red pout made all men turn their heads. Danielle, with her bright red hair, her cropped fishnet top, short leather skirt and platform heels did likewise. A couple of the men make inappropriate comments, but the girls don't bat an eyelid, so they continue on their way.

"I think Elaina's meeting up with that guy she's been seeing tonight," Danielle states as she stubs out her cigarette. The statement causes Alex concern.

"Have you met him yet?" she asks as she stubs out her smoke and they start down the alleyway.

"No, haven't met him but she showed me a picture of him, he's pretty hot. Looks a bit old for her though."

"Dani, we're vampires, does age really matter?" Alex side-eyes her. Danielle shrugs.

"Suppose."

"Did she say where he's from?"

"Na. She's been pretty tight-lipped."

"Did you even get a name?"

"Na. Hasn't mentioned that either. She doesn't want to jinx this by us knowing too much and asking too many questions."

"What a sudden change in the wind."

"What do you mean?"

"She was very vocal about the situation the other morning. Not much information but she wanted to talk about this incredible person."

"You don't trust him."

"Do I trust anyone?" Alex pauses as they approach the bar where it opens up into a decked platform, the smoking area of a club called Realm, a vampire bar. The smoking area is full of clubbers as Alex and Danielle approach the heavy black doors of the bar where the bouncer opens the door admitting them entry. Loud industrial music blares and multi-coloured strobe lights flash as the girls weave through the throng of dancers towards the stairs. A couple of chiselled guys in black clothing eye their pale, toned bodies and ethereal beauty as they ascend the wrought iron staircase.

Upon reaching the top of the stairs, the girls immediately descend on the bar to order Absinthe – blood cocktails. The upstairs bar is comfortably quieter with metal music playing at a volume that still permits conversation. The bar is a black marble slab. The décor is lush and stereotypically gothic but beautiful in a dark ethereal way. The Giovanni had funded the founding of this space as a refuge for young vampires who needed an outlet rather than have them wrecking havoc in the streets with humans. Taking their drinks the vampiric beauties sing along to the music as they make their way to where Catherine, Noelle, Elaina, Ten and Trente sit in a booth.

"Hey, guys." Alex takes a seat and removes her long leather coat revealing her incredible sculpted body in the tight leather dress.

"Are you on the pull tonight of what?" Trente teases then looks at Danielle in her fishnet and wolf whistles. "Looking good ladies."

"Why thank you, sir." Alex blows a kiss. "May as well make the most of being out of uniform." The group laughs awkwardly.

"Have you heard any more from Delin?" Catherine enquires, stirring her cocktail. Alex observes as Elaina who momentarily was interested is now distracted by a text she has just received.

"No. Nothing more." Alex watches Elaina reply.

"Nothing?" Trente asks.

"Well, she's pretty pissed but unfortunately for her she needs me so she'll have to figure something out fast." Alex takes a drink as Elaina finishes her text and returns, half attentive to the conversation at hand. "So Ira Tallon then?" Danielle, who observed the event first-hand confronts the elephant in the room.

"He's a Midnight Child?" she asks. Everyone's eyes bulge. Alex nods slowly, wary of eavesdroppers – unlikely in a club of this volume but Alex was always on guard. Trente shakes his head.

"I fucking knew it. There was always something odd about him. Remember that mission a couple of months ago? Me and Ten were sent with a unit of his? There was something about him. How did you find out?" Alex brushes the conversation off.

"Are we out for a night out or what?"

"Come on, Alex, this is the biggest drama of the year. Possibly ever, we want to know!" Noelle laughs.

"Julius told me," Alex reluctantly obliges, "He hunted each of us down, but Tallon is living in denial. I'll get him soon."

"I don't think you're off to a good start!" Danielle laughs. Alex pulls a face, after her last encounter with Tallon it was unlikely he would be very willing to play ball with her.

"You said 'each of us'. Is there more than you and Ira?" Catherine picks up on Alex's slip.

"Guys, right now it's best just to leave it." Alex brushes it off quickly. "You've fallen far enough on my behalf already." She raises her glass as a toast, "So, here's to a week off, for you lot at least. Let's get drunk!" the group cheer and laugh.

No sooner have the glasses clinked that Elaina receives another text. Danielle turns to Ten, who is as usual, at every opportunity, dressed flamboyantly in leather bondage-style garb and makeup. Having an industrial metal band had turned him a little eccentric. Danielle is commenting on his makeup when Elaina grabs her bag and stands. "Where are you going?" Alex's question is immediate, although she already knows the answer.

"I have a date." Elaina who is dressed in a pale pink mini satin dress, leather biker jacket and high heels shimmies past the group. Obviously dressed to impress, she rolls her eyes as Alex asks:

"Why don't you just tell him to come here?"

"What did you just say? Make the most of being out of uniform?" she pulls a naughty face. Noelle 'woos'. In a different circumstance, Alex would usually join in Noelle's teasing but not on this occasion, something didn't feel right. "Alex, it's a date." Seeing her suspicion, Elaina attempts to pacify her more experienced comrade, "Besides you lot, I feel would be a little overwhelming for him."

"Elaina, it's just that after everything," Alex is cut off as Elaina's phone distracts her again. "I've got to go. I've got to go now." Elaina flusters. "See you guys tomorrow!" she scrambles out as fast as she can in her heels through the sea of clubbers.

Alex turns to the group who are thrown by Alex's concern. She meets eye contact with Catherine for support. Catherine acknowledges. "I know. I know, Alex. But we can't stop her. It's her life. Her choice. We're probably just…it's been a weird week." Alex knocks back her drink. Trente decides to lighten the mood. "I know what we should do! Dance!" the group reacts with approval, but Alex declines.

"You do what you have to do. I'll be at the bar."

"Oh, come on!" Trente attempts to pull her on to the dance floor, but she fights him off.

"I'll be at the bar! I'll get you guys in a minute!" she shouts through the music as a new song starts. "I love this song!" Danielle shouts as she dances her way from the booth on to the floor. Noelle dances on to the floor with her. Alex watches as Trente and Catherine join in writhing within the lightening beams of the strobe lights. No sooner is Ten on the dance floor that he is recognised by two girls in short black dresses, fishnets with various piercings approach him. "Hey you're the singer from Hope Fails aren't you?" that line always meant one thing – Ten was guaranteed to go home with at least one if not two girls that night.

Alex weaves her way to the bar where a barman, seeing the beauty makes a beeline to serve her immediately. As the music blares, she leans over the bar to place her order and as she does so, the barman can't help but be struck by Alex's natural gothic beauty and powerful figure. There is an unnatural aura about her – unnatural even for the likes of himself. As he moves off to fetch the ingredients, Alex leans against the bar in wait. She glances over to where her group are dancing and having a laugh on the dance floor. However, Alex is distracted by a tall, attractive man who has noticed her at the bar. Seeing her long black hair cascade down the curvature of her leather-clad body as she leans on the bar, he can't resist. "You look like a dangerous woman." His flirting is scandalously blatant. The man is attractive, but Alex is not having any of it – she knows his type. "That's because I am," she smirks.

"Can I buy you a drink?" he slips in beside her at the bar. She cringes internally as the barman returns with her order and she passes him the money.

"It's fine, I've got it."

"Oh, an independent woman?"

"Is that so hard to believe in this day and age?" the man laughs. The barman outstretches his hand to offer Alex her change. "It's fine, keep it," she tells him. The barman's jealousy is apparent as he moves off watching the man who is attempting to chat up the gothic beauty.

"What's your name?" the man asks.

"Alex."

"Hi, Alex, I'm Nicholi."

"I didn't ask." The man laughs again, flicking his long, wavy hair.

"What's your deal, Alex?"

"You think because my pants haven't dropped to the floor at the sight of you that I have a deal?" the man is speechless. "Look I don't want to be rude, but please just go."

"Come on. You come into a bar wearing a dress like that, looking like you do, you're telling me you're not looking something?" he winks. Alex doesn't know whether to punch him or vomit, but instead, a lecture materialises. "Look, bud. Just because a girl puts on a nice dress and goes alone to the bar to buy herself a drink does not mean she's looking a cheap ride. Maybe she works very fucking hard and doesn't get much of a chance to socialise so when she does get the chance to wear a nice dress and go for a drink, she takes it. Maybe she just wants to look nice, go out with her friends, get a little drunk and have a good fucking night."

"Ah…" Nicholi surmises, "You're a lesbian. That's OK."

"Ah…" Alex's uses every inch of her restraint not to punch him in his well-groomed face, "You're insecure."

"Yeah, right," he laughs.

"It was nice meeting you, Nicholi, now fuck off." Alex grabs her drink, takes a sip and turns away from him. Cut off, Nicholi makes a derogatory comment under his breath that is drowned out by the music then skulks off looking for more prey.

Leaning with her back against the bar, sipping at her drink Alex observes her group dancing. The music pounds. The swell of clubbers cheer, laugh, dance and sing. The strobe lights flash and blind, turning everything to slow motion for split seconds. Between the strobe light freeze frame glitches, Alex sees Trente beckoning her to them. She gestures 'one minute' then turns to the bar to finish her drink. Catching her reflection in the mirror spanning the wall behind the bar she notices someone behind her. A pale, skinhead man in black combat style clothing with blood-red eyes stares at her in the mirror. A Renegade. An instant reaction, she bangs her drink on the bar, spinning around. He is gone. Alex scans the crowd. On high alert, she darts from the bar, barging through the crowd, drawing a gun she had concealed in her thigh – high boots. She grabs her coat from the booth, slips it on and from an inside pocket she draws her gun. She doesn't need to worry if her bullets are imbued with the Renegade's ligature, she knows they are, they always are. She looks to the dance floor – her group is unaware. She turns right to see another Renegade approach.

"Move!" she roars at a group of revellers blocking her shot. The Renegade draws a gun. The revellers panic and dash away. Alex shoots but misses. There are too many people. The Renegade returns fire. The blast of three gunshots startles the crowd. Alex darts for cover in the stairway. Panic breaks out in the club. Alex's group takes notice. Hopping up on to the railing Alex bounces around the pillar at the top if the stairs, hops from the next railing, landing behind the Renegade and shoots him in the head. Blood splatters the walls and clubbers in the splash zone. Screams ring out. The Renegade bursts into flames. The club descends into a chaotic frenzy. No one knows what is happening. Alex checks for cover then runs to her group.

"Alex! What's going on?" Danielle gasps. "Is it that guy again?"

"Renegades!" the group appears confused and rightly so, the Renegades had never attacked like this before. "Do any of you have weapons?" Trente, Ten and Danielle nod. "Imbued bullets?" She questions further. Trente, Ten and Danielle think then nod. "OK," Alex continues, "Danielle, come with me. Trente, Ten get to the streets, find Elaina!"

The music continues to pound as the clubbers in the immediate path of the incident scramble for an exit. Security staff step in to find the source of the commotion. Two more Renegades appear from among the frantic sea of clubbers who are scrambling for the exit.

"Shit!" Alex curses, raising her gun and firing. One Renegade uses a security guard as a shield. The security guard's eyes bulge as the bullet embeds itself in his heart. Blood gushes from the wound and then within seconds he bursts into flames and disintegrates on the ground. Ten immediately takes cover and fires. Trente grabs Alex.

"Go find Elaina!" Alex nods, glances into the blood-red eyes of the Renegades before grabbing Danielle and dashing for the nearest security exit.

As the two male members of the group engage the assailants, Alex and Danielle dash through the security exit and up a flight of stairs where they burst on to the rooftops, immediately scanning for danger. "Did she say where they were going?" Alex turns to Danielle as she hops to the edge of the building for a better view.

"No. But wait." Danielle gets her phone, using it to hack into Elaina's social media and her own mobile in an attempt to locate her.

"Come on, Danielle," Urges Alex as the phone continues to scan. Suddenly a map pops up. Danielle has managed to get a location for Elaina. She points to further down the alleyway, to the streets ahead.

"That way."

Without hesitation, Alex leaps from the rooftop on to the next. Drawing her gun, Danielle pursues. The pale blind eye of the moon emanates dully above them as they flit across the rooftops. On the ground below, human life continues in blissful ignorance. Flitting across the edge of the rooftops for a closer view of the streets below, the two preternatural soldiers close in on Elaina's position. As they leap to the next rooftop, the alleyways open up into a square. "Which way?" Alex scans. Danielle checks her phone. "That way." She points left towards a dark, quiet street beginning with a listed building, an old theatre in the process of restoration. It is the city's old quarter full of historical buildings and the National Museum. Danielle's forehead creases to a frown as she eyes the dark, cobbled street. Antique street lamps are the only source of light that cast a dull, yellow gloom on the street.

Without a word, Alex leaps from the lofty height of the rooftop and drops to the ground below, landing as light as a bird. Gun drawn she sneaks to the start of the street, sheltered behind the wall of the first building, an old-style sweet shop. Danielle quickly creeps to the wall of the old theatre. Two dark shapes have stopped in the street. Silhouetted by the dull lights they are still recognisable; it is Elaina…and Argon. Alex knows she cannot waste time on being tactful. There was just no time to lose. She barges out into the street, gun raised. Danielle follows suit. "Elaina, get away from him!" Alex shouts. Elaina who has been snuggling close to her date and flirting outrageously, on hearing Alex's voice turns around furiously.

"Alex, are you fucking kidding me? Have you lost your mind?"

"Elaina, I said get away from him!"

Elaina takes a step away from Argon only to stand in front of him to confront Alex.

"Alex, you are unbelievable! You are paranoid!"

"Elaina stop acting like a fucking teenager and listen to me!" Danielle's fear chills her blood. Alex's seriousness has rattled her, and she begs Elaina, "Please Elaina listen to her!" Elaina shakes her head in disbelief. However, before she can speak, Argon slides past her to approach his old friend with open arms.

"Alex Valentine. You leave me for dead then welcome me back with swords and guns." Elaina's jaw drops torn between jealously and shock. Argon, her date and Alex, her friend, know each other – they have a history. Danielle is equally taken back, making her momentarily lower her guard.

"Argon, do not take one more step or so help me God, I will shoot," Alex warns.

"God?" Argon stops just metres from her. "God can't hear us, Valentine. We are all alone. We are the outcasts of Heaven. The stain on Creation. But we Midnight Children are going to rectify the right of vampires to rule in this world." Elaina and Danielle are speechless. The man Elaina thought she knew has disappeared. The Alex both Elaina and Danielle thought they knew had just been made more suspect by this stranger's words.

Alex quickly scans the street for Renegades but can see no sign of Argon's bloody eyed henchmen. It is just him appearing as a ghost before her. His dark, tortured eyes, pale skin and dark aura have rendered him unrecognisable to his fellow Midnight Child and former companion. It dawns on her that her inability to cope with his death must have caused her to repress his memory almost entirely. Although she had never forgotten him, something in her mind had sought to protect her by shielding her from the truth. She hadn't recognised him because the Argon she had known and loved had been locked in her memory.

"Valentine, you're as beautiful as ever. Especially with that scar, I gave you."

"What do you want, Argon?" she grits her teeth.

"I want you to join my Crusade."

Alex laughs at his proposition. He moves closer to her, "We both want the same thing."

"And what would that be?" her gun remains on her target as he approaches, stopping only when he is centimetres from her weapon. The connection between them is magnetic. They are the moon and the sea. All she wants to do is throw her arms around him and never let go again. She wants to believe that the cruel past is gone and he has been returned to her to heal her wounds. But it is not to be. The change in him both pulls and repels her. Somewhere deep down, there is still love in both their hearts but somewhere deep and dark and unclear.

"Come on, Valentine, join me. Let's destroy the Authorities. Together again! We always worked so well as a team."

"And what would be your definition of destroy?" a smile creases across Argon's porcelain face revealing a glimmer of his fanged teeth. An attribute that still feels unnatural to Alex to observe on him. He shakes his head in a gesture that suggests she should already know the answer:

"You and I both know they don't deserve to live."

Alex's heart sinks. She had accepted the monster in herself, but she could not accept it in the man she once loved. She could see it now, physically, looking at him, she could see the Argon she had known and loved. However, in his eyes and his demeanour, her Argon was just a shadow. She considered for a moment that perhaps it wasn't that she had repressed his memory so deep that she had not recognised him, but perhaps she had not recognised him because she did not recognise the man he had become. Argon was talking about murder – a massacre – a massacre that wouldn't end with the Giovanni Authorities. She knew the Authorities needed to be destroyed, but Julius had a plan, an ethical, pragmatic plan; a plan she knew that Argon in his right mind would have joined in instantly. However, Argon was not in his right mind.

With a heavy heart, Alex speaks, "There was a time when I would have followed you anywhere. I would have followed you to Hell and never come back if you'd asked. But, I won't follow you now, Argon. I won't follow you into the dark." However, despite deep down knowing that Argon will not listen, Alex extends the offer in the vain hope that there is some shard of her Argon within him, "But join me. Abandon Belial and join me."

"Abandon Belial? The man who saved me? The Prophecy had me written off as a monster, something to be feared, derided and destroyed but Belial saw my potential. Without Belial, Julius would have the advantage. Julius would train you to kill me and you would succeed. All I would be, my life would merely be a stain on the Giovanni's history. A bug crushed upon a page." Argon smirks bitterly. Alex has no words or rather, she has too many. All her words, trying to escape at once, clog her throat. Elaina creeps closer in an effort to observe more clearly and understand the silence that has befallen Alex, a silence to her that seems incriminating. Danielle's hands tremble on her gun. She can't judge what way this will turn out.

Finally, Alex accepts that there is no going back. She aims her gun at Argon's heart, "So this is it then? This is the way it's going to be?"

"Are you going to kill me, Valentine?" his voice is slow, alluring. Alex longs for him and he for her but bitterness divides them. Alex forces words through her clenched fangs.

"I will not let Belial and the Ronakites take over Bodmin. I will not let the Hall of Vampires be ruled by more savages and thugs."

"Why would you protect the Authorities? The Giovanni Authorities who have betrayed me? That led you to betray me? You would save them and kill me?" Argon presses his chest against the gun. Alex's lip trembles as she grits her teeth, fighting back her emotion.

"I never wanted it to be this way!" she screams, "I don't want to kill you!"

"Doesn't matter." He places his hands on the trigger and quicker than Alex can react he pulls. The booming blast of the bullet echoes throughout the street. Elaina and Danielle scream. Alex's eyes bulge and she drops the gun. What has he done? Argon is silent for a moment, doubled over, his right hand over his heart. Then, he straightens, revealing his blood-stained hand. Other than that he is unharmed. "You'll leave a scar on my heart, Valentine. But now you see, you can't kill me. Not yet. Nor I you." Before Alex can react, he turns her gun on her and shoots Alex in the heart.

Again, the streets echo with the boom of the gunshot and the screams of Danielle and Elaina who for all their training as soldiers are reduced to instinctive fear. Alex doubles over. The blow has winded her. Pain ravages her chest just long enough to cripple her to submission then dissipates. She stumbles then rises. Argon tosses the gun at her feet. "We could be locked like this for eternity, Valentine." He moves towards Elaina, with a gentle hand outstretched. "No hard feelings?"

"You used me," Elaina's voice quivers.

"Not without reason. I needed to send a message." He steps close to her. The darkness of his presence in contrast to Elaina's pretty face, pale pink dress and blonde hair make her appear human. At his proximity to her friend, Danielle once again raises her gun at Argon. "Argon. Step away from her." She warns. Alex moves closer.

"Argon don't touch her!" Alex screams. Elaina flinches as he moves around her.

"Elaina, Alex isn't who you think she is." Argon whispers in her ear as a demon sowing doubt. "You only think she loves you, but she would do anything to save herself. Isn't that right, Valentine?" Argon turns to her. Ignoring him, Alex looks into Elaina's tear-filled eyes brimming with fear and doubt.

"Argon, please. Don't do this." Alex knows what is coming and is powerless to stop him.

"What, Alex? What do you think I'd do?" he pauses. Sickness fills Alex's stomach like a knife in the gut. Suddenly, Argon pushes Elaina out in front of him as he draws a sword from beneath his coat and plunges it through Elaina's back, piercing straight through her heart.

"No!" Alex screams. Danielle screams, dropping her gun and dropping to her knees. Elaina's eyes bulge. Blood gushes from her mouth. She chokes.

"Was it this?" Argon pauses. In the blackness of his eyes, Alex sees in that instant that all trace of her Argon is gone. The monster he spoke of has taken possession. He pushes Elaina from his sword with one hand and pulls back with the other, drawing his bloodstained sword from her body. Elaina stumbles forward as blood gushes from the wound. She chokes for breath as more blood clogs her throat. She falls to her knees. As flames engulf her body, the girls look on in horror. Argon disappears into the darkness as Elaina's body is consumed in flames.

The streets fall silent. On her knees, Danielle sobs, shocked and horrified. Tears stream down Alex's face as she timidly approaches the charred shell that was her friend. She kneels on the cobbled ground, reaching a gentle hand out to touch Elaina's immortal remains. Dust to dust. Too many emotions fill Alex's saturated mind. She wants to grieve for Elaina's death but already knows this is all her fault. All she feels is guilt. Elaina died because of her, and she knows it's only a matter of time before Danielle realises this too. Will the seeds of mistrust that Argon dared to plant in Elaina's mind before he cruelly murdered her find a place to grow in Danielle?

As the hot embers of Elaina's remains slip between her fingers, Alex fails to find words. She had already grieved for Argon. The Argon she loved had died. She knew she would never recover from it but she had accepted that he was gone.

Yet, he was not gone, not physically anyway. Now he stands before her, a dark phantom-like figure from a nightmare.

A soft breeze blows Elaina's ashes along the street. But, the girls have no time to grieve as the piercing wail of sirens fill the air. The gunshots and screams have gained public attention. "Shit." Alex curses under her breath, dashing across the street to grab her gun. She races back to Danielle, grabbing her arm, urging her to her feet. "Dani, we have to get out of here."

"We can't leave her here," Danielle sobs.

"Dani there's nothing left." Danielle shrugs Alex off and rips a thick strip of her top off then hastily scrapes up as much of Elaina's remains as she can, wrapping them in the material. "It's not much, but she deserves some sort of burial, some acknowledgement than just left on the street like dirt." Danielle insists. Alex looks to the material filled with Elaina's remains and nods. "You're right. But we really have to go." Alex drags her away into darkness of the nearest alleyway.

No sooner have Alex and Danielle made their escape that an ambulance and police cars arrive on the scene in a frenzy of red and blue lights. However, they find no crime. All that is found is a dark, deserted street where the soft breeze blows away any evidence of violence.

Chapter 19

The streets are rammed as a contentious march moves through the affluent quarter of the city. Here the historic and intricately designed buildings host financial companies, solicitor's offices, architects' offices, five-star hotels, political institutions, banks etc. Police line the streets as the protestors campaign against government corruption, poverty and class divide. Businessmen stand in the doorways of the secured buildings to observe the mayhem.

The street is a sea of red as crowds of marchers parade along the thronged street chanting socialist slogans and waving banners and flags. Party supporters brandish election posters of party elects that include Alex and Argon. Mounted police fight to control their horses amidst the raucous crowd. Armoured riot vans attend the event where the riot squad with batons and shields await intervention.

Two young students film the rally on their phones. A rowdy protestor attempts to spray-paint a socialist slogan on a bank wall but is quickly arrested. At the front of the march, Alex and Argon take the lead to promote their agenda, moving towards a platform to make their speeches. As the main speakers take their positions on the platform, Alex and Argon glance at each other delightedly. As they halt at the foot of the platform, Argon squeezes his partner's hand, "We can do this, we're winning," he kisses her softly.

"Argon, we did it," Alex clutches him tightly, "Look around you. We are in government. The people are behind us. The tide has turned," she beams.

Behind them, shielded by shadows they are being watched by a predator – a vampire. Julius Silverstone observes the ringleaders from the cramped crowd with a concerned expression. He watches them kiss and celebrate as the crowd of raucous marchers file in around them. As the noise levels escalate, Julius slips back into the crowd and disappears.

Alex and Argon had always been together. For as long as they could remember, it had always been the two of them. They had grown up in a monastery in the South of France. There they were educated predominantly by an old teacher who prioritised philosophy and ethics above all else. Why they were in a monastery had always been a mystery to them. Any questions on the matter were never answered. So, when they were old enough they left, travelled anywhere they felt like going until they received word of the death of their former guardian. The news came while they were in Dublin and it came as a wakeup call. With so much of their life a mystery to them, they decided perhaps it was time to make a life rather than running the world for answers.

With funds in short supply, Alex began to work in a local bar pulling pints while Argon worked in a munitions factory. They worked long hours to cover the rent in their basic apartment above their local bar where she worked. The apartment block was nothing more than a neglected tenement block for the working class. Mostly inhabited by those on and off benefits, separated families, families who just about made it by and elderly residents. Among these were those who felt let down by 'the system'. Alex frequently met the residents and others in similar situations down in the bar as she worked.

Alex and Argon were educated – all they had had in life was education – their teacher had been adamant they should be well versed in all the great texts. Now, while working in the bar, engaged by the trials of the working class, Alex took an active interest and formulated an agenda with Argon to create a campaign strategy and eventually a party. Alex believed that the government had a policy of choosing nature over nurture. Those in power seemed to believe that those who committed crimes and those who didn't 'achieve' – it was just their nature to do so and thus they were left to rot in the lowest level of the socio-economic pyramid of society. Alex ardently believed that this needed to be changed and so she vowed to work for the rights of workers and for a fairer distribution of wealth, for more transparency within the government and to create more employment and educational opportunities for the young.

Argon was always at her side in everything. He believed in Alex's passion, and he knew that if he supported and encouraged her, they could achieve anything because they had each other. One was nothing without the other. And, so together they canvassed for support. Starting small at first they recruited those within their immediate vicinity and used them to outsource. They held meetings and liaised with likeminded individuals in positions of power – particularly the media to promulgate their agenda. They were young, but they were passionate, and they were clever and prolific, and this meant that they drew hordes of supporters within a very short space of time. Within a year, having created bonds with various charities and organisations they had created non-profit food banks and youth clubs. Within five years, they had effectively undermined every government policy and shown them for fools. The people warmed to their empathy, to their opinions and to their unflinching devotion. Eventually, the government had to acknowledge their influence within the community. Alex and Argon's Socialist Party were encouraged to stand for election. And they took it by storm.

Alex and Argon couldn't imagine a life without each other. They had always loved each other; they had always been aware of this. If anyone showed hostility or aggression to Alex, Argon was there to defend and vice versa. They were inseparable. Always the rebels, they had always proved popular within the so-called 'outcasts'– gothic and grunge kids in particular. If Argon liked a girl, Alex always put in a good word for him and again, vice versa. However, if Alex and Argon were in a club and a guy was pestering Alex, Argon would step in. Argon knew Alex could handle herself, but that was their deal, and she did the same for him. Alex was growing into a beautiful woman and Argon into a handsome man, and so they were often objectified and targeted with unwanted attention. There was just something different about them.

As they grew older and entered the 'real' world, dating became an option – it was a societal norm. Alex and Argon would go to clubs together where they met friends. Alex dated a few guys and Argon a few girls but no relationships manifested into anything meaningful. Until one day, Argon came to the sudden realisation that the reason no relationship proved meaningful was because none of these girls were Alex.

Neither had wanted to admit it to themselves before that they would get jealous if one brought a date home. However, Argon couldn't fight it anymore. Terrified but knowing Alex would be understanding even if it were a rejection Argon decided he needed to tell Alex how he felt. He knew he would have to make the first move – Alex buried her feelings deep. He knew this was mostly to protect those she loved and to spare them from unwanted knowledge.

Going to Alex this night, Argon had never been so nervous. It was such an alien feeling to him. This was Alex – this was his Alex. Hiding in the bathroom, gathering his thoughts and emotions he brushed back his undercut dark brown hair away from his face before rolling back the sleeves of his crisp white shirt and splashing cold water over his flushed sun-kissed face trying to cool down. His nerves were burning, prickling his skin. Uncomfortable, he loosened his collar around his neck where his tattoo sleeve ended on his left side. Taking a deep breath, he looked at himself in the mirror, deep into his dark ocean eyes and exhaled slowly. A buzzing sound signalled a text as it appeared on his phone that was sitting on a shelf above the sink. Reluctantly, Argon acknowledged it. Opening the text, he saw that it was from Abigail, a girl he had been dating for the last month. With a heavy heart, he read, "So what? Is that it?" he didn't answer. He couldn't. He hated the idea of hurting the girl, but he couldn't bear for the break up to string out any longer by getting into an argument with her or worse, an explanation. All the girls he had ever dated had been jealous of Alex – they envied her relationship with Argon and were always intimidated by her beauty.

Unlocking the bathroom door he emerged, expecting to find his companion in the living room sorting party leaflets where he had left her but she was gone. "Alex?" he called as he moved down the hallway. No answer. He checked her bedroom, but she was nowhere to be seen. He paced back into the living room/kitchen staring at the tidily arranged party leaflets, campaign posters and forms on the coffee table. After a moment the apartment door opened and in she walked with a shopping bag and a pizza.

"Oh, I thought you were going out with Abigail?" Alex asked when she saw him.

"No," he shook his head. "I changed my mind," Feeling his anxiety, Alex enquired.

"Is everything OK?" Argon hesitated then shook his head. He was cute in an awkward sort of way. She knew he'd come around when he was ready, and she had just the way to settle him, "Well, I thought I was home alone tonight and expecting to be a total pig which I shouldn't be anyway. So 'mon have a drink, help me tackle this bad boy and if you want to talk about it then talk about it." She passed him the pizza box before producing a bottle of whiskey from the bag. Conflicted, Argon accepted while Alex went to get two glasses. Moving to the sofa and flicking on the TV, the words were on the tip of his tongue but fearing he'd pick the wrong moment or say what he wanted to say and get the wrong reaction he chose to hold back.

Alex was going to fill the glasses at the kitchen but when she saw how nervous Argon appeared she abandoned that idea and just brought the bottle over and filled the glasses there before extending one to Argon who accepted and was obligated to 'chink'. "Slainte," said Alex. For a moment, Argon just studied the glass in his hand, swirling the contents. Alex said nothing. Clearly, her friend was in some sort of turmoil that he had to brood over. She wouldn't push him for an answer until he was ready. Perhaps a drink would help. Grabbing a slice a pizza and taking a drink, Alex kicks off her boots and curls up beside him on the sofa. "Right, what are we watching?" she asks. Argon laughs.

"You're actually letting me pick?"

"What?"

"You must feel sorry for me."

"No, I don't," she lies.

"What were you going to watch when I wasn't here?" asked Argon, waiting for her to lie and say she was going to watch something good.

"I don't know I was thinking Rambo or something. What do you think?" she lies through her teeth.

"You're full of shit, Valentine," Argon teases.

"I am not," Alex blushed, knowing fine rightly he could see right through her.

"You were going to watch pure trash, weren't you?"

"Was not."

"Spit it out."

"No."

"Aleeeeex."

"Fiiiine," she blushes again, flicking the channel to Sex and the City.

"I fucking knew it," Argon judges her as she giggles, busted.

"It's not trash!" she defended, but Argon rolls his eyes. "You'll see," she turned up the volume. "I suppose we're having a girls' night then. Fuck me." Argon kicks off his shoes and grabs some pizza.

The next couple of hours were everything he needed to settle his nerves. Slouched there on the sofa watching TV feeling completely comfortable with Alex was all he ever wanted. No one could ever compare. Finally, as the hours passed and the clock crept towards the early hours of the following day, Alex brought it up. "So, what happened?" Argon could feel the tension gripping his stomach again, but he knew he had to say it. He couldn't let it go on any longer.

"Alex, I don't want to go out with Abigail. I don't want to go out with anyone. It just doesn't feel right."

"Are you coming out to me?" she teased, causing Argon to laugh nervously at her question. "It's OK if you are. You're my best friend." She comforts him although she was really hoping for her own desires he wasn't.

"That's the problem, Alex. You're my best friend."

"So?"

"So…" he hesitated, knowing if she didn't feel the same, he would be lost. These feelings had been growing for a long time. They wouldn't depart so easily through lack of reciprocation. "Alex, I love you," he finally confessed.

"I love you too." Argon shook his head, she hadn't understood.

"No, Alex. I'm in love with you." The words whisper from his lips so honestly that Alex is stuck by their purity and simplicity. She knew that Argon would never speak without deep thought. He would only speak what he truly believed and truly felt. The implications of this confession meant that she would have to accept her own feelings – a mental and emotional act which she was not comfortable with.

By Alex's silence, Argon feared he had upset her. "I'm sorry, Alex, I shouldn't have said anything."

"No. No. I just… I never thought…" her sentence trailed off as their eyes met. She stared into Argon's honest, innocent eyes, longing to say the words but was rendered speechless by the onslaught of emotion in her mind and gut.

"I shouldn't have said anything," Argon whispered, fearing he'd ruined everything and removed himself from the sofa to give her space.

Alex could not find the words. All she could do was look to him as he leaned on the counter, attempting to process his thoughts. He was everything she wanted but could this be the happy ending she had always dreamed of? Or would it be the death of the dream if it all fell apart? She and Argon had always been together. She had always known that she'd loved him, but this was different. This was romantic love. This would put them in a romantic relationship. This could ruin them. Her biggest fear was losing him, her best friend and now possibly, her lover… But, she did love him. She wanted him in every form. She knew they belonged together. She knew she couldn't be parted from him. "I love you," she finally uttered, rising from the sofa. The confession was partly an acknowledgement to herself. Argon felt a weight lift from his shoulders as she approached him. There were no more words. She just allowed him to pull her close in a long embrace.

After a moment she felt Argon's hands slide around her waist. His forehead rested on her shoulder. The touch was delicate but so relieving. She relaxed into it. All tension left as she finally accepted the feel of his warm body against her. "So what does this mean?" she whispered, "Where do we go from here?" her eyes closed as a light gasp emitted from her lips from the tingling sensation of a soft kiss on her neck.

"Remember what you always said, Alex?" she could feel his breath on her neck and slowly she looked up to face him, looking deep into his sapphire blue eyes. "You always said, 'to hell with the world – as long as there's you and me, that's all we need." Pulling him closer, they kissed, soft to start, still nervous at this new sensation. Butterflies fluttered in their stomachs. However, within moments, their kiss had deepened. As Alex was pressed against the cabinet by Argon's body, her hands slid up his sculpted back. She gasped again as Argon became more comfortable, more confident, sliding his hands upwards from her waist along her spine. The moment was escalating and it felt right.

Finding the collar of his shirt, Alex began to undo the buttons on Argon's shirt just enough so that she could pull it from his toned body. Alex had started it, so Argon went for it. Argon's former nervousness was obliterated as their bodies connected. All former fears and doubts Alex had felt were quickly cast aside as she felt Argon's skin against hers. She loved him. She always had done. And when Argon looked into her smouldering gaze, he knew that his heart belonged to her entirely – forever. He would die for her.

The transition to being a couple was easy. After the initial confession life continued as normal. Until one day, that changed everything.

Alex was lying in bed, half asleep. The shimmering beams of summer sunlight twinkled in through a slit in the curtains. Curled up within the blanket, Alex could sense she was being watched. "Stop looking at me, you creep," she muttered with her eyes partly opened.

"I can't help it," Argon laughed, caught out. He sunk back down on the bed as Alex, snuggled closer to him. He embraced the moment and savoured it – the touch of her skin as her leg entwined around his and her body pressed against him; the fresh rose scent of her soft hair that shone like an obsidian stone in the sunlight.

Running his fingers up her leg, the firm curvature of her body beckoned him. Rolling on top, he bent down to kiss her pale skin. Never in her life had Alex ever felt so complete. As his kisses reached the delicate skin of her neck, she couldn't wait any longer, taking his head in her hands to kiss him and pull his body down upon hers. "Never leave me." She whispers.

"I'm not going anywhere." He promises, "I couldn't live without you."

It had been almost a year since they had decided to be together as a couple. Their party was going from strength to strength so much so that they had just been elected to parliament. Argon had decided that once the chaos of their working political lives had died down that he would propose to Alex. They had never talked of marriage and it was an idea Argon was sure Alex had never even considered but to be able to call this woman his wife filled his heart with indescribable joy. He had always imagined Alex being in his life – he had never known a life without her. He wanted to grow old with her. He wanted to give her everything he could. He wanted to do everything he could to protect her. He already had the ring carefully concealed in a box in his bottom beside drawer. However, that morning he took it and placed it in the inside pocket of his coat above his heart. He had planned to propose to Alex after the finale of their election campaign – a Citizen's March through the city later that evening. In the days to follow, at the right moment, he would ask Alex to be his wife.

Later that night as the crowd of socialist party marchers marched down Kildare Street towards Leinster House where journalists and news reporters with TV cameras flocked, tension was growing. Politicians and business types had gathered around to observe the spectacle, cast taunts and sneer as the speakers made their speeches. As the party reps including Alex and Argon turned right into Molesworth Street, the journalists and news reporters flocked closer.

Some drunken politicians had stumbled out from the Shelbourne Hotel around the corner with the aim to stand and judge the party of underdogs who had dared to challenge the system – and succeed. A makeshift stage had been created by an open HGV. The party members took seats on the stage while Alex took to the microphone to introduce the main speakers. Quickly, the street was flooded with a crowd that surpassed anything they believed they could have assembled. No sooner had Alex introduced the main speakers to a chorus of cheers and the party Chairman, a sixty-two-year-old socialist veteran called James was making his speech that the drunken businessmen began to antagonise.

Those in their nearest vicinity attempted to ignore them at first. Then, they tried to tell them to 'catch themselves on' but it was no use. A group of young male socialists offered to politely remove the businessmen from the area, but the businessmen were more than pleased to treat and accept this as the fight they instigated. Seeing the fight about to happen, the Gardai moved in.

As the squabble intensified more police stepped in, but instead of intercepting the fight, they exacerbated it by hustling the protestors from the crowd of marchers and dragging them to the armoured vans. Seeing the biased behaviour, more marchers joined the conflict. James cut short his speech in the middle of making some solid points about the housing crisis to plead with the marchers to remain calm. The news cameras pushed closer towards the scene, antagonising the situation. Soon the shouts and roars rose within the sea of red flags and banners.

As the police continued with their heavy-handed tactics, a group of young male marchers began to taunt them – accusing them of protecting the rich and ridiculing their numbers and weapons to monitor what was intended to be a peaceful demonstration. One young man who had had too much to drink hurled a beer can at the riot squad. As the riot squad moved in to detain him, a squabble broke out. A police officer was injured in the fray and as a result, more police were called in and the violence escalated.

James is forced away from the microphone as bottles are hurled towards the stage. Alex and Argon are appalled as they observe the news cameras swarming around the now violent scene. Their former exhilaration had quickly turned to outrage. “Fuck this shit.” Alex makes a start towards the microphone, Argon reaches out to grab her arm but just misses her. However, James grabs her as he retreats to the back of the lorry. His grip is forceful but protective as he urges her towards Argon.

“Do not feed the dogs,” he warns.

“But James, this is exactly what they want! The media is going to ruin us!”

“There’s nothing you can do,” he insisted.

Despite his warning, and despite knowing he was right, the urge to intervene was causing Alex’s heart to pound in her chest. Seeing a police officer produce a baton, Alex again darts forward, however, this time she is dragged back by both arms by Argon and James. Before her, missiles pelt the stage. She turns to Argon and James, who says, “Get out of here, you two.” Argon knew not to argue, but Alex being Alex couldn’t resist.

“James, no. We can’t.”

“The police are going to shut us down and if you intervene, if you do anything that’s exactly what they want. Arresting you will be a triumph for them.

Go. I will handle this." His words rested uneasily in Alex but she accepted his reason, looking to Argon for reassurance. He knew this was killing her – but she knew James was right. He'd been doing this gig for forty-five years. Although she was reluctant to follow his orders and abandon her post, James had been her mentor when she first began campaigning – she trusted his judgement. Accepting with a begrudging nod she allowed Argon to lead her from the riotous crowd.

Clutching Alex's hand, Argon dragged her from the crowd where they raced into the gloomy backstreets where the noise of the crowd gradually faded to muffled roars, cries, crashes and bangs. Sheltered from the commotion Alex stopped suddenly in the gloom of an alleyway between two old graffiti stained Edwardian houses. Hearing her halt, Argon turned warily. "This is wrong," she spits, kicking the wall. Argon knew there was nothing he could say to comfort her – he felt the same way. "I'm going back." Her decision was instant. She started off back towards the fight. "Alex!" Argon hissed darting after her. Although he agreed with her – he wanted to be there too but more than that he wanted to protect her from ending up in a jail cell and also from the potential physical violence.

However, as Alex approached the top of the alley a man appeared. Alex stopped in her tracks. Dressed all in black from head to toe in an expensive suit and black gloves with pale corpse-like skin and deep green eyes with an inhuman gleam, the man stilled an immediate chill in Alex's veins. James had warned her that it was common practice for threatened parties to send 'hitmen' to their opponents to send a message – basically an offer they couldn't refuse. It seemed likely to her that this man had been sent to shut her up. "Alex Valentine," the man stated her name so matter of the fact that she hypothesised that her hitman theory was correct. Fearing the same, Argon slipped his hand into Alex's, urging her backwards. It wasn't the first time someone had been sent to sabotage their efforts.

"Come on, Alex." Argon pulled her backwards.

"Alex Valentine we need to talk," the man stated, stepping forward.

"Not a chance, mate!" Argon shouted, forcing Alex in the opposite direction and forcing her to run.

As they ran into the next street, sirens wailed as police cars whizzed past on the road towards the march that has descended into chaos in the business quarter. Seeing an old, dilapidated townhouse, Argon saw an opportunity to take cover from the threat and broke through the bottom window. Jumping through, he turned to help Alex through after him. The flashing lights of police vehicles flitted past the window as Alex took cover in the gloom of the abandoned building. "Come on." Argon led Alex through the neglected formerly affluent dwelling. It was just like the former residents vanished leaving everything behind – a ghost house. Pictures remained on the grimy walls of peeling wallpaper. Dust and cobwebs sat thick on the tables, chairs and shelves. Alex observed the remnants of former family life as they passed across the rotten, creaking floorboards into the hallways. Stopping in the entrance hall, Argon turned to Alex protectively, "Wait here. I'm gunna make sure there's no one in here." Kissing her cheek he crept off and disappeared into the next room.

Alex remained for a moment in the silence, listening to the ambient noise. The house creaked and groaned as Argon's footsteps tread on its ancient bones. Naturally curious, Alex was drawn to the spindled staircase and began to ascend carefully as not to cause the building more pain. Stepping from the staircase to the landing, she treads carefully towards a spacious bedroom, now just a neglected shell with torn voile curtains fluttering in the broken windows.

Hearing a creak behind her, she turned her eyes to a large broken crucifix lying on an old rustic dressing table. Above this part of a poem had been engraved into mildew – smudged mirror – 'The Stolen Child' by W.B Yeats. Alex read it aloud in a whisper as she wiped the gunk from the engraving, "Come away, O human child, to the waters and the wild, with a faerie hand in hand, for the world's more full of weeping than you can understand." She pondered the words and their meaning for a moment – they had struck a chord within her, a chord that hit a note in her heart that reverberated through her body. She shivered at the feeling of an icy cold chill down her back – as if someone had walked over her grave, as the saying goes.

Shaking the feeling from her body, she began to study the old perfume bottles and various female effects before easing open the old drawers of the dressing table to find old handwritten letters barely legible due to the degradation of time. As she sifted through the letters, she began to notice something out of the corner of her eye. Glancing to the mirror, she caught sight of a man standing behind her, a sight that provoked instant panic in her. She jumped to her feet in defence. It was the man from the alley. She hadn't even heard him enter. Surely his feet would have caused the floorboards to creak. She glanced to the door, her only escape route. "It's all right." The man assured her however, it was a hollow statement to her. He stepped forward. Alex shifted towards the door. "Alex, you are in serious danger." The man warned.

"Who sent you?" her voice quivered.

"Alex, someone is coming for you. You need to listen to me. We need to talk but not here."

"For fuck sake! You're all so afraid of sharing power! Who sent you? We were elected legally! You can't shut us up!"

"Alex, it's not about the party. You need to understand." Julius' statement was cut off as Argon, upon hearing Alex shouting, called to her. Alex hesitated. She did not want to acknowledge Argon's call for fear that a reply would draw him towards danger. Trembling, she challenged the man before her.

"Who are you?" the man stepped forward again. "My name is Julius Silverstone." The name startled Alex. She knew that name. She had known it all her life. He approached, "I'm not here for politics. I'm not here to hurt you. I'm here to save you."

"Who is coming for me?"

"Alex? Alex, where are you?" Argon's voice called from downstairs. The sound of his hurried footsteps caused Alex's heart to pound. She decided that if this man was here to kill her he would have done it by now, so she decided to respond to Argon's call.

"I'm upstairs, Argon!"

"Alex, you need to listen to me. Come with me. I'll explain later." Julius stepped forward again. Alex held up her hand as a gesture for him to stop, "Who is after me? Tell me now."

"Alex, where are you?" Argon called again, his voiced now closer. Alex heard his footsteps clatter up the stairs. "Soon you will understand, Alex. I'm sorry." Alex is confused by Julius' statement but feeling the seriousness in his tone a sinking feeling arose in the pit of her stomach.

Faster than Alex could comprehend, Julius was upon her. He grabbed her tight to sink a pair of razor-sharp fangs into her neck. As the blood was drained from her body, she fell limp, defenceless. She was too weak to fight him. This is it she thought. Just as everything was going right in her turbulent life, she was going to die. As the energy left her body, her head hung on her shoulders. As her strength gave out, she slumped to her knees with Julius releasing his grip to set her down. She was barely conscious but just alive enough to see Argon appear in the doorway. "Alex!" he exclaimed, panic-stricken at the sight. It was the last sound she heard before she collapsed to the floor.

Argon immediately shot towards Julius, hurling him against the wall. Julius did not fight him. He could have defeated him easily but wanted to see Argon up close. He wanted to feel his aura to verify his doubts. Argon raised his fist to strike the attacker but hesitated as their eyes locked. Argon immediately realised that this man was not natural. This man was not of this world. Terrified by the intensity of Julius' unusual hazel-gold vampire eyes, his fear was further reinforced as within the vampire's unnatural eyes he caught a fleeing image of himself screaming in agony as the monster he would come to know as Belial tears into his neck. Gasping in horror, Argon relinquished his grasp, stumbling back in disbelief. "I'm sorry, Argon. I can't save you," whispered Julius.

Argon remained horrified as the Julius moved to the broken window. "We'll meet again." Julius' words chilled Argon to the core, and he was left in a state of shock and despair as the man jumped from the window, leaving the cancerous mutation of vampirism to ravage Alex's body. He had to do this. Belial was coming. He had to intervene. He had to take control and speed up the Midnight Child's metamorphosis. He had to force Alex's body to turn. He didn't have the strength to turn both of them in one night but having seen into Argon's eyes and into his soul, Julius knew that there was no saving Argon. It was his destiny to fall to Belial. Julius could smell the sickness in his blood. Even if he did 'awaken' him, Argon would always have turned to Belial.

Argon stood in shock in the silent, sombre aftermath of violence. The ragged curtains flickered in the broken windows. Suddenly, snapping back to reality, he rushed to Alex who lay lifeless on the rotten wooden floor. Cradling her in his arms, tears streamed down his face. The thought of losing her was too much to bear. Barely conscious, her eyes fluttered, and her neck was smeared in blood. "Alex, wake up. Wake up, Alex. Alex, please wake up. Please don't leave me," he begged her, clutching her close as he quickly dialled the number for an ambulance. He was not about to lose her and if he did, his only thought was that he would have to die too.

Argon had remained by Alex's side all day in the intensive care unit of the hospital. On the table beside the bed rested a daily newspaper, the front-page story of which has been dedicated to the 'violent and disastrous march' and that 'ringleader Alex Valentine was subsequently rushed to hospital after being involved in a brawl at the protest'. The truth had been subject to much creative licensing. Argon had expected the onslaught of media bias, but he never imagined how deep it could cut him in the midst of everything that had happened that night. Turbulent thoughts thundered in his mind as the machines beeped and nurses carried out their duties. With his eyes dark and heavy with pain, Argon watched Alex breathe, her chest rising and falling slowly. His best friend, the love of his life was on a life support machine. He couldn't believe it. Everything had changed so suddenly. He couldn't process it. The doctors couldn't process it either. They had never seen anything like it. He feared they would ask him to make a decision, a decision he couldn't make. He couldn't bear the thought of letting her go. If she had to leave this world, he would have to go with her.

Earlier the doctor had come to check on Alex's condition. "It's a miracle she's still alive," he had told Argon to his great despair. "She's strong, but her body needs to produce more blood before there's any permanent damage, at the least. But with the amount of blood she's lost, her body will not be able to replenish that quickly." His diagnosis felt condemning. Argon couldn't cope with it. He couldn't hold back his tears.

"What about a transplant?"

"She has a very rare blood type. So rare in fact that it isn't a type."

"What do you mean?"

"Her blood group doesn't exist. I have never seen anything like this. I've called in an expert for advice because it's a situation I have never encountered the like of in my life." The doctor's pessimistic tone was so hopeless it only furthered Argon's despair.

"Try me." He was desperate to save her, "I don't know what group I am. Please. I'll try anything." The doctor seemed reluctant. He lifted a chart from the bottom of the bed.

"We need to keep her stable." He passed the chart to Argon to read. "In her condition, I do not want to cause her body any more stress." He watched as Argon's eyes widened in horror. He gasped and looked to Alex then to the doctor as the doctor returned the chart to the bottom of the bed, "We need to keep her stable. We don't want to lose both of them."

Argon couldn't believe it. Alex was pregnant. He was going to be a father. No. He thought bitterly. No. He would not let them be taken away from him. "Try me. I'll do anything." The doctor nodded, understandingly, "Come with me." Before following the doctor, Argon kissed Alex on her forehead and glanced down to her belly, imagining the fragile life that was growing inside her.

Wiping away his tears, he hurried off with the doctor. This had to work, he thought. He craved the thought of being a father. He longed to be able to call Alex his wife. His entire life, his entire world hung in the balance. He would not lose everything.

To the doctor's absolute incomprehension, Argon's blood matched. The doctor stood in his office comparing Alex and Argon's charts, and when he returned to the ward to tell Argon the news, he honestly didn't know if it was good or bad. He had never in thirty years of working in medicine came across such a case. "It is a match," he told Argon, a statement that filled Argon's heart with hope but he quickly considered the implications of the results. Both he and Alex had exactly the same rare blood type.

"What does that mean?" he asked.

"It means that both of you have an alien blood group. In fact you have alien DNA." The doctor was matter-of-fact, but Argon could see the perplexity on his face as he continued to study the results. The doctor pulled the curtains closed and folded his arms, a gesture that troubled Argon intensely. "Not only do you and Alex have the same alien blood and alien DNA, yours are exactly the same." The doctor's words induced a sickness in Argon's stomach.

"Does that mean…we're…related?" he asked, not really wanting an answer. The doctor shook his head, letting out a sigh.

"Not even identical twins have the exact same DNA. You do. Not even identical twins have the same fingerprints. You do. I am having the results further analysed because going by these results you are not twins, you're exactly the same person." Argon had absolutely no idea what the doctor meant by this and didn't bother asking because he had a feeling the doctor didn't know what this meant either. "I'll be back later when we've looked into this further. You should go home and get some rest. She'll be well taken care of."

Argon nodded as the doctor departed; however, he had no intention of going home. He would not leave Alex's side. The doctor's bafflement disturbed him. If the doctor couldn't make sense of the information, how could Argon? He tried to think back as far as he could. He tried to think of where they had come from, but he had very little knowledge. He had grown up in the Institute. That was all he could remember. He knew they were not related. They had different birthdays, so they weren't twins. They were born in two separate places. He had seen their records once when he went snooping in the monastery. He had seen their birth certificates. Argon's train of thought stopped in its tracks. Both he and Alex had a guardian, a trustee who they had never met. Someone called Julius Silverstone had been privately funding them and signing off on their medical forms and anything else that was required. The birth certificates had a strange seal on them, a sort of brand. Also, on everything signed by the elusive Julius he would stamp the page with the same crest – Giovanni. Argon's mind raced. Was it plausible that he and Alex were somehow part of a cult? What if their parents had been part of a cult and had been killed and thus they were entrusted to the care of Julius? Argon had given himself a headache. He thought too much and cried too much. He needed to rest. Leaving the curtain closed, he slumped into the chair beside Alex again and watched her as he let the weight of his exhaustion pull him to sleep.

As the clock hit midnight, Alex shot awake. Panic-stricken by her surroundings and the wires she had been hooked to she quickly scrambled to free herself. Woken by the commotion, Argon jolted awake. Seeing Alex, he immediately darted to calm her. "Alex! Alex!" he soothed her from her confusion. Looking deep into her eyes, he could see they had changed. Even in the clinical gloom of the ward, he could see that her usual dark ocean blue eyes were now tinged with green with a back ring around the iris. He remembered the unnatural eyes of the man who had attacked her. He wanted to attribute the change to stress, but something within him told him something was wrong. "How do you feel?" he asked quietly.

"Like shit," she took his hand softly.

"I've been so worried." He watched her in silence. For a moment they just gazed into each other's eyes, relieved to be together but sharing the knowledge that they were not out of danger yet. Eventually, Argon touched Alex's stomach. "When were you going to tell me?" Tears filled Alex's eyes as she looked back to Argon.

"When everything had calmed down," she laughed bitterly. "Argon, promise me. Promise me that if anything happens to me, you'll save the baby."

"Alex, I…"

"Argon, promise me."

"I promise." It was a grim vow. It tied him to a situation he didn't even want to consider. "How long have you known?"

"About three weeks."

"Three weeks? Why didn't you say?"

"I wanted to tell you when the election and everything was over. When there was nothing else to think about."

Alex was quiet. Her mind was in torment. Argon had wanted to wait for the perfect moment but now finding out that he was going to be a father, he wanted to be a family. Digging his hand into his pocket, he produced the ring box. He was nervous again, like the night he told her he loved her. "Argon?" Alex gasped at the sight of the box. "I've had this for a while," he started.

"Alex, I love you. I always have. I want us to be together forever. I want to call you, my wife. I want us to be a family." Alex started to cry. Her mind was awash with emotion. "I want to spend the rest of our crazy lives together. Will you marry me?" Alex nodded through her tears.

"Of course, I will."

It was a platinum trilogy ring with three white diamonds and inside was engraved the word, 'forever'. Slipping the ring on her finger, Argon leaned in and kissed her softly. For a moment, all worry was forgotten. The fear of everything that had happened was momentarily displaced by shared happiness. However, Alex fell silent again clutching Argon's hands in hers. "Argon. That man. He said his name was Julius Silverstone." The revelation caused Argon to sit upright. He couldn't believe it. "Argon, I don't know what's happening." His cult theory was becoming more plausible. "Who or what is he?" Argon can't answer her. The evidence had gotten too strange. Everything he had learnt was just causing him more confusion. "I think I'm losing my mind." Argon touched her comfortingly as she slumped. "I need to get out of here." Argon eased her back on to the bed as she tried to make a break for it. "You can't leave."

"I need to go and get clothes. This hospital shit is driving me mad."

"Look," Argon levelled with her, "I will go home and get you clothes. You stay here until the doctor sorts this out. I know you're not happy about it, but you have something else to protect now."

"But Argon what if he…"

"Alex. I will be fine." He assured her with a kiss to her forehead. "I'll be back. Don't move. I'll get a nurse." He smiled, slipped through the curtain and left the ward.

By the end of the night, Alex would become fully aware of the fleeting transience of happiness.

Alex rested back into the bed, exhausted. Her body felt different. Her sight had changed. Even in the gloom of the ward, the colours seemed much brighter than they should be. The beeping of the machines screeched in her ears. Even the dripping of the IV fluid in the tube was unbearable, every drip like a gunshot in her head. She tried to block it out. She tried to focus on the silence, but even the hum of the ambient noise drove her mad. After a few minutes, the sound of footsteps cut through the maddening sounds. Assuming it was the nurse she waited. However, the person who appeared through the curtain was no nurse; it was Julius.

"What do you want?" Alex sneered. Her fear was gone. She was too exhausted, too weak to fight him. "Come to finish what you started?"

"I told you, Alex, I am not here to hurt you."

"Clearly!" she laughed, gesturing around her.

"You don't understand," he moved closer to the bed where Alex sat up. "You need to come with me."

"Yeah, 'cause that's going to happen!"

"Alex, you are in danger. What I've done is an attempt to save you not to kill you. You need to come with me now."

"Who are you?"

"You know who I am."

"What are you?" Julius hesitated at the question. There was no time to explain. He looked over his shoulder to where the doorway would be behind the curtain. "Alex, I know how this sounds, but you need to trust me. I have cared for you all your life." Alex noticed he was carrying a rucksack. "Please trust me." Alex could see a fear in his eyes that confused and disturbed her.

"Prove you are who you said you are." Julius glanced over his shoulder again. Clearly, someone was after him. Quickly he moved closer to her, revealing on his hand a ring emblazoned with the Giovanni Crest. A wave of nausea washed over her. She thought back to her records at the monastery. It was real and she could barely understand it at all. Satisfied that she now understood, Julius pulled clothes from the rucksack. "Put these on. I will explain everything later. We just need to get away from here. Where is Argon?"

"He went home," Alex answers, worried why Julius was asking this question.

For a moment, Julius stood in contemplation. Alex broke the silence, "What did you do to me?"

"I'll explain later."

"I'm not moving until you tell me." Julius succumbed to her stubbornness by gratification, "Get changed and listen." He moved behind the curtain, offering her privacy. Alex slowly pulled clothes from the bag-black leather trousers; black boots; a black bulletproof bodice and under armour; gun straps and a long black leather coat. She held the gun straps warily in her trembling hands.

"I am a vampire," Julius spoke from behind the white curtain. The sentence sent shockwaves through Alex's transforming body. She dropped the gun straps. She wanted not to believe him, but everything was too strange. It made sense in a nonsensical way. "And you are a vampire." She eased off the bed, numbed by a shock. She just about managed to hold herself upright to slip on the trousers.

"You have always been a vampire, Alex. Your body would have turned soon, but I couldn't wait any longer. I have already been waiting for centuries." Behind the curtain Julius, sensing danger, drew his gun, his eyes locked on the doorway. "There is a growing danger to you. You are of immense importance. I had to force your cells to mutate, to change. A monster is coming for you." Alex had slipped into the bodice and gun straps. She pulled back the curtain, startled to find a gun in Julius' hand.

"What do you mean 'monster'?" seeing that she was dressed, he moved to the bag and produced a bag of blood.

"Drink this." Alex was immediately repulsed. "You need to," urged Julius. She pushed it away.

"Julius, I'm pregnant." Julius's green eyes widened with shock. This had not been part of the prophecy.

"What? How can this be?"

"Well, you know, things happen." Even in her predicament, she retained her sarcasm. "Drink it quickly." He pushed it back towards her. It was her turn to yield. She took it from him and with a grimace ripped the bag and drank expecting it to be disgusting. However, to her disbelief, it tasted rich with a slight bitterness like a fine wine. As she drank, Julius slipped two guns into her holsters.

Suddenly, from beyond the doorway, the sound of crashing and banging echoing down the corridors caught their attention. Julius immediately turned defensive. "We need to go."

"Argon. I need to make sure he's safe, and then I leave. I'll go away until this dies down. I need to know he's safe." As shouts and screams penetrated through the crashing and clanging, Julius paused a moment, discontent flooding his body like a burst dam. Alex didn't understand, and he had no time to explain. "We need to go," he said again, as he pulled her towards the window and flung it open.

"The door's the other way." Julius turned to her.

"We can't use the door."

"Well, I sincerely hope there's a very long ladder in that rucksack, Mary Poppins." This was no time for sarcasm, Alex would have to learn and adapt quickly. He urged her to the window, "Trust me." The intensity of his eyes proved to Alex his sincerity. She moved closer to peer down to the hard ground of the car park far below.

"Julius, I can't," she touched her stomach.

"Julius Silverstone." A deep, growling voice caught their attention. Julius and Alex spun around, guns drawn to find the monster in the doorway. Belial. A towering figure, he was dressed in a worn, ripped, dirty green military uniform with straggled hair, dark, piercing red eyes and corpse-like pale skin the creature was a startling image. His hands were stained in blood that smeared across the walls as he leaned in the doorway. Julius instinctively moved in front of Alex to shield her. "Belial." He spat, "You can't have her."

"You've done well so far, Julius. I'll give you that much. It took me a long time to catch up with you." He swaggered forward, "But, Brother, be warned. If you stand in my way, I will kill you."

No sooner was the threat off his tongue that a bullet embedded itself in his shoulder. The wound sizzled. Belial roared out in pain. Smoke rose from the wound. Julius snapped around to see Alex with a smoking gun in her hand. "OK, I'm ready to jump." She hopped up on to the ledge, turned to Julius, who nodded reassuringly. Blessing herself, she took a deep breath and jumped. She hated herself for taking the chance and threatening the life of her unborn child, but it was the lesser of two evils. She plummeted towards the ground and was bracing herself for certain death, but suddenly some animal instinct kicked in. She spun in the air and landed in a kneeling position. Awestruck, she glanced to the sky, upwards to the window from where she had just leapt. She could barely believe it. Seconds later, Julius landed like a bird at her side and immediately hopped over to take her arm and lead her to safety.

"He will follow," Julius warned as he led her through the car park as alarms wailed from the building. As the commotion escalated, Julius and Alex hurried from around the corner to the darkness where Julius had concealed his car.

"Where are you taking me?" she asked as they jumped into the slick black Porsche.

"Somewhere safe.."

"I'm not going without, Argon."

"Alex, my main priority is you," he revved up the engine.

"And my main priority is not disappearing and leaving my best friend at the mercy of a mad man!" Julius wasn't pleased about it. He believed in the prophecy and therefore, what Argon would become. But, perhaps there was a small chance. "Make it quick!" he decided to take that chance and zoomed the car out past the oncoming police cars and into the night.

As Julius and Alex raced off into the night, Belial marched through the hospital with a group of rogue vampires – the bloody eyed Renegades. He dug the bullet from his shoulder as staff and patients fled from the terrorising Renegades. The bullet, imbued with a supernatural seal, gleamed in his hand. It wasn't enough to kill him, but it did sting. The dishevelled general flung it across the lobby as he lunged for a cowering nurse. Police arrived on the chaotic scene to be brutally slain by the Renegades.

As the Renegades tore the building and the police apart, Belial, grabbing the terrified nurse by the neck, shoved her across the reception desk. "Alex Valentine. Her address. Now."

In Alex and Argon's flat, Argon was quietly packing a bag of clothes for Alex when all of a sudden the door to the flat flung open. "Argon?" he heard his name called in a panic.

"Alex?" he couldn't understand how she could have gotten from the hospital so quickly. She had been in no fit state when he left her. He rushed into the living room, where he found her and Julius. He slammed to a stop, confused by Alex's militant appearance and her companion. "Alex, what's going on? Are you OK?"

"We need to get out of here."

"Alex?"

"Argon there's no time to explain." The fear in her eyes unnerved him, but more than that was the change in her appearance. She had been so close to death – so fragile and haunted, but now she stood before him like a gladiator. She was strong and radiant. There was a glow in her porcelain skin and despite the fear in her beautiful eyes, he could see something different that had not been there before. More than that even, what unnerved him most was the hint of elongated incisors peeking behind her pouted lips.

Argon was frozen in confusion. He looked between Alex and Julius. Seeing his gaze gravitate to Julius, Alex grabbed his hand. "Argon, it's fine. He saved me. We need to go." Reluctantly, Argon allowed Alex to lead him from the flat.

They rushed behind Julius towards the end of the dingy hallway, where Julius, with his gun drawn, checked the staircase. It was clear. They started to descend. They merely made it down two flights of stairs before footsteps resounded throughout the stairwell. The sound of loud, booted footsteps alerted them to looming danger.

Julius glanced over the staircase to see a pack of skin-headed Renegades in dishevelled black clothing tramping up the staircase. Julius forced Alex and Argon to retreat. Back on the level of their apartment, Julius turned to them, "Where are the other exits?"

"Lift." Alex pointed down the corridor to the elevator, "Or fire escape." She pointed in the opposite direction and to Argon's horror, she drew a gun from her holster. Julius immediately looked towards the fire escape. It seemed like the safest option.

"Get back," he gestured for his precious Midnight Children to hide behind the wall as he hid behind the other and as the Renegades reached the top of the staircase he engaged them one by one, moving at a speed Alex and Argon could barely keep up with.

Of course, the residents of the building did not emerge from the safety of their flats as the gunfire resounded through the corridor. As Julius took out each Renegade one by one, blood splattered the corroded, paint flaking white walls before their inhuman bodies burst into flames. Argon impulsively closed over Alex to protect her. However, no sooner had Julius dispatched of the last Renegade, the lift doors opened with a gritting metallic screech. Julius barely had time to react as Argon was snatched backwards. "Argon!" Alex screamed as he was torn from her into the hands of the monster, Belial. Julius just managed to catch her as she attempted to dart to her lover's aid.

It was too late. Julius had lost. With one swift and brutal bite, Belial sunk his jagged fangs deep into Argon's neck! "Argon!" Alex screamed as she struggled against Julius, who was momentarily transfixed by the horror of the truth. The prophecy was being fulfilled before his eyes. He had for the first time, attempted to flout it but to no avail. As prophesised centuries before, Argon would fall to Belial. The war would come.

Argon's body fell limp as Belial bled him dry. Dark, crimson blood gushed down Argon's neck and shoulder and sprayed the walls and floor. Julius needed to save Alex from the horror of the sight and to protect her from also falling to Belial's hands. Julius, her guardian angel, threw her over his shoulder and descended the staircase, gun still drawn, wary of the continuing threat of Renegades. She continued to struggle against him, screaming and crying Argon's name and shooting her gun back towards Belial. Yet, her bullets were wasted. She did not have the angle. She thrashed against Julius, but he was too strong. Tears ran down her face blurring her sight as in seconds they had burst out into the darkness of the night where Julius bundled her into his car.

The last image she saw of Argon, her best friend, love of her life and father of her child was of him falling to his knees blood-drenched and drained of life at the foot of a monster.

Chapter 20

"Ahhhhhhh! Fuck! Fuck! Fuck!" Alex wakes from a nightmare. Her memories tormented her. She had been crying in her sleep. Confused, disturbed and haunted she falls from the couch in Julius' study to a heap on the blood-red carpet on the floor.

Julius, who had been working at his desk immediately comes to crouch on the floor beside her, offering a glass of blood that she accepts shakily. "Parasitic memories. Your body's trying to flush out those associations you wish you could forget," he advises.

"I wish I could forget them. They'll never let me go."

"You have been asleep for almost twenty-four hours. You arrived in here, collapsed on the floor and you've been suffering a constant nightmare since."

"My life is a nightmare."

"I found out from Delin what happened."

Alex falls silent for a moment. She can't talk about it. Her memories had wounded her and the clash of past and present disturbed and saddened her too much to be able to process her emotions. She takes a drink to relax then inhales and exhales slowly. "He killed her, Julius. In cold blood he killed her… because of me. My Argon is gone." Her lips tremble. This time Julius is lost for words. There is nothing he can say to comfort her. "Maybe he's right. Maybe the Authorities do deserve to die." She ponders darkly.

"Alex! Don't say that! Those words spoken by Argon are Belial's words. He has brainwashed him. They will get the justice they deserve, believe me." Alex is unconvinced by Julius' assurance.

"Julius, Elaina died feeling used, feeling betrayed, feeling alone. She died as a pawn in our stupid 'war', a war for which the Authorities are to blame. Argon must have felt like that when we left him – confused, alone, betrayed. The Authorities started this. I'll end it with their deaths. They deserve to die. They deserve to die for all that they have done to him. I don't even recognise him anymore! I loved him!"

"The man you knew is gone! You have to understand that. Killing the Authorities will not save him; it will only get you killed and make you a monster along the way," Julius urges, understanding of the turmoil in her mind.

"I don't care. I don't care, Julius. They took Argon from me, they took my child from me, they took my life, and they will rape and kill everything that threatens their thrones. I will rise against them. I might lose this war, I might die trying, but I swear to fuck I will not go quietly."

Silence falls between them. Julius knows Alex is resolute. He knows he cannot stop her if she is determined to follow this path. All he can do is protect her along the way. After a few minutes of quiet contemplation, Alex whispers, "Why?" it was a hollow question she was asking for she knows she will never get her answer and 'fate' as the usual answer was unacceptable to her. "I gave them my trust. I gave them my oath because I had nothing left and look at what the Authorities have done. This was all their doing. So I vow to be their undoing completely. I will kill them if I have to. I will kill them all."

Her spearing vow plunges into her mentor's heart – he is losing her. Before he can offer any words of advice or consolation she jumps to her feet. "I need to go to Ar Novad's."

"You can't, Alex, you've been suspended."

"Convenient."

"Alex, you need to rest."

"Julius, I am so sick of everyone telling what I need to do and what I can't do! I know you come from a good place, Julius, really but I can't play their game anymore. What I need to do is to even the score! It's time Tallon and I had a little talk! It's time 'His Majesty', Ira Tallon got his hands dirty!" noticing something on Julius' bookshelf, she goes to it.

"Alex, please," Julius rises, "Please just be patient a little longer – with me. Trust in me." Drawing a book from the shelf, she gazes at it solemnly as the sight of it calms her. She traces the name on the cover, 'The Three Musketeers', the book Elaina had been reading.

"They took everything from you, Alex, I know that," Julius levels with her, "I want you to get your justice, but I need you to remember to control yourself. Spontaneous and reckless actions will be your undoing, not the Authorities." Alex listens to him as she clutches the book to her chest. She understands him.

"Elaina's death has marked the end of any trace of innocence left in my life. The blood on Argon's hands is on mine too. This is my fight, and Elaina took the fall. I deserved her death. She was too young – naïve, still too human perhaps but innocent. She didn't deserve this. I suppose it's always the innocent who get caught in the monster's crossfire."

Again her words sting Julius' heart. She deserves to be bitter. She deserves her revenge, but he is afraid, afraid her recklessness and the fire within her will draw her down the wrong path. He does not want her soul destroyed by acting on malicious intent. Revenge could ravage and destroy her.

He can see she is deep in thought. Something is stirring in her mind. "Alex, we will win this."

"Yeah. We'll win this when I kill Argon, right? When I kill Argon for them." Alex has absolutely no intention to do so. She has no intention of killing Argon. They share a common understanding, a common bitterness and a common enemy. Perhaps he can be persuaded to come back to some sort of middle ground. Perhaps there is hope for him – after she kills Belial.

"I need to go to Ar Novad's."

"Alex. No."

"Don't worry, Julius. I'm not going to start fights. I need to speak to Delin. I don't think Ar Novad's is safe."

"I should go with you."

"No. It's fine." She tosses him the book as she heads for the door then stops in realisation, "Although I may need to borrow your car." She winces. Rolling his eyes, Julius tosses her the keys.

"Treat her kindly."

"But, of course." Winking she exits. Although her mood has elevated significantly, Julius knows the particle accelerator in her mind is sending little jolts of electric through her brain. All the electrons and protons are smashing together forming a plan – a plan he knows will secretly aid her own agenda.

Chapter 21

It is quiet in the early hours of a Monday night as Alex pulls off the main street in Julius' precious Porsche and into the side entrance to Ar Novad's Institute. The crisp spring air still clings on to the chill of winter as the starry night fades to an inky blue morning.

Alex rolls down the window as she pulls up to the armoured gates of the fortress. A soldier behind a bulletproof screen requests her ID as a security camera scans her face triggering a 'warning' on the administration computer system. A voice emanates from the intercom, "Alex Valentine you have been suspended. We cannot permit you entrance."

Furious, Alex emerges from the car, drawing her sword. "I need to speak with Delin, immediately."

"Alex Valentine, stand down."

"You tell Delin to let me in now or so help me God, I will break down these doors." The intercom goes silent. "I'm not kidding." She raises her sword to the gates.

"Alex Valentine, return to your vehicle." The voice comes through the monitor. She is not backing down. Gripping her shining silver sword, its glistening blade imbued with inscribed incantations; she slashes it across the gates like a red-hot poker cutting through ice leaving a gaping wound.

An alarm sounds. She casually returns her sword to its sheath and pushes the two slits of the wound open to slip through into the heart of the fortress. Guns drawn, two sentry soldiers block her path. "Get out of my way." She attempts to move past. They defend their position. Without drawing her own weapons, she rolls her eyes. She isn't in the mood for Delin's lackeys; she only wants the boss. Unarmed, she slips from their sight, faster than they can compensate for. She quickly disarms them before rendering them unconscious with just her hands.

Marching onwards into the courtyard, she doesn't get far before she is surrounded by more of Delin's gun-toting, right-hand command. She knows she doesn't have to fight them. She is inside. She has got their attention. She raises her hands in surrender. "Where is she?"

"I'm right here, Valentine." Delin's voice booms from a doorway where she has stepped into the courtyard. He boots bang on the stone slabs as she swaggers towards the surrounded rebel. "Your arrogance, Valentine, is appalling." She enters the circle, her beige uniform appearing ghostly white beneath the courtyard lamps. "We need to have a talk," states the steely General.

"No. You need to listen." Alex snaps, "Elaina Hart. You killed her. Argon. You destroyed him. You made him a monster. You and the rest of the Incumbents."

"Alex Valentine!"

"You and the Incumbents, you started this war! This blood is on your hands and there is more to come!" Alex's eyes glow fierce green with fury. The soldiers guarding the General stir with worried interest at Alex's words and the uneasiness they stir in the General.

Alex eyes Delin's guards, directing her warning to them, "It's time you all knew. The Midnight Children were created by Evelyn Delin and the rest of the vampire nation's Incumbents. We were created for one purpose alone." Her eyes lock on Delin's where a green fire burns within. " – To keep them on their thrones." She digs the knife in. "But there will be blood." Alex continues, "It's time everyone in this Institute knew – Ar Novad's is not safe. You are pawns. A monster is coming." She turns again to Delin to look her square in the eye, "Belial is coming." Delin is silent for a moment. Fury rises in her gut, twisting and burning.

"Arrest her," she commands. The guards hesitate. However, after a moment, the OIC and his second in command take the troublesome Midnight Child by the arms. Alex allows herself to be taken. She has a plan.

As she is escorted away, Delin shoves a hand against her breastplate and leans in close – an intimidation tactic. It doesn't work. "You will learn your place, Midnight Child." Alex holds eye contact until she is led away. The remaining guards escort Delin back to her office.

Alex is led through the courtyard towards the military prison, a block of cells outside the main compound of the Institute. In comparison to the grandeur of the Institute, the prison block was more like a POW bunker. To her guards' surprise, Alex easily complies with their escort. However, they don't notice that she is planning her escape.

As they pass from the light of the main buildings and enter the straight gravel path towards the prison block, Alex pulls back with a swift jolt and slips from their grasp. She has fooled them with her compliance and caught them off guard. They spring to raise their weapons, but Alex is too fast. She quickly disarms them. With the butt of one guard's rifle, she knocks the other unconscious. The second guard attempts to engage her in unarmed combat. Smirking, she relishes the opportunity to show off her skill but does not have time. He attacks. She blocks, catching him in a lock and quickly knocks him out. Dragging them from the prying eyes of the CCTV cameras, she conceals their unconscious bodies in a dark corner and slips into the shadows.

Taking a leap, she lands on the rooftop of a lower building then darts across, close to the wall as not to be seen. Dropping down by the entrance to the dormitory doors, she slips inside.

The corridor is quiet. Many of the soldiers are still offsite. She creeps through the shadows, sneaking past a soldier who exits an administration room and ascends the staircase to the male dormitories.

The names of the soldiers assigned to each dorm room are listed on the outside. Luckily it doesn't take her long to scan the names and find Ira Tallon. She glances down each end of the corridor for intruders. The corridor remains silent. She tries the door, but it is locked. A sharp bang of her fist on the door commands the attention of the soldier within who is taken back by her appearance in his doorway. "Where is Ira Tallon?"

"He's ummm…" the soldier stutters, "He's in the military archives."

"Thank you." In a flash, Alex is gone. The soldier emerges into the corridor to see Alex disappear lightning fast down the corridor. He had never seen the Midnight Child up close before. She definitely had an intense aura, even if he had only encountered her for a split second. There were also rumours passing around that Ira Tallon was also a Midnight Child. He knew something was stirring in the Institute and the morbid curiosity of it all was being spread like Chinese whispers.

Alex doesn't take long to get to the archives. She has no time to lose. She knows it is only a matter of time before Delin discovers her guards never succeeded in assigning the Midnight Child to a cell. The door to the military archives is coded, and Alex knows that if she enters her own code, her location will be flagged. Also, her pin is most likely blocked. Only one thing for it she thinks, before she quickly rips the keypad from the door, just enough to fiddle the wires and undermine the system. Ar Novad's might have trained her as a soldier, but Julius had trained her to be a spy. Her skill for espionage is beyond soldier.

Within seconds the vaulted doors slide open with a pneumatic sigh. She quickly slips inside before they slam shut behind her.

The expansive military archives are an encyclopaedia of ancient vampire history. Carefully and clinically laid out in rows of itemized bookshelves and computers the soldiers had access to a vast supply of intelligence. It was making sense of the centuries of information that required a keen eye for detail. Inside the military archives, Ira is carefully scanning an old bookshelf. He works alone. His coat and bag are laid on a desk he has claimed for his research. He moves along the bookshelf, the top buttons of his shirt undone and shirttails tucked out. The military archives were often quiet at this time of night or rather the morning. Soon as the sun would rise, the fortress would go into lockdown. Luckily he enjoyed the privileges of being a Midnight Child –immunity to the burning light of the sun.

As he draws a hefty volume from the shelf, he flicks through the old, rough pages to the index. From the information Alex had acquired, provided to him by Julius, Ira had detected a clue to where the Lanuonin had gone underground with underground being the keyword. He believes that the Lanuonin have actually created their own subterranean city.

From the corner of his eye, he suddenly becomes aware of a figure at the end of the bookshelf. He jumps, dropping the book with a loud bang as he catches sight of Alex leaning between the two bookshelves. "What are you doing here?" he composes himself, bending to lift the book.

"Whatever you're looking for make it quick," she warns.

"Weren't you suspended?" he sifts through the book to find the page he was looking for.

"Indeed, I was. Tallon, we need to get out of here."

"I'm not going anywhere with you."

"I thought you would say that." She moves closer, "You think hiding in here's going to save you?"

Ira is disgusted by Alex's statement – she was judging him. He slams the book shut. "What do you want, Valentine?"

"I want you to come with me. We need to talk."

With a sigh, he leans against the shelf, "Unfortunately I agree with you." He is Alex's reluctant ally and even more reluctantly, her partner in crime. However, he knows for better or worse they have a common goal – the destruction of the Giovanni Authorities, so he knows he must find some sort of way to work by her side.

"So what?" he asks, "How did you get past the guards?" Alex rolls her eyes. Dumb question, he realised. "Did Julius tell you about me?"

"He did – eventually – but not enough. That's why we need to talk."

"The third Midnight Child, he found us."

"It's not a case of finding us, Tallon. Ar Novad's is pretty obvious. The problem is, he's here now. It's been over four years. You know what that means? They're ready to fight. We have no idea the extent of Renegade recruitment. All we know is that there are at least three other clans out there for their recruitment agency. Many, many vampires harbouring much bitterness and hostility towards the Giovanni – rightly so but that does not bode well for our agenda."

Tallon falls silent. He has not faced the Renegades yet. It suddenly dawns on him how sheltered his existence has been. However, his contemplation is interrupted by a bang at the door. Delin's guards have found Alex. The door is jammed, but the loud bang of a sort of battering ram means it will not take them long to penetrate the steel doors.

"We need to get out of here." Alex starts off, "Take that with you." She refers to the book in Ira's hands. There is no time to be a librarian.

"Where are we going?" he slips the book into his bag and throws on his coat.

"The Hall of Vampires," Alex replies. Ira's eyes bulge at her statement:

"Alex, we can't! We haven't been invited!"

"We don't need an invitation, Tallon but we do need answers." Wary of the danger, they quicken their pace as the steel door begins to buckle and cave. Ira quickly hurries through the desks of computers and glass case displays towards the opposite end of the room. "This used to be a chapel." He ascends the raised platform of what once was an alter but now boasts a large reading desk.

"This way." He motions to the doorway to the next room. They dash through to what used to be the priest's sacristy but is now a storage room. Once through, Alex grabs a book laden case and shoves it with ease against the doorway. At the other end of the room is another bolted doorway. Ira rips it open to reveal a dark spiralling staircase. Alex dashes after him up the old stone staircase leading them upwards into an escape route, an ancient passage running above the alter and across the length of the building. "They're going cut us off. They know about this passage." As the words leave his lips, he realises Alex has stopped running. He turns to see her digging something from her inner pocket.

"Would you say we're about the side entrance?" she asks darting past him.

"Close enough." Ira watches in confusion as she sticks something to the ceiling and runs back towards him. "Good." A split second after Alex arrives back beside him an almighty bang brings him to his knees. A huge blast demolishes a section of the roof sending shrapnel shards of wood and stone crashing down around them in a plume of fire and smoke. "Are you out of your fucking mind?" Ira roars at her.

"Probably." She passes him through the smoke and debris. "Come on." She urges hopping up through the flames to perch in the hole as the flames billow around her yet she remains unharmed. Ira emerges through the smoke, gazing up at her, flames licking his porcelain pale skin. "You're entirely as I expected, Valentine," he mutters. Fire alarms screech through the building.

"This is my idea of Shawshanking out of this shithole," she mutters.

As Alex moves off Ira leaps through the hole. He takes a moment to observe the breath-taking view of the city beneath the morning spring sun as it rises above the skyline. "Tallon!" His attention is taken by Alex, who he turns to see dashing across the rooftop. He bolts after her. Of course, his first escapade with Alex Valentine would be to turn fugitive. He can only imagine the repercussions of betraying the Incumbent General. Chances are he would also face a sentence in military prison. Chances are, he faced worse – Court Martial for desertion.

Reaching the end of the rooftop, Alex leaps into the air like an eagle and soars towards the ground below. Ira halts at the edge looking down as in the distance a fire engine races along the waterfront. Following suit, Ira leaps to the ground below. Luckily the sunlight inhibits the pursuing vampiric soldiers to hunt their prey any further. Alex and Ira have a safe getaway. However, as Ira reaches Alex's car, which she has abandoned outside the gates, he notices she is looking through the gates with a smirk. He follows her gaze to see Delin, Shanay and a handful of guards peering from the safety of the shadows. Arms folded, Shanay's gaze is piercing. His eyes burn bright green with rage. Ira knows his association with Alex has now stained his reputation. No longer will Delin believe in his compliance and obedience. There is no going back.

Somewhat shameful in his actions, he jumps into the car with Alex at the wheel. Slamming her foot down Alex reverses backwards into the street and then accelerating forward, they flee from the fortress like a charging knight just as a fleet of fire engines arrives on the scene. The Midnight Children are headed to the Hall of Vampires without invitation and without permission. Arriving on the Authorities' doorstep unannounced would be a shot in the dark, but it is Alex's plan to catch them off guard. She expects a scripted performance from them, but she knows the lines. The answers she seeks she knows she will only get from their lies.

Chapter 22

Pushing Julius' car to its limits, Alex and Ira speed out of the city boundaries and into the quiet countryside where the morning sun has broken into a light drizzle as the grey clouds close the sky. Ira has fallen to silent contemplation as he watches the raindrops trickle and stream down the windows. His irritation is apparent as Alex blares loud rock music and smokes out the window. The rhythmic window wipers swipe left and right.

Eventually, as they veer off the country roads and on to the motorway where Alex follows the sign for the airport, Ira slams his hand against the audio button on the dashboard, shutting off the music and plunging the car into silence. Alex side-eyes him curiously, takes one last puff of her cigarette then tosses it out the window. She pauses a moment to allow Ira time to speak, yet he doesn't, so she decides to break the silence.

"What's wrong with you?" she asks the question to which Ira takes umbrage. He turns to her indignantly as if she should know better.

"What's wrong with me? What do you think is wrong with me?"

"I think that stick up your ass might have something to do with it." She knows she is antagonising and she means it. She wants Ira to bite.

"You are unbelievable," he mutters, "However, you said we needed to talk, and you were right. Why are we going to the Hall of Vampires?"

"Because I want to watch those spin doctors lie to my face. But, back up there a little. You're not getting away that easily. What is your role in this tragic little play?"

After a long, uncomfortable sigh, Ira caves. "Julius has been providing me with the evidence you acquired. I've been collating it and using it to create a case against the Giovanni Authorities."

"We do not need a case. We have evidence enough."

"That's not what Julius believes. Nor I. We believe that our mission will culminate."

"Our mission?"

"We believe that our mission will culminate," Ira ignores her sarcasm, "In a trial against the Giovanni Authorities. We will convince the other clans to hold a court. There we will present the evidence, and the Giovanni Authorities will be accused of war crimes and sentenced to imprisonment."

"Imprisonment!" Now it is Alex, who is appalled, "Imprisonment is not good enough!"

"It is justice we seek, Valentine and that is what they deserve. They will be stripped of all titles and luxuries and imprisoned for eternity."

"No. Oh no, Tallon. You've cowered in a corner. If the Renegades haven't come for you yet, they will. This is what the Authorities have done to our lives and the lives of everyone who encounters them. They create slaves. The Authorities took everything from the other clans including the rights and liberty of those in their own. They took everything from us. They cursed us from birth. You witness the people you love killed and destroyed before your eyes and then tell me what they deserve."

Tallon again falls silent. He knows she is right. The Renegades had not come for him because they didn't know he was the Midnight Child; no one did. No one he loved died for or because of him because he didn't love anyone. He had always kept himself to himself, especially after Julius turned him. After Julius turned him, he had become more reclusive. He focused on his work alone. Even dating women, like he had done in the past, he tried to avoid for fear bloodlust would consume him.

"Who else did they kill? I mean apart from Elaina?" He finally asks. Alex lights another cigarette.

"They killed my best friend. He was the only thing I had in this world." She observes the scenery as they drive past an old, abandoned wreck of a factory. She studies its ruin and dilapidation considering the ruin of her own life and dilapidation of her body. Despite the grudge she holds against Ira, she has lost the will to fight him. "How did you come to this? How did Julius find you? Where did you come from?" she asks. Ira is reluctant to think about it, but despite his wariness of Alex's volatile temperament, he knows they must accept their differences and work together. Seeing her packet of cigarettes sitting below the dashboard, he helps himself, "Do you mind?"

"Would it matter if I did?"

"You're the one that wants answers." He accepts the lighter she passes to him.

"You know Delin's probably warned the Authorities. It's a wonder they haven't sent the cavalry after us," Ira states after a long drag.

"They can arrest us all they want; we're still getting in." Alex remains staunch and continues her interrogation, "You're very good at diverting the subject, Tallon. If I didn't know any better, I'd take a guess you were a lawyer in a past life."

"I was a lawyer in a past life. In a wonderful life before where we are now."

"Oh, I get it. I get it. I'm the fucking patsy here. I take the risks, I take the fall. You swoop in and save the day. I'm just not intelligent enough to parlay with the clans."

"That's not it. Julius formed a plan and fitted our strengths to suit."

"Fine. Divulge your histoire."

"Julius came to me about three years ago." Ira rests back in reflection, turning his gaze again to the rain as the cigarette burns slowly between his fingers.

His memories return in a flood. In his mind, he sees his former life flashing before his eyes. A charming bachelor, Ira had his pick of beautiful women. With a flourishing career as a human rights lawyer, he was taking on more cases and reaping the rewards of successfully closed cases. He was young, intelligent, good-looking and rich. He had it all. He had just moved into a stylish penthouse apartment in the centre of London and just about to open his own firm when Julius waltzed into his life to ruin everything.

As Ira opens his heart to Alex, she knows better than to take advantage of his honesty by passing comment on his privilege in comparison to her own. But Alex sees an opportunity. She can see Julius' logic in a way – Ira knew the rich, he knew how they worked, how they spoke and how they thought. Alex knew passionate defiance and chaos. Alex knew how to put a spanner in the works.

As Ira speaks, the cogs begin to turn in Alex's mind. She could play her part as a patsy, and all the while play them at their own game. Oh, she could be the spanner in the works all right. She could let Ira be the face of reason – of hostile compliance – the ice to her fire while she played her own game in the shadows.

"So how did it happen?" she asks, taking Ira from his thoughts.

"I was coming back from a meeting, well not meeting…"

"You were in the pub."

"I'd just won a case. Done a couple of interviews. Then I went for a couple of drinks with some colleagues to celebrate. It was a case I'd been working on for ages. Discrimination against refugees."

"Fair play."

"I had a meeting in the morning, so I couldn't stay too late. I left around ten. Got a taxi back to my apartment. A girl I had been dating had text to say she was going to come over so when I got home, I just poured another drink and waited. Around half ten there was a knock on the door. I assumed it was her. But, when I opened it, there was no one there."

"Suddenly there came a tapping/ As of someone gently rapping/ Rapping at my chamber door," Alex rhymes.

"Sort of," Ira continues, "I checked the corridor. There was no one. But, when I turned back into the room, there was a man. At first, I assumed it was because of the case. I figured someone was sent to even the score." Alex empathises with Ira's situation. Both she and Ira had chosen controversial careers which made hitmen and the like a valid threat.

"Before I could react properly, the man told me not to panic. He told me his name was Julius Silverstone. This name, I couldn't believe it. I had been adopted when I was just a baby, and they told me my godfather was the only family I had – a man called Julius Silverstone – but he was always away on business, and that's why I had never met him. Although he always sent money and was extremely interested in my education." Ira paused in thought. "I thought surely this couldn't be this man. Why now? He told me I was in danger. Someone was coming for me. I didn't know what to believe. But I didn't have long to think about it. He apologised for what he had to do and then he turned me. I woke up the next morning on my couch, and I knew there was something wrong. The anxiety that comes from waking from a bad dream, that's how it felt, but I knew it wasn't a dream. I knew there was something different."

Alex turns the car off onto a slip road heading towards the sea as Ira finishes his story. "Long story short, I ran. I couldn't explain what happened. I couldn't go to the police because they'd think I'd lost my mind. I wasn't prepared to hang around to find out if Julius was telling the truth that someone else was after me. I phoned my office, told them I had an emergency and I wouldn't be in. I packed up whatever I could, and I ran. I used a fake name and rented a place for about six months before Julius eventually tracked me down again. This time he explained everything, and we made a deal. I would come with him to Ar

Novad's, but I wanted nothing else to do with the so-called 'Midnight Children'. I could barely accept what I had become and the life that I'd lost.

"Julius had invited me to live in San Lorenzo with him as you do, but I wanted to put distance between Julius and myself. I couldn't forgive him. I didn't want to face reality. But here we are now."

"Yes, here we are. Tallon, I need you to face reality. I need you to fight." Alex slows the car as she nears a small aircraft hangar.

"Valentine, I will fight them but not by your definition. Doing this, creating this case and seeking justice for the life I lost is the closest I've got to re-creating some sense of that life. But, I don't want their blood on my hands." Ira's tone is mournful. Alex stops the car, turns to Ira knowing that to him she is warmongering – knowing that to him she must seem relentless in her bloodlust to bring the Authorities down, but she knows she needs Ira to face the truth. He will get blood on his hands.

Alex jumps out of the car, and Ira follows. The rain has desisted and given way to a pale sun. "Tallon, as I said before, the Renegades will come for you. They've come for me. Argon will come. Belial will come. You can't fight them with words." Finishing her sentence, Alex turns to pull Ira's sword from its sheath, a movement so abrupt it startles him. "Easy Tallon." Alex purrs as she inspects the blade. Removing it completely she extends it towards the sun. The cold steel shines as normal, however, worryingly, without inscriptions. She returns it to him. "What's the problem?" he asks.

"The problem is, Tallon," she produces her own sword for him to view the inscriptions imbued into the fabric of the weapon, "You may be armed, but you are not dangerous."

"I have ligatures," he insists.

"Do you have the Ligature of the Renegades?" she raises her eyebrows to which Ira shakes his head.

"No."

"Why?" she questions.

"I refused to go to Bodmin. I told you."

"Tallon, you idiot, you could have…" she trails off. It suddenly dawns on her why Julius had given them their roles. Julius didn't want Ira fighting until he was properly armed to take on the Renegades. It wasn't because he was smarter than her. "Been killed…" she finishes with a smirk.

“That’s funny, is it?” Ira questions, unaware of the epiphany that has just repaired her ego.

“Nope,” she replies, punching the code in the keypad to open the hangar before quickly jumping into a small military cargo plane with Ira hopping in beside her.

“So what you’re saying is kill everyone?” asks Ira. It wasn’t really a question.

“What I’m saying is give as good as you get,” she replies.

As Alex starts the engine and pulls the plane out of the hangar, Ira means to speak but decides against it. There was no point in arguing with her. Before she dragged him into this, he had believed that she was her own worst enemy, that it was her own personality that got her into trouble, but now he was considering that it was a product of her environment. He hadn’t encountered Belial, nor the Renegades, or even the Authorities for that matter. He hadn’t borne the brunt of their threats and attacks, so for that reason, he could forgive her somewhat. Perhaps he would understand her better after he experienced the Authorities first hand himself.

However, something about this journey isn’t sitting well with him. His optimism for the Midnight Children’s endeavour continues to flicker, and as they take to the sky en route for the elusive land of Bodmin, a sinking feeling grows in the pit of Ira’s stomach. For the first time, he gets the chilling sensation that Alex might be right.

Chapter 23

Black clouds fill the death cold night as the Midnight Children enter the Bodmin airspace. Below them, a wheezy wind blows the gnarled trees in Moor Falls cemetery as the edges of scattered, sinking tombstones are illuminated by the full moon. Alex's gaze remains stern as they approach the bottom of the mound of black earth that rises into the night to where it levels to the plateau. There the Hall of Vampires leers high above the once-thriving city of the supernatural. Ira cannot believe what he is seeing. Never had he imagined Bodmin to be so morose. He had always envisioned this to be the epicentre of the Giovanni empire, not the macabre fortress it was in reality.

Below them, the sentries at the gate inspect the plane with suspicion. The main guard looks to the sky, using the cat-like night vision capabilities of his green vampire eyes to inspect the approaching vehicle. The wings are stamped with the Giovanni Crest, however, there are no visitors expected, a fact that makes the guard suspicious. He turned to his colleagues, motioning for them to stand to attention.

Alex lands the plane on the landing strip at the base of the mound. Usually, any visitors would be greeted by an armed escort and taken by car to the Hall of Vampires. Alex and Ira, having arrived unplanned, expected to be greeted by gunpoint, however when they step from the plane, they are met by nothing but the eerie silence of the ethereal island. Around them, the bleak, black streets are empty. Their presence appears not to have caused any disruption. Nothing stirs. However, from the corner of his eye, Ira notices a silhouette peaking from behind a curtain in an end tenement block – one sign of life in a miserable place. All he can think is, this is a tomb.

"Come on." Alex starts up the wide cobbled path towards the towering black gates. As the guards see them approach, they raise their weapons. Having never experienced Bodmin before, the intimidation Ira feels is overwhelming. It is a sensation he had never expected. He had never imagined that Bodmin would be so bleak and decrepit. Behind the gates, he looks through to view the ruins of what once was a grand empire. The cobbled streets are lined with ancient beautifully constructed, albeit time tarnished buildings. At the very top of the sloping street is the imposing Hall of Vampires and while it is the most extravagant and dominating building on the plateau, its dark façade screams decades if not centuries of neglect.

Alex and Ira reach the gates and stop before the guards. "Who are you? What's your business here?"

"I'm Alex Valentine. This is Ira Tallon. We're the Midnight Children, and we need to speak with the Authorities." Reluctantly the guard, Chiron, lowers his weapon. He studies the Midnight Children with noticeable suspicion in his bright green eyes. He is a stoic character, a proper soldier, never relaxing his stance. His strong jaw sits tight and his thin lips are tensed as he sizes the so called 'visitors' up. He gestures to his second in command to alert the Hall. Alex doesn't have time for games, "Don't pretend that you weren't prior warned from Evelyn Delin that the Midnight Children had fled Ar Novad's."

"Yes," the guard agrees, "And we were told to arrest you on sight should you arrive." The guards close in on the Midnight Children. Ira is startled by the hostility, but Alex draws her sword.

"You may try to arrest us. One way or another I'm getting through that gate, whether I take you down one by one, or somehow you win and drag me through in chains. One thing's for certain; I will not go quietly." The guards hesitate but remain poised for conflict. As neither party appears willing to stand down, Ira draws his sword. Alex was one threat to the guards but with another Midnight Child to contend with, they know the odds aren't good.

Reluctantly Chiron raises his radio to his lips, eyes remaining locked on the armed assailants before him. The Midnight Children were a special breed, or so he was lead to believe. Like the entire vampire nation, they had heard of the prophecy. He truly believed as many did that the Midnight Children would either be their salvation or their ultimate demise.

"This is Chiron. The Midnight Children are at the Gate. They seek counsel with the Authorities. Permission to arrange an escort to the hall? Over" the radio clicks and beeps. As he awaits his orders, the guard does not let his attention slip from Alex and Ira whose hands remain clenching their weapons. The beeping of the radio breaks the silence. A calculating voice comes through the mechanical medium.

“Permission granted.” The guard pauses before replying then decides against it. Taking a step back, he turns to the command hub beside the Gates where access is controlled and all movement closely monitored.

“Open the Gate. Bring the jeep.” The guard in the command hub immediately obeys his superior’s orders while two move to arrange vehicles for the escort. With a simple tap of a red button, the enormous gates grind open revealing the dark ascent towards the Bodmin Plateau.

A sentry in swat team clothing rolls a jet black armoured jeep towards the gates. Chiron takes note and turns his attention back to the Midnight Children, “Your weapons.”

“What of them?” Alex shrugs.

“Hand them over.”

“Over my dead body.” She snorts then pauses as a smirk curves her lips. Acting obliging, she offers up her sword, “OK, fine. Take it.” Wary of her gesture, Chiron hesitates. Ira watches closely, what is she up to? With all eyes on him, Chiron decides to accept the weapon that he had demanded her to relinquish. However, as soon as the hilt meets the flesh of his pale hand, he cries out. With one touch, his skin blisters and burns forcing him to release his grip. The sword clatters to the ground. As Alex moves to take it, all eyes are now on her. “You did ask for it,” she shrugs, “And putting on a glove isn’t going to change the outcome should you try again.” The, humiliated OIC has no patience for Alex’s games but having a feeling this is a fight he will not win, he caves.

“Do not take my leniency to mean me a fool.” A guard runs to open the back doors of the armoured jeep. Chiron stands aside to allow the Midnight Children to pass. With Alex leading, Ira returns his sword to its sheath and follows eyeing Chiron as he passes. One thought troubles his mind, this is a trap.

Chiron slams the rear door behind them as the ‘guests’ settle uncomfortably in the back. As an armoured support jeep pulls up behind them, Chiron checks his weapon, little comfort, he thinks. Supposedly these creatures in his custody were indestructible…or so he and those like him had been led to believe.

The thick tyres spin on the worn cobbled streets as the armoured escort starts up the macabre mound. Rumour had it that the mound was built on an ancient burial pit. Pure bloods don’t burn but not all were of high enough rank to deserve an eternal rest in Moor Falls so many were interred in the civilian cemetery. However, there were so many bodies from the clashes of the clans that soon this resting place could hold no more. So, rather than grant all soldiers a decent burial they were tossed in unmarked graves. Plus, the Giovanni's human victims obviously didn't deserve proper burials…

Bodmin's history was steeped in pain. War had brought the authorities from each of the four clans to call a truce and settle their differences. However, the Giovanni Authorities were always plotting behind the scenes. Bribery and intimidation and suspicious deaths forced the other clans out. The truce fell to ruin and Bodmin along with it. The Giovanni Authorities' lust for power could not be satiated. Eventually, it was fight or die, and the Lanuonin and the Teva decided they would leave Bodmin forever and find their own way. The Ronakites retaliated. Being the Giovanni's biggest threat, the Giovanni showed no mercy and effectively obliterated them. However, a few managed to escape. The Ronakites like the Teva and Lanuonin went underground. While the Teva and the Lanuonin went on to live in obscurity and where merely whispers and rumours of their whereabouts remained it was widely known that the Ronakites were amassing. Old wounds and old scores needed to be settled and for the last few centuries the Ronakites were growing in numbers, waiting for their moment, waiting for a turning point – waiting for the Midnight Children. Many vampires believed that Bodmin was cursed. Many believed the Hall of Vampires itself was cursed. Many believed it was something to do with the Midnight Children… But, of course, they were wrong – Bodmin and the Hall of Vampires along with it was scourged by the Giovanni Authorities.

As the armoured escort winds around the once brilliant city – the vampire empire – Alex and Ira observe the sombre stillness through the dark tinted windows. They wind around the hill until the jeep reaches the straight climb towards the plateau. Nothing stirs. Bodmin is a ghost town of beautifully crafted sculptures left to rot. A shudder runs down Ira's spine. He turns to Alex, whose eyes are fixed on the road ahead. No one speaks a word. The only sound is the rolling tyres on the cobbled street.

Higher they climb along the desolate mile passing a grim time-worn prison with moss, grit and grime clinging to its stony skeleton. This is medieval, thinks Ira. Whether Alex had seen it before and is desensitised to the icy inhumanity of the place or whether she is too dead inside herself, Ira cannot tell. Her expression remains blank and unreadable. Climbing further along the mile, he views an old courthouse where visions of torture and execution as a public spectacle disturb his already morose mind. But, he has little time to brood as soon the street levels out to an expanding courtyard. Before them, the Hall of Vampires with its yellow beady-eye like lights sneers down at them. Its façade appears charred as if some hellish blaze had engulfed the stone completely and left this scarred carcass. Ira shudders once more.

The armoured jeeps grind to a stop. Chiron's radio clicks as he opens the conversation with his elusive superior, "Chiron. Escort has arrived at the Hall. Over." Immediately he throws open the passenger door and hops out, gun in hand. Through the tinted windows, Alex and Ira watch as the gate soldiers in the support van debark and stand to attention, awaiting orders. The loud pop and click of the door handle calls Ira back to focus. Looking to Chiron, he remains composed as he climbs from the vehicle into the cold night. Ira knows he has a reputation to uphold, well, perhaps not reputation but myth. No matter how nervous he is, he cannot show it. Act the part, he thinks, taking a deep breath and striding into the centre of the courtyard, surveying his surroundings in circular movements. Somehow the air itself smells singed. Ira recoils at its bitterness and as if on queue a pale grey fog flows in across the courtyard like a lost soul.

Through the fog, Ira can just about make out Alex's figure as a plume of fog engulfs her. His eyes begin to adjust to the gloom as though the fog he sees a small red glow as Alex lights a cigarette. He knows what she is doing. As she takes a few steps through the fog where he can see her clearly, he knows that it is just an act. Like Ira, she too is doing her best to appear apathetic and nonchalant. Neither of the Midnight Children wants to appear shaken in front of the Giovanni authorities and their lackeys. Alex's tactic, Ira deducts, is to make an appearance that she has no respect for any of them. Well, he thinks, perhaps it's only half an act.

Alex's voice in almost a whisper pierces through the fog.

"I went to the Garden of Love,
And saw what I never had seen:
A Chapel was built in the midst,
Where I used to play on the green."

Chiron watches as Alex paces the courtyard, the Executioner to the Witch. He fears the stillness in her voice and the calmness in her presence. His heart thuds dully like the heels of her boots, hitting the cold stone ground and echoing in the abyss.

Alex slows to a stop, noticing something disturbing smeared along the grey ground – blood. She mulls the image in her mind, silently scanning the monstrosity before her – the bleak landscape and abandonment of what once was beautiful. She looks up to the wind-beaten, time-worn walls of the hall and to the sneering, snarling gargoyles high above and rolls her eyes, what a cliché you are…

She continues pacing, circling Ira and moving towards Chiron, whispering her enchantment:

"And the gates of this Chapel were shut,
And 'Thou shalt not!' writ over the door;
So I turn'd to the Garden of Love,
That so many sweet flowers bore."

Heart full of discontent and his hand on his weapon, Chiron watches the Midnight Children from the short set of steps that lead up to the Hall of Vampires. His sentries observe from the base, ensuring never to let the Midnight Children slip from their sight. If rumours were to believed and these creatures were as smart, and as fast as they were supposed to be, then it would only take a split second for them to disappear through the fog like ghosts.

However, it was clear, the Midnight Children have no intention to disappear. They stand bold before the Giovanni guards, unafraid. Alex takes a long draw of her cigarette and stops at the bottom of the stairs where she whispers the last lines of the poem:

"And I saw it was filled with graves,
And tomb-stones where flowers should be:
And Priests in black gowns, were walking their rounds,
And binding with briars, my joys & desires."

Another chill creeps down Chiron's spine, and the sentries too stand in silent disturbance. Fortunately for the Giovanni infantry, a thunderous boom suddenly reverberates around the cold, stone walls of the courtyard so loud that the cobbled ground below them trembles.

The colossal mouth of the Hall of Vampires groans open to spew out the crème-de-la-crème of the Giovanni army. As they step into the night, they are silhouetted by the Hall's burning throat. The commanding officer flanked by two corpse-pale, green-eyed lieutenants descends towards the Midnight Children. Despite his youthful, handsome appearance with his pale chiselled face and long black hair, the sternness in his features and in his manner age him. The condescension in his black eyes repulses Ira and likewise, Alex who, in order to equal the officer's apparent despite, waits for him to reach the second last step before dropping her cigarette to the ground and crushing it beneath her boot.

The Major 's green eyes are so dark they appear black. He stops at the second step. He stares at where the cigarette had been distinguished then slowly peels his gaze to stare at Alex dead in the eyes. "So is this the welcome party?" she chirps. His gaze lingers on her a moment, sizing her up before panning towards Ira where he locks his sights, reading his target. The Major's stare is so deep that Ira feels its weight upon him like someone just signed his death warrant. However, despite his discomfort, he knows he cannot show weakness. He must mirror the Major's demeanour. It is a standoff. Seconds of silence seem like a lifetime as nothing moves but the wind rustling through their effects. No one is giving in.

Eventually, Alex decides to cut the bullshit. Fuck this bravado. "So what's the deal here? Are Heaven's Gates locked to us Heathens or what?" Although the Major's expression remains unwaveringly grim, the speed that he snaps his head to her attention leads Alex to surmise that she had struck a nerve. At last, he speaks:

"The Giovanni Authorities in their graciousness have permitted you an Audience. I would expect you to be appreciative and…" he trails, judging their appearance in their black customised military uniforms, "Standing to attention." He finished. Alex and Ira make no attempt to make themselves 'presentable'. "Lieutenant," calls the Major without turning. His second in command, Chiron, immediately steps forward.

"Yes, Major Sinclair."

"Relieve the Midnight Children of their weapons," the Major orders. Alex rolls her eyes and Ira sighs. They both look to Chiron who appears sheepish. The Major averts his gaze to the Corporal who steps forward.

"Major," Chiron explains, "We have already requested their weapons."

"And yet they retain them." The Major points out to him.

"Yes, sir, I know." Chiron's face is flushed with embarrassment. Known locally by the troops as a 'sarcastic prick' the Major was not one to look a fool before. However, on this occasion, the Major was in no mood to make an example of him. “Return to your post,” the Major orders the Gate sentries.

“Yes, Major,” Chiron calls his men, shooting Alex and Ira some shade as he and the Gate guards return to the armoured vehicles. Alex smirks, turning her attention back to the Major, “I’m not going through this again.”

“Let me get this straight.” This time the Major cuts the bullshit, “You two who are due to be court martialled for fleeing the custody of the military police and breaking out of Ar Novad’s Institute turn up here without formal arrangement and now expect us to allow you, armed, access to the Giovanni Authorities?” Ira sees the Major’s point, but Alex once again smirks.

“Major, if we were able to escape the custody of the military police and break out of Ar Novad’s, doesn’t that say more about them than it does us?” this time Ira smirks. Alex was being a smart ass. Now it is the Major’s turn to roll his eyes. He turns his back on the Midnight Children and starts up the steps.

“Enough. Lieutenant, escort the Midnight Children inside the Hall.” The Lieutenant accepts his orders, signalling his men to action who form an escort around the Midnight Children. The Major throws open the enormous black doors of the Hall where the burning lights that illuminate the blood-red walls of the Hall of Vampires burst into the night. He turns back to the Midnight Children, “The Authorities are waiting for you in court.”

Suddenly the two Midnight Children don’t feel so smart. Suddenly that trap Ira was worried about seems all the more a reality. Regardless of whether he was a trained lawyer or not he knows he is well out of his depth where the Authorities are concerned. He is not ready. The plan was to gather the evidence to put the Giovanni Authorities on trial, not himself! He attempts to look to Alex for empathy, but she has already started up the steps. Fuck them she thinks, they don’t scare me. She pouts her way towards the Hall’s cavernous mouth, but as she is engulfed she fights to suppress the sensation that perhaps she has bitten off more than she can chew. Own it, she tells herself, or you’ll get eaten alive. Retaining her composure, she strides through with Ira in tow, and the huge doors are slammed shut behind them.

Chapter 24

Inside the Hall, Alex and Ira are marched by armed escort through the lavish atrium of the Hall of Vampires where the Giovanni aristocracy mingle and ogle the suspicious guests. If there was a vampire 'upper class', this is it. Women in formal gowns cosy up to men in tailored suits drinking classes of the rarest blood mixed with absinthe and various liquors – vampire alcoholic indulgences. Rhesus negative blood had always been a vampire favourite and one the Giovanni drank by the gallon.

Along the blood-red carpet the Midnight Children stride heads held high past copious works of art and lavish adornments, tapestries and trinkets. The Midnight Children glance at historical paintings of battles, portraits of the past and present Authorities, the Incumbents and more disturbingly an artist's impression of the ceremony in which the Midnight Children were created. However, with no time to linger, they ascend the antique and intricately carved mahogany staircase and march along one of many extensive hallways towards the Authorities' Court.

The hallway opens up into a circular chamber informing the Midnight Children that they have now reached the North West tower of the Hall of Vampires. Gone are the rich tapestries, portraits, arched windows with thick crimson damask print curtains, gilded picture frames and priceless embellishments. Here, the artistic palette is sombre, morose even morbid. From biblical depictions of the Fall of Adam and Eve, the Day of Judgement, the four Horsemen of the Apocalypse to the Inquisition, the Salem Witch Trials, the Scales of Justice and Victorian public hangings and torture. The theme of this chamber Alex and Ira surmise is intimidation.

Apart from this so-called 'art' there is no need for superfluous embellishments in this chamber. At the press of a button, the windows could be shut by steel slides embedded within the window frame that slice down like a guillotine to cut out the sun's deadly rays. There is no rich mahogany staircase here, just a black wrought iron craft spiral staircase descending to the lower levels. The only furniture is a black, varnished coffee table and a couple of black couches for those awaiting the Authorities' coveted attention.

The Midnight Children are brought to an abrupt halt in the centre of the chamber flanked by the Giovanni guards. With a flick of his thick black hair, the Major steps to the Chamber door which resembles something akin to a steel vault. To keep something in or out? Alex wonders. The Major quickly types in a code and a light on a security camera above the 'vault' flashes. Content with the visual, there are three loud clicks, and metallic screeches as the door unlocks from the inside before a loud boom signals to them that they have been permitted access. The Major pushes the door open.

As the guards usher them towards the Authorities' Court, Alex and Ira look to each other, both silently doubting the other's integrity in this situation. Ira enters the dimly lit chamber determined to spot inaccuracy, contradiction and corruption in order to build his case against the Authorities. Alex too enters in search of those incentives; however, her end game is not to gather evidence for a trial. With gritted teeth, she enters knowing that all she will hear are lies and deceit. These were politicians, lawyers, military and clerics. Not one of them could be trusted. Not one of them could be allowed to live. While they are both here to challenge the Giovanni Authorities' lies and hear for themselves the narrative the Authorities' have weaved around the Midnight Children, Ira is determined to put them to justice by means of law while Alex by means of execution. The human in Argon is dead – the person he was once, obliterated and she would make the Authorities pay. An eye for an eye…

They descend another black wrought iron skeletal staircase where they arrive on to what appears to be a black marble stage. Only when they reach the centre and survey their surroundings, they realise that they are standing in an amphitheatre. Under her breath Alex laughs to herself, catching Ira's attention. He frowns wondering what could be so funny at this current point in time. This is Alex Valentine, and for all, he knows she has something up her sleeve. She had a reputation that he had recently come to learn was rightfully earned.

He watches her stroll across to stage right as if walking about to rhyme off a passionate, bittersweet monologue. In her mind she recalls Shakespeare's famous lines, 'Life's but a walking shadow, a poor player /That struts and frets his hour upon the stage /And then is heard no more: it is a tale/ Told by an idiot, full of sound and fury, Signifying nothing.' An omen? She contemplates the quote for a moment before brushing it off with a bitter smirk, sure we knew that anyway.

A loud boom from somewhere above calls their attention to the stalls. The thirteen Giovanni Authorities have entered the dark court, filtering from their procession to their assigned seats while armed sentries take up their position. The Major stands, arms folded, at close range by the side of the stage. If the Midnight Children were going to pull some stunt, he would be close at hand to engage them. While it was a rumour of high regard that the Midnight Children could not be killed, with his gun in a holster at his side, his sword in a sheath on his hip and a dagger beneath the breast of his coat, if any move was made the Major would be ready to fight.

Zanned Delin, the leader of the Giovanni Authorities and oldest Incumbent vampire, takes his seat in the middle of the balcony facing centre stage. To his right sits Caros, the vile and ruthless General of the Giovanni army. To Zanned's left sits Farius, the priestly figure of the Giovanni Authorities. Although his green eyes are so pale they appear to be blind, he peers down on the stage with a poise of self-righteous judgement that boils the Midnight Children's blood.

"You have arrived without invitation" a voice finally booms in a gravelly English accent. It is Zanned. "Either you have arrived in arrogance or desperation." He accuses. Alex and Ira side-eye each other.

"Arrogance." Another voice snorts. Caros, the hypocrite has seen fit to spit insults from the get go and Alex is not having any of it. "In fact it's neither," she steps forward. The Major's hand twitches towards his gun but hesitates. "On our part anyway." She smirks.

"I'm sure you are aware that the Ronakites are amassing." From Zanned's right-hand side, Caros snorts again.

"Of course we're aware." Zanned replies. Alex shrugs and challenges him.

"So I am sure you are also aware that Argon has finally emerged to lead the Renegades and they have attacked Ar Novads and have actually penetrated its walls."

"As I said, we are aware," Caros eyeballs her in disgust – how dare she address so boldly an Authority of his rank. "I believe the Renegades are planning an attack on Ar Novads and I believe they have done a deal with the Ronakites. What I want to know is firstly, is there anything in Ar Novad's of any value to them? And secondly, what do you plan on doing about this?" Alex finishes.

"Well, firstly, Miss Valentine," starts Zanned, "That is quite frankly none of your business."

"Not my business? Oh, you are wildly mistaken." Alex struggles to restrain her rage. "When my life is dictated by your mistakes and I live to suffer the consequences, when everything I love is taken from me and twisted and torn apart because of the actions of the Incumbents and the Authorities, I would say that is my business."

"Order in this court!" shouts the Major, revealing a flicker of concern in his expression.

"When the Renegades attempt to take my life and the lives of those who have nothing to do with this fight die just for being close to me! When their only crime is being made a Giovanni, it is my business!" Alex shouts.

"Enough!" Zanned stands. "Have you come here for answers or accusations Midnight Child? You might have escaped the confines of Ar Novad's Institute, but I will assure you if I make the call, you will not escape our cells." Before Alex can dig their grave any deeper, Ira steps in hoping that flattery will better suit their intentions.

"I implore your attention, sirs. We do not wish to cause injury or insult, but we do need answers. We do have reason to believe that what Alex has told you is the truth. We have seen the Renegades within Ar Novads and Argon, and we do have reason to believe an alliance has been made between them and the Ronakites." Ira is playing along with Alex. While they have no substantial evidence to prove this allegiance Ira understands Alex has attempted to provoke the Authorities through their own fears. They know, despite all self-righteousness and bravado that they could not withstand an attack by both the Ronakites and Renegades.

Hoping to say his piece without interruption, Ira continues, "We have reason to believe that Ar Novad's is no longer safe. We cannot be certain if Argon's intentions are to find information hostile to the cause of peace or to simply cause nothing but terror to the lives of those inside the walls." For a moment the Authorities remain silent. Zanned turns to Caros for silent support. Caros nods with approval, knowing his leader will take the political approach. "We have two thousand soldiers stationed at Ar Novads. This incident was no more than a security breach and caution will be taken."

"It is not the time for caution. It is the time for action," Alex seethes, "How many need to die before you see that?"

"May I remind you, Valentine, that you are still suspended from duty. You have no business in Ar Novad's Institute until General Delin states otherwise," Zanned reminds her.

"Should you disobey any further orders I will have a cell here with your name on it." Caros peers smugly down at her. Alex can feel the disgust rising in her stomach.

"Sirs," again, Ira intervenes sensing their appeal about to descend into an argument, "You need to trust us."

"We do not need to do anything of the sort," Snorts Caros.

"War is upon us. Ar Novad's is the first step," Ira speaks softly. He understands the precariousness of the situation, so does not speak as a threat but as a warning.

"It is a mere provocation. Argon and his Renegades are no match for Giovanni forces." Rolling her eyes, Alex steps forward, disgusted by Zanned's denial.

"That's all very well for you to say from your gilded throne. But when Argon, the Renegades and the Ronakites are done with Ar Novad's, when they've got what they came for they will come for you."

"Alex Valentine, you are in no position to be making threats!" Caros rises to his feet, ready to order an arrest. "Deny it all you want, turn your blind eyes, but this is the truth!" she engages.

"You are nothing but a war-mongering whore!" Caros roars, signalling to his guards, "Arrest them both!" Caros' guards with the Major leading the assault immediately react to their orders and close in on the stage. The Midnight Children immediately raise their swords. "Drop your weapons!" Caros yells as his guards move closer.

"Not on your life," Mutters Alex before engaging the Major. Faster than he can react, she has him knocked to the ground. Astounded by her sheer speed and force the Major stares up from the ground in disbelief. Winking, she turns her back on him and is immediately set upon by another soldier who she easily overpowers also. With ease, she renders two more unconscious then sets her sights on the next target. Behind her, Ira reluctantly engages the guard before him. Neither are fighting to kill but ready to do so if appropriately pushed.

Bearing witness to the agility of the Midnight Children who quickly overcome each of the Giovanni's finest armed guards, Zanned decides that enough is enough. Rising to his feet, he appears as a brutish, dominating figure backlit by the dark and sombre glow of the amphitheatre. "Halt!" he bellows in his rough accent, "Cease! Enough of this debacle!"

"With all due respect, sir, we didn't start it." Ira shoots Caros a menacing glare from beneath his dark fringe as he returns his sword to its sheath.

"Well, I'm ending it." Zanned sinks back into his throne. He has seen potential in the Midnight Children, something that his absent presence in Ar Novad's has not witnessed before. Caros is right to be wary he thinks, but Zanned was not fool enough to waste an opportunity – the Midnight Children were assets. If he could keep them close, he could cast a cold eye on them and better to do this as a friend than a foe for Zanned knew that imprisoning the Midnight Children would only succeed in turning them against the Authorities. We may not be able to kill them he postulates, but we can keep them close enough to try.

The Giovanni's defeated guards drag themselves from the floor and return to their positions flanking the stage. As he moves past, the Major's eyes appear to stare right through the Midnight Children's souls with a bitterness so strong Alex can almost taste it. High above in the balcony, Caros too seethes with spite. The Midnight Children have made a mockery of his best-trained soldiers, and he will not forget it.

The stage falls silent. Refusing to relinquish her grip on her sword Alex steps up, "You can fight us, and you can imprison us all you want – well, you can try – but that does not change the fact that Argon and his Renegades are plotting as we speak."

"And what would you have us do, lieutenant?" Caros exaggerates the word 'lieutenant' to emphasise her inferior rank.

"Well, first of all, I'd climb up there and kick your ass and then you could kiss mine." Again Alex and Caros are on the verge of a clash, so again for the cause of damage control, Ira steps in.

"I would have you take us seriously. Arrogance will not keep Argon and his army of monsters out of Ar Novad's."

"Calling us arrogant now, Tallon?" Zanned pushes. Seeing the engagement about to stumble into the same argument as before, Ira sighs. This time Alex intervenes.

"Look. The Renegades have attacked before – specifically they've attacked me before. And, you know where they've attacked? In the darkness, in the shadows. They come out of nowhere, they attack and very few of them have lived to tell the tale. The Renegades are guerrilla fighters. They attack quickly and in locations with a getaway. Since Argon's appearance, the Renegades are getting bolder. He's instilled something in them. Only when you have a good plan in place can you be that content and can you be that arrogant."

"Speaking as someone with experience in such?" the Giovanni leader interrogates.

"I don't know, Zanned you tell me. You appear unnaturally relaxed for someone on the brink of war."

"I do not fear Ronakites."

"Our numbers greatly outnumber theirs and our army is greatly superior, better equipped and better trained." Alex can't believe what just came out of Caros' mouth. She glances back and forth to the sheepish soldiers standing guard around them with her eyes lingering on the Major.

"So you've demonstrated." Alex remarks. Caros grits his teeth.

"Midnight Children," Zanned rises again taking a moment to look to the rest of the Giovanni Authorities, not for support or approval but to make sure they are paying attention, "Do what you must to ensure the safety of Ar Novad's. If what you say is true, we would not want it falling to the wrong hands." Zanned acquiesces not to appease the Midnight Children but to keep them distracted and out of Bodmin. "I will inform General Delin of your reinstatement, and perhaps you could come to some sort of civil agreement about how best to protect the Institute."

Disregarding his usual obedience to the Giovanni leader, Caros jumps to protest, "Zanned you can't be serious. After everything they have done? She broke the Ankh! She attacked General Delin! She neglected her duties which resulted in an entire section of her platoon being suspended from duty! Then! Then while on suspension she broke back into Ar Novad's Institute, got herself arrested, broke out by bombing the Institute and went on the run!"

"Yeah, to here!" Alex can't help but smirk at Caros lists her various deviant achievements. It appears as if Zanned is about to go back on his word when Ira speaks up:

"Sir, Zanned, Alex may have done all those things, but she has done them for the love of her Clan. Alex tried to warn General Delin of an attack before it happened. She is trying to protect this Clan." Zanned considers Ira's words until Caros interjects with derision.

"Perhaps she only knows what's coming because she's planned what's coming."

"Sir, that's absurd!" Ira argues.

"Is it now? Why was Valentine not in the weapons locker as General Delin had ordered on the night that Argon infiltrated the Institute? Would it be entirely out of line to suspect that Valentine herself could have let Argon in?" Caros makes a good point, one that hits Ira hard. He knows little about Alex, in fact, he knows little about all of this mess at this point. All he knows is to subdue his doubt and stick to his argument. From the corner of his eye, he catches Alex's looking to him with her dark, piercing eyes. She can sense his doubt.

"Yes, sir," he turns back defiantly to address Caros, "It would be entirely out of line."

"We'll see." the wretched warrior vows. A silence settles once more. No-one moves. The hollow eyes of the Giovanni Authorities peer through the darkness like demons to the two fallen angels below. No more words need to be said.

However, Zanned always having to have the last word cuts through the silence like a sledgehammer. "So, Valentine, Ira Tallon would have me believe that you are working in the Giovanni Clan's best interests?"

"Is that so hard to believe?" she questions. Zanned's paranoia, like all the Giovanni Authorities' is palpable.

"Well, you've appealed to us to protect Ar Novad's. What I am giving you is a chance to prove that's in your true interests. I give Ar Novad's Institute to you and Tallon to protect. Should Argon have conspired with the Renegades and Ronakites to attack Ar Novad's I want you to prove your sincerity. Are you willing to die for the Giovanni Clan?" the question Zanned has put to the Midnight Children is not a question, it is a challenge, and they know it. Having charged them with this responsibility, any failure damns them. "Die for this Clan?" Alex finally responds forcing Ira once again to wonder where she is going with her words.

"No Zanned, I will not die for this Clan," Caros beams with the expression of 'I told you so' but is cut short with Alex's following words. "I will not die for this Clan. I will die because of this Clan."

There was so much more Alex wanted to say. She had a whole speech planned. What she really wanted to say was, "Why would I die for this Clan? Haven't I already given my life to this Clan? Why would I fight and suffer and die? Would you even care? Would you even have a shred of respect for anything that I had done? Where will you be fighting? Will you grip swords and face the blood and the mutilation and murder against the Ronakites? Where will you be standing when I lay dying? Where? Will you be there so I can look up and ask 'Why? Why am I lying dying? Why have I been stained with all this pain and hate and suffering?' No, I will not die to keep you on your thrones."

Alex says nothing. Words were worthless in this stand-off. Losing patience and desperate to avoid going around in another circle, Alex returns her sword to its sheath with a high-pitched screech. She turns to Ira, a signal for them to depart. In silent understanding, Ira nods. Turning to the Authorities, he asks, "So are we free to go?" the Authorities and armed guards immediately look to Zanned who pauses, claps his hands sharply then extends his right arm with two fingers raised in the gesture of a 'pardon'.

"Go." He speaks no further but rises, tugs his suit into place and starts towards the exit. The rest of his coven fall into their unholy procession and follow him out. Caros hangs back to command his guards, "Escort the Midnight Children to their plane immediately. Get them the Hell out of Bodmin."

"If we are to protect Ar Novad's Institute, we would need to be suitably armed." Alex's statement stops the Authorities in their tracks. She can see by their questioning looks she has hooked them, "You want Argon dead. Tallon can't do that without his sword."

"He has a sword." Snorts Caros.

"You know what I mean," she snaps, "You want Argon dead. Do you trust me to do it?" it is as if the collective Authorities sigh inaudibly at once. They know she's got them good. Zanned can feel Caros' eyes burning on him. Caros had him under pressure to hold out until the Alchemists could find a way to overcome the swords' enchantments. Zanned, notoriously the master of impromptu lying, in this case decides it is his better judgement to acquiesce.

"Major, escort the Midnight Children to the Chamber of Perfidia."

"Zanned!" Caros erupts inciting Zanned's eyes to glow fierce green with rage. He glares at his right-hand man. Caros immediately yields, "I'm sorry, sir. I will not obstruct your decision."

With that, Caros turns his back, sulks his way into the darkness ad exits the 'court'. As the guards move to form their escort, Alex and Ira, this time go quietly. Neither Midnight Child is quite convinced they have got what they came for, but there are many things they couldn't reveal about their mission, not even to provoke the Authorities. The Authorities know the Midnight Children are up to no good and the Midnight Children know the Authorities are up to no good. The important thing is, who will make the first move.

Alex remains silent as they make their exit because not only does she have to hide the truth to the Authorities, but she must hide the truth to Ira also. She needs him to trust her. If Ira lost his trust in her, he could lose his trust in their entire mission and out of that there are only two scenarios she can see; one where Ira abandons all hope and gets himself killed and one where Ira joins Argon and helps Argon kill her. I have enough enemies, she acknowledges, and for that reason, she keeps her lips sealed.

Chapter 25

Major Blaine Sinclair leads the way through the palatial Hall of Vampires. Flanked by the Giovanni's finest armed guards the Midnight Children meander through the long crimson corridors further from the glamour of the social gathering and into the silent corridors of marble floors, vivid paintings, tapestries, busts and statues where only those of significant rank and privilege are permitted.

As they near the back of the Hall, the Major orders his soldiers to stand guard at strategic points. As they enter the Chamber of Perfidia the last two soldiers, those of the highest rank are ordered to stand guard at the top of an exquisite wide, gently winding spiralled staircase within a circular chamber. Alex and Ira peer over the edge of the balustrade, absorbing the majesty of the craftsmanship. Ira is awestruck. It is as is the entire chamber is carved seamlessly from a single entity. There are no steps. The staircase simply slopes, or rather snakes downwards. At the very bottom, on the ancient mosaic floor is a large stone baptismal font that looks as if it has simply grown out of the ground. Above him is an oculus allowing the moon to line up perfectly with the font at a certain moment in time. Despite the artistic and architectural grandeur, it is a chamber the Authorities rarely frequent. The oculus is their security for at night, sentries would be posted to guard the only entrance and as the sun came up in the morning, the deathly light of day would prevent any vampire from leaving the chamber alive.

Despite the darkness of the night, the Major is taking a huge risk descending into the chamber alone with the Midnight Children. All his senses are on high alert as he leads the way to the bottom. Despite having a quick hand to his sword, he could not defend himself if the Midnight Children chose to attack, he could put up a fight surely, but he couldn't kill them. Accepting the role he is playing is the only thing driving him forward and keeping his composure.

As the Midnight Children follow the Major downwards, memories flood Alex's gut in a sickening wave. As they close in on the ground floor, she eyes the finely engraved font with a mixture of sadness and hatred. An image in her mind casts her memory backwards to her first time at the Hall with Julius just months after she was 'turned'. Back then, she had been so overwhelmed by the life and love that she had lost. And, it was no sooner that she lost her baby and her last connection to her human life that she was forced to come to this desolate place and pick up a sword. The precious mosaics, the artistic elegance and architectural splendour, are now all lost on her. Her memories leave her eyes and heart closed to the magnificence of her surroundings. How quickly the hollowness in her heart had turned to hatred when she took up that sword. From the moment she gripped that sword in her hand, she knew what she was going to do. Now it is Ira's turn.

The Major reaches the ground floor and moves straight past the font and directly to an intersecting hallway along which are further chambers each sealed shut by golden gates. He halts at the largest gate immediately facing the font. Producing a long golden key from the inner breast pocket of his leather overcoat, he unlocks the gate with an echoing clank. He urges the hefty iron gates open and steps into the vast vault followed by the Midnight Children. Their ethereal eyesight adjusts quickly to the gloom however the Major flicks a switch illuminating the room with artificial light that draws their sight to a mound of earth in the centre of the room. Ira had expected the room would reflect the grandeur of the walls outside it, but this was more of an excavation site than a shrine.

Below their feet was an old First Century brick road, and the walls that held up the vault were little more than crumbling frescos. Before them upon the mound of the earth stands a concrete tomb and upon the concrete tomb, plunged into the centre are two glistening swords. Having seen it all before, Alex remains stationary by the doorway. Ira proceeds towards it, stalked by the Major. As Ira arrives at the foot of the tomb upon which lays an effigy of a person, he asks the Major, "Who is this?"

"No-one." The Major replies solemnly as Ira runs his fingertips along the slab.

"No-one?" Ira questions.

"It was built to be the tomb of the First," the Major answers. Ira notices a thin wound in the effigy close to the others from which a third sword has been pulled. He looks to Alex who draws back her coat to flash the rose-design hilt of her sword confirming his unspoken question. “The First is in here?” Ira questions. He is captivated by the idea that his Creator is so close. If he was really to believe the prophecy, then he was the living embodiment of the First’s soul. A chilling sensation creeps over him at that thought – it is like looking upon his own tomb. “No, The First is not here,” the Major steps closer, “It was made for him ceremoniously before his death. Throughout the ages, there were tales of monsters who slept in coffins so he thought a tomb would be a fitting monument. Perhaps he had a sense of humour or, maybe he saw it as a sort of symbol of the death of humanity. It has various interpretations. It was planned to be placed in Moor Falls Cemetery, but it never got to that point.”

“The war broke out?”

“No. The Incumbents got to him.” Alex cuts in to answer Ira’s question. Ira looks from Alex to the Major whose gesture Ira reads as confirming Alex’s statement.

“So where is he?” Asks Ira.

“Only the Incumbents know that. Probably the Authorities too.” Alex’s judgemental gaze connects with the Major’s. “And the swords?” Ira continues to question.

“The swords are an accident,” The Major cuts in before Alex can speak; however, she draws closer. Ira is surprised that the Major is offering up his information so easily but surmises that it is an attempt to get in with his version of events before Alex can. The Major continues, “The First and the Incumbents got into an argument. It was a setup. It was a plan to corner him. The First was so enraged that he plunged his sword into his ‘tomb’.”

“Then Balthazar stabbed him in the back – literally,” Alex cuts in again. The Major is unimpressed. Ira turns to read the Major’s response to her interjection and finds truth in his expression.

“When the First died.”

“Was murdered,” Alex corrects.

“His sword split into three parts, just like his soul. Three embryos, three swords, three Midnight Children. The swords have remained set in that stone ever since. No-one has been able to touch them let alone remove them except…” the Major trails off as he side-eyes Alex, expecting her to interrupt. Knowing the Major is giving her the opportunity to speak, she remains silent on purpose, forcing him to finish his sentence. “Except for the First Midnight Child, Alex

Valentine," the Major completes his sentence. Alex beams childishly at the mention of her name.

The Major's words settle in Ira's mind, and he struggles to accept them as facts. However, he is staring at and touching the evidence. After a moment, his gaze moves from the stone slab beneath his hands to the shining steel bodies of the swords. He studies them carefully. "How do I know which one is mine?" He asks.

"Remember, at the gate?" Alex replies. Ira recalls Chiron's hand burning at the touch of her sword. He nods and returns to studying the swords. As he leans closer, he can see the inscriptions shining within the steel – the Midnight Children's Ligatures. His gaze ascends to the hilt of the one to his left. On the pommel rests a design akin to a crown of thorns surrounding a blood-red stone. The grip appears charred and twisted as if left in fire. Below it appears an array of symbols that seem to be etched into the steel. Turning to look at the sword to his right, he knows this belongs to him. He doesn't need to touch it to know it belongs to him. The grip is quite plain, but just below this laurel wreaths are etched and the pommel itself if the head of an eagle. Without hesitation, he grabs the hilt of the sword and pulls it from the tomb. He looks up from the sword in his hand just in time to see fear fill the Major's dark eyes. There is one sword left. Alex, Ira and the Giovanni Major all look upon it with trepidation. Argon will come for it.

The Major quickly composes himself, "Are we done here?"

"Do you think you can stop him?" the Major appears offended by Ira's question.

"Ira Tallon, I will not have to stop him if you keep up your end of the bargain and use that sword for its intended purpose."

"You also won't have to stop him if the Authorities allow him to waltz right through their doors." Alex passive-aggressively accuses.

"That will not be happening," the Major snaps. Alex pulls a face in response and shrugs her shoulders. "Be under no illusion that you are untouchable." Warns the Major, "It could have been Argon waltzing in here to collect his sword, not Alex Valentine or Ira Tallon."

Alex and Ira know the Major is right. The Authorities could well have done a deal with Belial, the Ronakites and Argon, unlikely but possible. They were in a perilous situation isolated in Bodmin and despite their hubris; Alex and Ira knew the Authorities knew it. The Authorities know that Argon will come for the sword one way or another, sooner rather than later.

The Major, having said his piece takes off out of the chamber before Alex or Ira, particularly Alex, can speak. Alex watches as Ira's gaze descends to linger on the sword in his hand. She can see the sorrow in Ira's eyes. Suddenly, holding this sword in his hand, the reality of the situation feels more tangible. He looks to the one remaining sword yet to be pulled from the tomb – the sword that is his only destruction. The thought of dying by the sword sickens him. The thought of Argon plunging that sword through his chest, compels his heartbeat to fall out of rhythm. He takes a deep breath, wondering if this is really the way it has to be.

"Let's get out of here," says Alex, sensing his discontent drawing Ira in a dangerous direction. Clutching the unique sword in his hand, he looks to his comrade before nodding lightly. Hoping that she has broken Ira's train of thought, Alex makes a swift exit from the chamber where the Major waits to seal the gate. As Ira leaves the chamber and they start to make their way back up the winding staircase, Ira looks up to the moon staring through the eye in the ceiling. At that moment, he thinks; if there is any way to escape this reality and this inhuman war, he will take it.

Chapter 26

Closely surrounded by their futile military escort the Midnight Children are marched down the war-worn cobbled slope from the black plateau where they emerge from the mist and move straight towards the landing strip where their plane awaits. Chiron, still bitter about being made a fool of, along with his Gate sentries have all paused to observe the spectacle from their post.

With the Major's eyes burning their backs, Ira asks, "So what now? How do you suppose we win Delin over? I think it's going to take more than a bunch of flowers and a sorry card." Walking closely behind him, Alex pauses for added effect then replies:

"Actually, I was going to act like nothing ever happened." Ira half stops in his tracks, glancing back at Alex and causing her to nearly walk into him. Seeing his expression of disbelief, she shrugs, "Well, she's getting no sorry from me. And I want no apology from her for that matter, 'oh Alex, I'm so sorry to hear about Corporal Hart. I'm so sorry I didn't listen to you'. I'd rather have a lecture than a painted apology."

"Alex," Ira stops as they approach the plane, "Elaina would have died regardless whether General Delin had listened to you or not." It is a fact Alex did not want to accept. The soldiers form around them and stand to attention. The Major listens intently as Ira takes Alex's hand loosely in his own, "Alex, you couldn't have known that the guy who attacked Ar Novad's would be the third Midnight Child. You couldn't have known that he was the same guy Elaina was speaking about. Warning her was all you could do. She chose not to listen."

"I should have known," Alex whispers.

"How could you?" he asks, shaking her hand lightly, "You can't save everyone." Alex knows Ira means well, but that statement was like a knife in the gut. How many more would die and take part of her with them, she wonders. She concealed the death certificates she found in the vault. She saw Argon's name. Albeit, she didn't look long enough to see any detail, but she should have put two and two together. Seeing Argon's name had haunted all sense from her. In her attempt to erase Argon from her mind, she had abandoned all logic, and as a result, she had failed Elaina. The mere mention of his name would have been enough of a warning to Elaina, but Alex could not bring herself to say it.

Seeing Alex drift and her demeanour drop, Ira lets go and turns to the Major, "Goodbye Major. I'm sure we'll meet again."

"Indeed, we will," the Major declares. Taking this to be a statement of warning Ira grimaces and moves to enter the plane. Alex lingers, sensing some semblance of softening in the Major's stance. She had seen that look before, that sadness in his eyes – that sadness is mine. Finally, the Major speaks:

"Will you do one thing for me, Valentine?" curious, she remains silent and nods in response. "Will you tell Julius I send my regards?"

"Yes. But who will I tell him sends his regards?"

"Tell him Blaine does." With that, the Major swivels on his heels and makes a start back towards the Bodmin plateau with his squad of soldiers in pursuit. Alex watches him walk away, wondering what must have happened between Julius and the Major, Blaine, to waken this sadness within him – a disagreement? An allegiance? Fate?

Through the darkness far above, little yellow lights pierce through the fog, not like stars in the night sky but like spiders in a nest. She lingers longer as Ira starts the plane behind her with a loud rumble. The gust of the small but powerful engines blows her long black hair across her face and causes her long leather coat to flap against her boots. Drawing the strands of her hair back from her face, she spares one last glance to the Major as he ascends towards the mountainous domain and is swallowed whole by the darkness. Once again, she wonders if this is just another enemy who would once again cross her path. With any luck, she hopes, Blaine does not hold any bitterness towards Julius or their cause. Hopefully, she wonders, that Blaine will not prove to be Julius' Argon.

Chapter 27

It is early morning when their small Giovanni branded plane touches down on the coastal landing strip, and of course, as Alex had imagined, Julius' Porsche that she had abandoned by the aircraft hangar is nowhere to be found. As the two Midnight Children emerge from the hangar, having returned the plane to its rightful position, Ira squints in the light of the morning sun. When his eyes engage, he gazes out towards the twinkling sea as the sunlight sparkles and rolls with the waves before crashing against the rugged coast. Ira inhales the fresh air. Beneath the light of the sun with the warmth on his pale skin and the smell of the sea air, he feels like he has just stepped through a parallel dimension. However, reality strikes as he turns his attention from the sea and suddenly realises that their vehicle has gone AWOL.

"Alex."

"Yes, Tallon?"

"The car."

"Yes, Tallon?"

"The car is gone."

"I see that."

Ira turns to her, arms flailing in question. In response, Alex produces Julius' car key as some sort of proof of innocence. Ira pulls a face, "Very good, Valentine." He sighs, "Now how do you suppose we get back? Bus it?"

"Nope." Alex gestures to the security cameras on the outside of the hangar. Seconds later, as if on cue, a fleet of Giovanni crested armoured landrovers with blacked-out-windows roar up behind them. Ira shakes his head, "I don't know whether I feel like a celebrity or a criminal."

"I suppose it depends on whether you're getting handcuffed to a bed or a radiator." Alex shrugs; a reply and gesture that seem incomprehensible to Ira in their current situation.

Giovanni guards in riot gear, gloves and masks with a gauze over their eyes jump from the vehicles, guns raised. Not a millimetre of skin shows. In their attempt to shield themselves from the menacing light of the sun, they appear more like robots than humans – well, somewhat human. "Alex Valentine. Ira Tallon. Get in the vehicle." The Commanding Officer orders. To his and the rest of the guards' surprise, the Midnight Children accept his order without resistance. Believing it to be some sort of scheme, the convoy leader holds his command for the squad to return to their vehicles. Instead, he stands his ground, poised for combat that never comes. Alex and Ira saunter on past the line of guards and hop into the back of the leading landrover. After a moment of deliberation, the Commanding Officer orders his squad back to the vehicles.

To both Ira and the Giovanni soldiers' surprise, Alex remains silent throughout the journey back to the city. Ira isn't sure whether she is tired, worried, deep in thought, plotting or otherwise but he decides to leave her be. With his own mind swirling with thoughts and questions, he relaxes as much as possible back into the seat to enjoy the silence.

Both Midnight Children gaze through the blacked-out windows watching the world drift by through the translucent divide. As they journey closer to the city, the rural roads turn to motorways, and the vast green fields and ancient trees turn to the cold stone of buildings and the suffocating bustling of human traffic. Alex turns away from the window, assuming they will be veering off the road towards Ar Novad's, however, curiously, they drive on through the city. Alex's anxiety heightens – a trap? She wonders. Could these Giovanni soldiers actually be Renegades in disguise? Or, would the Giovanni have sold them out? As Ar Novad's passes by, even Ira becomes alert to the possibility that something might have gone wrong here.

From the corner of his eye, he sees Alex reaching within her coat to pull out a tidy 9mm gun she had taken from Julius' armoury. There is no point in moving too hastily she thinks; no point in jumping to conclusions, however, she keeps her finger carefully on the trigger just in case. If she got the right signal, she would have no problem sending a silver bullet through the back of these bastards' brains.

The Midnight Children pay close attention to the direction the driver is taking them. Unable to read the driver's expression in the mirror due to the mask, Ira leans over slightly to observe through the front window as they veer away from the river that intersects the city and take the side streets to bypass the traffic. Alex is just about to question the driver's intentions when she sees a road sign for directions that the driver instantly follows. She softens slightly – the road sign reads, 'San Lorenzo Mansion' – they are being taken to Julius.

The Giovanni soldiers drive Alex and Ira directly to the enormous sandstone palace that seems so pale and sallow in the sunlight. The Commanding Officer disembarks and opens the back door to free the Midnight Children. Unable to see behind the soldier's mask, Alex eyes him warily as she emerges into the sunlight. Her boots crunch on the stones beneath her as she takes a few strides forward, carefully scanning for anything amiss. Nothing seems askew. The wild and ancient grounds surrounding the mansion are quiet, and still, not even a breath of wind stirs the grass nor ripples across the pond. The only noise she can hear is the gentle cascading of the fountain, a stone sculpture of John the Baptist. Julius had told her it was an original Da Vinci who used to be an old friend of his, but Alex had never believed him.

"What's going on here?" Ira finally addressed the elephant in the room. He stares at the Commanding Officer, silently pushing him for an answer.

"Just following orders," the Commander replies.

"Yeah, but whose orders?" Ira's question is permeated with mistrust.

"General Delin's orders." The Commander replies before re-entering the vehicle and driving off down the long stone driveway with dust in his tracks. Alex and Ira turn to look at each other. This was not the welcome they were expecting. Instinctively, Alex reaches for the rose gold hilt of her sword and slides it from its sheath as she starts towards the mansion, ascending the steps and sneaking towards the arched castle gate-like doors stealthily as a cat. Ira creeps closely behind. They should probably go through another door, Alex thinks but in reality if there was an ambush inside waiting to happen, whoever was inside probably already had all bases covered.

Deciding to throw tactics to the wind, she quickly unlocks and flits through the huge wooden doors. Inside she stands, sword in hand, surprised to find only silence. She turns back to Ira who shrugs. "Julius?" she calls carefully as she starts down the hallway and into the cavernous atrium. The Midnight Children scan high and low for signs of trouble. Nothing. No furnishings unfurnished; no signs of struggle; no signs of stealing. Nada. Ira is the first to return his sword to its sheath. "Perhaps we're being a tad paranoid," he suggests.

"Alex?" Julius voice echoes down the corridor from the lounge. Alex immediately rushes towards it with Ira in pursuit. Throwing open the lounge door, prepared to find a hostage situation, Alex almost drops upon finding Julius and Delin apparently sitting having a quiet chat. All the blackout curtains are closed, permitting no shard of natural deadly light through. However, the enormous room is warmly lit by the finely crafted chandelier hanging high above and numerous vintage Tiffany table lamps.

"I'm sorry, if I'd known, we had company I would have dressed." Alex replaces her sword and moves into the room. Julius and General Delin both know she is being sarcastic but let it slide; they have business to discuss.

"Blaine sends his regards by the way." Alex relays the message to Julius to test his reaction. Julius tries to remain composed, but Alex knows the name has struck a nerve like the same hold Argon had on her.

"You spoke with Blaine?" he questions. Delin watches him.

"Not exactly. Although I did kick his ass." Julius smiles softly at the thought of it.

"What's going on here?" Ira comes closer into the room.

"Alex, Ira, come sit. General Delin has a proposition for you." Julius gestures to the seat beside him. As they approach and sit, Julius pours two glasses of blood from a crystal decanter and passes them to Alex and Ira. "Would that proposition be that if we kindly fuck off, she'll kindly ask the Authorities not to try to kill us?" General Delin tightens her lips, not amused and fixes her glasses. Alex had always wondered why Delin chose to wear them – what the hell would a bloody vampire need with glasses? She contemplated.

"I am done playing games with you," Delin speaks, "I am removing both of you from your posts."

"General!" Ira cuts her off.

"And I am allocating your platoons to other officers." Ira shakes his head at this apparent insult. Alex figures she's finally pushed Delin's buttons enough and she's getting cut loose – result, she thinks. However, the steely General continues, "I am allocating the both of you a task force." Now the Midnight Children are taken by surprise. She's doing what? One minute she was having them arrested – now she was giving them a task force?

"What's the catch?" Ira questions. Delin removes her glasses.

"I am giving you a task force comprised of Alex's Delinquents."

"Great." Ira rolls his eyes.

"Can I trade Holly in for no-one?" asks Alex.

"Don't worry, Valentine, she wanted nothing to do with you anyway."

"Ah, win-win." Alex drinks.

"I don't want anyone else involved," Delin continues, "The only reason these soldiers will make up your task force is because they were already involved in one debacle."

"Careful now, General," Alex warns. Without a blink, Delin presses the play button on Julius's 70" LCD TV, and in full definition, Alex watches her and her section on CCTV camera footage dashing through the vaults beneath Ar Novad's. There was no denying it. It was there in full HD; she had been caught red-handed in the act. Ira shakes his head at her – of course, Alex would have known there would be security cameras in the vaults, she was just being arrogant.

"You were correct, Valentine. Ar Novad's was breached and going forward we need to ensure the building is secure. However, I do not want to instil panic or excitement within our ranks. We need this to be covert."

"To be clear, we're not the one who breached it," Alex pouts.

"I figured that out all by myself, Valentine," Alex half appreciates Delin's sarcasm. The General again presses play, choosing a different camera angle. After a moment, the breach is confirmed; a squad of Renegades in shabby combat attire rush down the tunnel in Alex's section's direction. Delin pauses the footage, "We have precious materials in those vaults. The Ankh of the Dead is in those vaults. We need to secure them."

"Who's this 'we' you keep talking about?" Again, Alex is being sarcastic, but Delin needs the Midnight Children to trust her. The General looks to Julius who gives her the signal to blow her cover. For the first time since the night, Argon attacked Ar Novad's the ancient commander appears nervous, vulnerable even. "It was a grave night when the call was made to murder the first of our kind." Alex is intrigued, Delin has just admitted to murder with Julius just sitting there. Holding up her hand for the Midnight Children to view the weighty signet ring emblazoned with the Seal of the Incumbents on her finger, she continues, "I am an Incumbent of the Giovanni Clan. However, I was an Incumbent for the entire nation, not just the Giovanni. I never wanted it that way. Zanned held sway. Zanned and Caros manipulated and intimidated the other Incumbents into believing this was our only salvation. He made us believe that it was kill or be killed; that the First was a monster who had turned on his own creation and for that he had to die.

"When Zanned had his plan in motion, he held a 'vote' to give the charade an illusion of legitimacy. No-one would have spoken out against him. They were too afraid of what Caros' thugs would do to them. Crucifying them and leaving them to the sun was a particular passion of his. Caros was the Head of Defence. Zanned had fixed his cards so that when the election came, Farius became Chancellor of the Exchequer with control of all the finances of Bodmin. He flooded the Council with Giovanni. Money and status equals control and power."

"Neither lasts forever," Alex mutters.

"We completed the ritual in Moor Falls Cemetery," Delin confesses.

"Ritual murder," Ira interjects.

"Balthazar descended into the Hall of Perfidia and killed the First with an imbued dagger and when the flames became embers and the embers became ashes there within were three glowing embryos – the Midnight Children."

The Head of Ar Novad's allows the Midnight Children a moment to reflect on her words before continuing, "I begged him not to do it but Zanned, of course, tried to have the embryos, you, destroyed by fire, water, sunlight, everything. Nothing worked. Only when all his attempts seemed to prove futile, he considered locking you away forever. This time I persuaded him to give you to me. I told him there was no use in locking you away for someone to inevitably find when I could keep you and study you. When the clans split and war broke out between the Giovanni and the Ronakites I kept you hidden."

"Wait," Alex postulates, "Julius broke us out of Bodmin." Julius smiles, he knew Alex would fixate on that detail. She continues to her question, "Were we given or stolen?"

"A mixture of both," Julius admits. "The prophecy" – he is cut off by Alex and Ira pulling faces at the mention of the word. Despite their dubiousness towards the prophecy, he continues, "The prophecy foretold of the Midnight Children's arrival before the act of killing the First was completed. The Incumbents were warned. That's why they so clung to your destruction. After the war, I saw the bloodlust rise in the Giovanni Authorities. They killed indiscriminately – Ronakite, Renegades, Teva, Lanuonin – even Giovanni – anyone who spoke against or up to them. I had sworn to protect the Midnight Children. The prophecy needed to be fulfilled to regain order."

"Could you not just have gone to the Teva and Lanuonin yourself without us and committed them to your cause?" seeing a loophole, Ira attempts to question Julius' reasoning.

"No." Julius shakes his head, "This was the way." Unfortunately, Julius was steadfast in his adherence to the prophecy and Ira was getting no more of an answer.

Having had Julius teaching her for the past number of years, Alex is unwilling to allow Julius to take over the story; she was well educated in his version of events but not at all familiar with Delin's role in this tragedy. "So, what then? Julius stole us from you?" Alex looks directly at Delin, who has lost her nervousness and regained her prim and factual manner. "No, Valentine. I gave you to him."

"How come?" Ira is straight in.

"Because I too swore to protect the Midnight Children, I too believed in the prophecy. So, when Julius gathered me among others to solemnly swear this I did." Surprised by Delin's declaration the Midnight Children turn back to Julius who explains:

"We are a small society known simply as the Guardians. Unfortunately, we were a small and secret society until Caros sniffed us out. He doesn't know who we are, not all of us but simply that we exist."

"Although they're bound to know that you and Julius are the main culprits?" Alex argues.

"That's correct." Delin agrees causing an expression of confusion to cross the Midnight Children's faces.

"General Delin and I were banished from Bodmin. I lived here in exile for twenty-seven years until I caught wind of Belial. I knew the time had come, so I went searching for you. In order to protect you, there was no choice but to shatter what you believed to be reality."

"This is exile?" Alex interrupts, unable to hold it in; she gestures around at the grandeur surrounding them. Julius sees her point but cannot say any more on the matter, not at this point in their journey anyway. "You two must have got booted out the Hall's doors with your pockets full." Alex pulls a face then grabs a bottle of wine from a side table and fills a glass.

"In fact, the only thing I took with me was the key I gave you for the vault below Ar Novad's which General Delin directed me to find," Julius informs her. Alex's jaw almost hits the floor. "Oh, and my car." Julius continues, "I took my car. This place has been in the bloodline for centuries and I have more than enough Giovanni gold to keep me invested for a few centuries more."

"Not only were you a Guardian and stole the Giovanni's most precious asset, you were Head of the Giovanni's Archives, surely then they'd have you tortured, even killed for what you've done and the information you hold?" Ira suggests to which Delin and Julius nod accepting of his point.

"Have you considered I'm also an asset to them?" Taking Julius to mean he is an asset due to his vast knowledge of Giovanni affairs and the 'prophecy', Ira nods in acceptance.

"What about you, though?" Alex directs her question to Delin, "OK, you might have got booted from HQ, but you still landed quite comfortably in a position of power. Why didn't they just kill you? It's not like they haven't killed an Incumbent before."

"True, but I am his wife," Delin states.

"Sorry to burst your bubble, General, but I don't think that matters to him," Alex warns before removing herself from their circle leaving Delin to ponder her words and whether she believes them or not.

After a moment of silent reflection, Ira looks to the two more experienced rebels before him. "You left us with the Guardians, didn't you? When you took us from Bodmin?" Julius nods in response. Ira continues, "You must have a list somewhere?"

"We do. We have a signed Covenant of all the original Guardians, many of whom are now deceased." Julius appears sombre, "However, new Guardians have taken the vow and joined our ranks throughout the years. We keep their names secret. Too many have already died to protect the identity of the Midnight Children."

"Well, the secret's out," Alex steps in, "Our identities have been revealed, and yet the Guardians remain guarded. We're going to need more than this room and a seven soldier task force to take on Argon, the Renegades and the Ronakites. They vowed to protect us, so; it's time for them to fight."

"And the Teva and Lanuonin," Ira adds.

"We need to find the Teva and Lanuonin first," Alex reminds him, "Unless someone else has inkling?" she looks towards Delin.

"Whispers and rumours only," she admits.

"Whispers and rumours are good enough for me."

"First thing's first," Ira rises, assuming his role of lawyer, "Whatever material we have in the vaults we need out before it falls into the wrong hands."

Alex produces the ankh key hanging on a chain around her neck from beneath her bodice.

"I'd argue it's already in the wrong hands." Delin attempts a sly joke which impresses Alex.

"We will assemble the task force tonight and clear the vaults." Ira continues before turning his attention on Julius, "Julius, you know more than any of us about Giovanni history. Dig out what you can on the Teva and Lanuonin." He turns to the General, "General, you are the face of Ar Novad's. You are who everyone turns to. Therefore you need to be aware of everything on the surface. You need to keep control."

"I thought I was the one who gave orders around here, Captain Tallon?" Delin smirks causing Ira to smirk bitterly in response, "It's our war, General."

"I'll raise a glass to that." Alex raises her wine glass. Julius, Ira and General Evelyn Delin copy her action. "To the Midnight War." Alex cheers.

"To the Midnight War." They all toast and down their drinks. In the warm glow of the Tiffany lamps and crystal chandelier, an icy chill grips them like claws down their back. No Covenant is signed. No vow is voiced, but they all know they are about to embrace a war they aren't in a position to win.

Chapter 28

Night has once again set on the city. Despite the green leaves in the half bloom of mid-Spring, the cold chill of winter still clings to life in the night air. As humanity continues to live and sin and sleep, Alex watches from the roof of Ar Novad's. She observes as cars slither along the road like eels on a river bed. She watches drunks stumble from bars, smoke, sing and laugh. She gazes longingly out at the horizon to the oil-painting black mountains against the navy blue sky. She wonders what will become of her. She wonders what she must keep buried and the fear of what will be unearthed. I don't want to kill you…her heart breaks as she thinks of Argon and the man that he was. If there was any chance to save him, she would. She couldn't let the Authorities, the Incumbents and the goddam prophecy win.

"Alex," calls Ira from behind. She turns. "Let's go." He gestures for her to follow. As she turns to follow him, she looks across the rooftop to where a group of soldiers had been given the unenviable task of repairing the roof she had destroyed. For a moment she understands why she hadn't won much favour within the ranks.

Back inside the corridors of Ar Novad's Alex and Ira having gathered their 'task force' in the weapons locker have set up a command post – back where it all began. Fourteen screens have been set up to monitor the CCTV footage of the tunnels, the main building and the exterior. The small unit of humbly ranked soldiers have assembled in combat gear, although neither Danielle, Noelle, Catherine, Ten or Trente really understood why. In fact, they were surprised to have been called back to duty within less than a week of suspension, and more surprised to see Alex and Ira back within the walls after what they had done.

"OK, here's the brief." Alex starts as Ira sprawls a map of Ar Novad's across a few tables they have thrown together, he then overlays the map with a clear sheet showing the layout of the tunnels and vaults. Those gathered within the room may not have known where this was going, but they had a fair idea it was nowhere good. "Delin has decided to use us as a task force. The task is, to ensure the tunnels are clear and that there is no unauthorised way in or out of Ar Novad's."

"For us or the Renegades?" Danielle asks.

"Renegades," Alex answers.

"How can you be sure this isn't a trap?" Trente is the next to question.

"I can't," Alex shrugs.

"Then why agree?" questions Catherine.

Alex sighs, "This could well be a trap. Delin could trick us all into descending into the tunnels where we will all be killed by Argon and the Renegades."

"Well, we could be," Catherine points out, gesturing to the soldiers around her. The Midnight Children look to each other guiltily.

"You don't have to be a part of this if you don't want to," Ira speaks plainly although he knows that this statement is rich coming for him for he was the Midnight Child who had absconded and tried to get away from it all but in the end couldn't outrun it. Alex decides to level with her squad.

"You don't have to do this, but Delin has revealed herself in a very convincing fashion that she is on our side and has been since we were created. There are secrets in those vaults that we need to ensure do not make it into the wrong hands. With this, I agree whether I trust Delin or not. Those secrets should be in my hands. Could Delin be a double agent? Possibly. Could she be setting us up? Possibly. The fact of the matter is that the Renegades were in those tunnels and regardless of what reason they were there for, which can't be good, we need to make sure they don't get any further. We need to exterminate these rats before they get to us and I'm not just talking Tallon and myself but every person within these walls."

The 'task force' silently consider their options. They were trained soldiers, so of course, they should accept their orders, especially when they came the whole way from the top and especially for all the lives that were at stake. However, when they were assigned to complete a task under the command of two creatures who couldn't be killed, it kind of made them feel expendable rather than essential. After silently weighing up their options, Danielle being Alex's feisty second in command and ready to get revenge on Argon for almost killing her on the night of the break-in is the first to cave. "All right then." She stands, "For Elaina." The name of their fallen comrade evokes the warrior within all of the soldiers. Noelle, Catherine, Ten and Trente stand to show solidarity for their mission. "For Elaina." They agree.

"Great." Alex wastes no more time and dives straight into action. She points to various doorways on the map. "These doorways are all the entrances to and from the tunnels into the building and vice versa, right?" The group nod in response, so Alex continues, "The only entrance slash exit that we will be entering and exiting through will be this one," she points to the back of the room at the doorway she had used on the night of her fight with Argon.

"You can't be serious," Trente objects, "So if we get attacked here, or here, or here, or here," Trente points to the various doorways, "we have no escape." The Midnight Children see his point, but unfortunately, there is only one answer, and Ira knows to reveal it gently:

"We can't risk the Renegades getting into Ar Novad's. We have to seal off all the doors." The task force appears to crumble.

"This is a suicide mission," Ten shakes his head.

"Not completely," Alex goes to the door and points to a small alarm system overhead, "On the other side of this door is a panic button. Should one of you make it to the door before the Renegades, you slap the button, whoever is watching from the Command Post," she gestures to the CCTV display, "Gets a signal from a silent alarm and opens the door remotely."

"And this works?" Catherine remains sceptical.

"Funnily enough yes and we know because you know the way it's very odd that Delin wears glasses even though she doesn't fucking need to?" the group nod even though they'd never really thought about it before. Alex continues, "Well, Delin's been wearing goddam Google glasses this whole damn time. We accidentally triggered the alarm that night, and she got the alert like fucking Robocop."

"Talk about four eyes." Noelle mutters.

"Delin's been suppressing the alarms, the footage, she's handled the media, the Authorities to keep this operation safe," Alex confesses to which the soldiers are amazed.

"What operation would that be?" Trente questions as Alex had never quite explained to any of them what exactly she and Julius and now Ira were scheming. Alex responds vaguely:

"We're going to destroy the Giovanni Authorities and unite the clans once again in Bodmin."

"Destroy?" Catherine is taken back.

"Not destroy." Ira steps in, "We've been gathering evidence to put them on trial. We wanted to present this to the Teva and Lanuonin, once we found them put the Giovanni Authorities on trial for war crimes and re-instate a more fair and diverse Council elected from the four clans."

"The four clans? Even the Ronakites?" Catherine is taken further back.

"Well, the arrival or Argon and the start of the Midnight War has made our mission slightly more complicated," Ira confesses.

"So we're at war?" Danielle turns to her leader, Alex, "Is this what we were trained for?"

"You were trained to protect the Authorities' interests." Danielle is torn by Alex's words. Technically, as a trained Giovanni soldier, having knowledge of a rebellion or even by association with such a scheme would brand her worthy of treason. Seeing doubt fill Danielle's features, Alex continues, "Evelyn Delin is a Giovanni Incumbent and Zanned's wife and even she turned on the Giovanni Authorities."

"General Delin ordered this task force to protect everyone inside this building. Whether we like it or not, we have been given orders by a Giovanni Authority. When this is over, you can walk away; you can have nothing further to do with our gunpowder plot. But now, right now we have a duty to fulfil for the safety of all those in this Institute." Ira's words are met with a wall of silence. The soldiers' hearts are heavy. Yes, they have been forced into an extremely awkward situation.

"Fuck it." Again it is Danielle who bites the bullet and draws out her Giovanni crested sword.

"Let's go."

Chapter 29

The small unit of preternatural soldiers descend into the dark, skull lined vaults and flank out to cover both sides. With the Midnight Children leading the charge, their unnatural eyes adjust to the gloom like cats. Under Alex's orders to inspect every vault, the soldiers move slowly. The newer vaults have keypad locks for which Delin had provided them the codes. They also required fingerprint scans for access. Each soldier checks a vault before methodically moving on to the next section. Ira, having been passed the keys to the older vaults by the General, conducts his investigation of each chamber.

It is hot in the vaults, a lot hotter than the soldiers had anticipated; hot and humid. How many of the books and papers had not been destroyed before the vaults were sealed and secured the soldiers didn't understand unless they hadn't always been there. There is one vault that Alex has her sights set on. Slipping away from the squad, she moves further through the gloomy subterranean passageway towards her target. She clutches the ankh key tightly in her left hand as her right is clenching the hilt of her sword. She pauses before pushing the key in the slot. She listens. She scans. Behind her, she can hear her soldiers systematically inspecting each vault. Nothing appears out of the ordinary just yet. Condensation or leaking water drips from the ancient brick ceiling above her on to the rough stone ground below her feet-drip, drip, drip.

She looks back towards her squad as they conduct their sweeps in a surprisingly professional manner. Alex knew, if her squad were taking something this seriously, they were nervous. On Ira's orders, Trente and Noelle clear the vaults on their side and then disappear down a connecting passageway within the warren of tunnels.

Suddenly, from the corner of her eye, Alex sees something slip past – or she thinks she sees something. Pulling the ankh key from the vault, she backs up and takes a closer look to where there is a wide-open un-gated vault and beyond that an old spiral stone staircase descending to the darker depths of the vaults. If there were Renegades in here, there were many, many places to hide.

Above ground, Catherine watches the monitor with fearful eyes as Trente and Noelle continue their search separated from the group. On the opposite side she can see Ira moving away from the group and towards a stairway to a higher platform. On another monitor, Alex steps closer into the open chamber. Suddenly the keypad of the door beeps loudly causing Catherine to nearly jump out of her skin. She fumbles for her sword but is relieved to see General Delin enter the room. "How are they doing?" she asks.

"It seems to be clear… so far." Catherine turns back to the monitors as the General crosses the room for a closer look. Catherine is surprised to see that the General is not dressed in her usual formal attire but rather dressed in combat attire. Wasn't the plan for Delin to stay out of this and keep up appearances?

Below in the vaults, Ten emerges from a vault and stops in the middle of the creepy corridor. "Smoke break," he lights up a cigarette. Ira stops half-way up the grimy steps. Looking downwards, he observes Alex in the passageway below him.

Alex carefully steps one foot in front of the other, trying not to make a sound. She stops in the long desolate corridor of dripping bricks and a worn grey stone floor which slopes downwards into some abyss. Drip, drip, drip. She notices something on the ground. She doesn't need to bend down for a closer inspection – she can already smell it, the sickly acrid smell of congealing blood. Whose blood?

Alex knows she needs to move quickly. She hurries back to the vault, opens it with the ankh key and steps inside. Nothing has been touched. This is how she wanted to find it. No-one else should be able to open the vault, not without the ankh key. What she had planned was to grab a few more documents, but just in case there was trouble, she didn't want them to get damaged, lost or stolen, so she decided that leaving the vault in lockdown was the best action. She turns on her heels, about to exit the vault when a figure rushes at the doorway. Alex instinctively adopts her fighting stance. "Alex!" it is only Danielle. "Alex, the Ankh! The Ankh is gone!" There is a fear in Danielle's eyes that Alex has not seen before. The full reality of their situation has now hit her hard. Someone or something had been down here and probably was still down here with them. She was there when Elaina was killed, and she had a good idea that Argon would kill her and the rest of them just the same.

Alex hurries after Danielle to the keypad and finger-print sealed vault where Delin had ordered it to be stored. Danielle was right; the vault is empty. Where once the broken Ankh of the Dead had been laid out on the floor in the middle of the room like a coffin, there is nothing. Fuck. "Someone knew what they were looking for," Ira speaks from behind Alex. Alex nods in agreement. Someone knew where the Ankh was being stored, meaning someone had been watching them for a while. Worse, however, is the fact that whoever it was who took the Ankh was able to open the vault that required a six digit password and a fingerprint scan. Alex and Ira's eyes connect, likewise did their thoughts, was this an inside job?

Above, in the weapons locker Catherine and General Delin watch closely where Ira, Danielle and Ten have gathered around the vault. Unable to see inside the vault to tell what is happening or what Alex's is doing, Delin realises something is not right. Suddenly from one of the top cameras, they notice movement. It is not Trente or Noelle because they are in the lower eastern section of the vaults. This movement is coming from the higher northern section. Delin moves closer to the monitor, eyeing the movement through a darkened stairwell – a shadow? No. It is a group of shadows. Renegades. Catherine gasps, there is movement on another monitor – a swarm of Renegades have emerged from a camera blind spot and are closing in on Noelle and Trente's position. General Delin immediately turns to the map still spread across the table to find a doorway closer to their position. She turns to Catherine as she rushes to the door, "Keep your eyes on those monitors. If the alarm is triggered, make sure you only open it if it is safe. Do not risk letting Renegades into our halls." Delin exits. Catherine stares helplessly. Her comrades were about to be ambushed, possibly killed and all she could do was sit and watch.

As Alex exits the room, she notices some cabling that she had at first overlooked considering she was concentrating on the documents in the vault. Her eyes track the wires that are running along the ground close to both sides of the walls. With a sinking feeling, Ira, Danielle and Ten follow her gaze. With their fear and suspicion mounting, they look to each other before following the cable that is lining every wall in the warren of tunnels. The four soldiers follow the main path until they arrive at a vast chamber where the steps down to it are just about hanging together. This chamber wasn't on the map. This chamber had been constructed or rather deconstructed from a series of vaults to weaken the foundations.

Alex is the first to go forward to the edge of the platform, "This is the heart of Ar Novad's isn't it?" she questions as she looks down. Her stomach churns in knots. Danielle nods, unable to speak, so Ira translates for her:

"Yes, it is." His heart sinks as he moves forward to stand with his fellow Midnight Child. Looking down suddenly, his stomach starts to churn also. The whole place is rigged to blow.

"Can we disarm it?" He whispers to Alex who can't take her eyes from the horror before her.

"Tallon, the entire tunnel system is wired. There's no time." She whispers in return, but Danielle, who has come closer hears. Once again, fear penetrates her features. Ten, who had before appeared calm now crumbles.

"Did you just say this place is going to blow?" he gasps. Alex and Ira give way to allow Danielle and Ten a view. Their jaws drop. Ar Novad's is going to go up in flames.

Suddenly a blood-curdling scream reverberates throughout the passageways. Danielle's eyes widen, "Noelle!" she is about to dash to her comrade's aid when Alex grabs her. "Run. Run back to the doorway. Hit the alarm. Get to Catherine and Delin and evacuate the Institute. Get everyone out of Ar Novad's." Alex orders.

"But, Alex," Danielle protests in despair.

"That's an order." Alex was not messing around. Reluctantly Danielle obeys and bolts back through the snaking tunnels. Alex, Ira and Ten likewise immediately dart towards the source of the scream.

As they bolt from the chamber and enter the eastern tunnels, they come face to face with a pack of red-eyed Renegades. Blood drips from the leader's hands and slices down the blade of his broad sword. Alex does not want to think about whose blood it could be. Instantly she engages them. While they are no match for her strength, skill or speed the Renegades outnumber the remainder of the task force.

Aware that they need to break through this barricade in order to support Noelle and Trente, that is if they are still alive, Alex batters the Renegades. Also aware of Ten's vulnerability in this situation, she attempts to steer their swiping assailants away and shield him from attack. She glances to Ira as she slices through a Renegade with her beautiful, imbued blade and breaks their formation. Ira handles himself well, but Ira is no warrior. Like a ballet dancer, Alex swivels effortlessly around the Renegades to engage two who are closing in on Ten like playground bullies. Ten holds his ground, but he is visibly scared. Taking a defensive position, he struggles to hold them back. However, as Alex parries in to join him they engage the hulking bullies together.

Taking on two Renegades at once as they cajole and slur him, Ira knows he has to fight not for his life but for Danielle, Ten, Trente, Noelle and everyone else in the Institute. He was not like Alex; he had never fought the Renegades before. He knows this is going to take every inch of his intuition and training. He uses the Renegades' arrogance against them. They are toying with him, teasing him, taking swipes but nothing severe. Ira strikes. Timing himself perfectly, he waits for both Renegades to close in then darts forward, drawing knives and embeds them directly through their lower jaws. The Renegades' eyes bulge. Ira quickly slips the knives back through the gushing wounds and plunges them through their hearts. Every Clan had a Ligature – a holding seal, all you needed was to perform the right ritual to imbue your weapons with the right words to kill. Luckily, Ira and Alex had done just this on both their weapons and those given to the members of their task force. So, as the ligature works its deadly magic, the Renegades are engulfed in a plume of blazing red fire before falling as dust on the cold ground.

Overwhelmed and fear flushed, Danielle slams against the doorway and immediately pounds her fist against the discreetly placed panic alarm. No sooner has she struck the alarm that searing pain screeches through her body. Crying out, she slumps to the ground. Where had they come from? As she pulls her pale hand away from her side, she gazes as the bright red blood dripping from it. She has been stabbed, badly stabbed. Above her two smirking Renegades look down at her, proud of the injury they had inflicted.

Inside the weapons locker, bold red letters flash on one of the monitors. The alarm has been activated! Catherine rushes closer to the monitor for a better look and to her horror, finds two Renegades on the other side of the door. She grabs her sword from the table, clutching it tightly. Catherine has never had to fight before. She had fought competitively within Ar Novad's but had never been put in a situation where it was fight or die. Although she is fairly confident that they are not getting through the door, the fact that she is all alone makes her uncomfortable. She feels so helpless. At least if the General was still in the room she could have sought direction, but it was not her call to break protocol, and the protocol was 'do not open the doors unless it is clear'. She turns back to the monitor just in time to see the Renegades draw back from the doorway and march back down the tunnel. They appear to be dragging something. Catherine looks more carefully. "Shit." She gasps – it is Danielle.

With the Renegades cleared Alex, Ira and Ten make a break for the eastern tunnels in search of their endangered comrades. A little bloody, but still breathing Ten keeps up with the Midnight Children as they race down a dark, narrow tunnel. Alex stops abruptly causing Ira and Ten to slam to a stop behind her. It is that smell again – blood. The floor is sticky with dark pools of blood that then smears into a clearing. Something or someone has been butchered and dragged. Carefully now, the three soldiers creep towards the clearing. In the gloomy light, two figures become visible on the ground – Noelle and Trente.

Ensuring the coast is clear, Alex, Ira and Ten hurry to their aid. Ten stands guard, scanning high and low as the Midnight Children inspect the two injured soldiers. They are still breathing but barely.

"Noelle. Trente. Can you hear me?" Ira hisses, "Can you hear me?" Noelle is fading rapidly. There is so much blood it is hard to tell where she has been hit. Trente attempts to speak, but even with their supernatural hearing, his words are inaudible. Ira leans closer. Trente's eyes flicker as he attempts to bring himself closer to Ira's ear, "Tra… It's a…"

"Trap" Ira finishes Trente's sentence as his life extinguishes. He looks to Alex who is now standing staring to the tunnel where Noelle and Trente were clearly dragged from. The three take up positions back to back as the sound of pounding footsteps grows louder and louder from all around them. On the ground, Noelle and Trente's bodies slowly burn, carbonise and disintegrate.

"We need to get out of here." Ira rapidly scans for a way out.

"You don't say." Ten grits his teeth, fangs bared like a wolf, knowing that he could be seconds away from joining Trente and Noelle. As the footsteps come closer, Alex grabs Ten and points towards a doorway about two stories up at the far eastern side. There is a half-demolished staircase that if he moves quickly, he can escape from. "Through there is a passageway. At the end, you'll find another entrance to Ar Novad's. If Catherine or Delin see you, they'll open the door. Go!"

"But what about."

"Go!" Alex cuts him off, urging him towards it. No use. Suddenly a knife buries itself in the back of Ten's skull. "Ten!" Alex just manages to catch up as he staggers and stumbles to his knees. The footsteps stop behind them. Whatever was coming has reached them. With Ten still in her arms, Alex holds on as he starts to burn. As she lets go, his body slips from her grip and crumbles to dust on the blood soaked ground. The knife that killed him clatters against the stone. Alex looks to her hands which are blackened in her comrades' ashes and blood. Anger boils the blood inside her. She picks up the knife as he rises to her feet and looks up to see a wall of Renegades blocking the tunnel to the east.

Slowly swirling back to face towards the northern tunnel system she sees the room flooded with Renegades and nowhere for her or Ira to run – even if they wanted to. There was no way to get a warning to anyone in Ar Novad's. With any luck, Catherine had seen the Renegades on camera and was alerting the Giovanni army within Ar Novad's. What Catherine might not be aware of, Alex surmises is that the whole foundation of Ar Novad's is rigged to blast them to hell. However, she thinks, there was no way Argon and the Renegades were going to blow the building while they were still in it. Best bet, she decides, is to bide their time and fight. Hopefully that will buy Catherine time.

The Midnight Children grip their swords. "I take it we're doing this, Spartacus?" Ira mutters. The question is rhetorical; he knows well; it's their only choice. "All for one and one for all." No sooner has Alex uttered her response that they charge towards the Renegades. However, they are halted mid-charge as Danielle is tossed like rubbish at their feet. It has become apparent that the Renegades are not here to fight but to taunt.

Danielle is wounded but alive still. She crawls towards the Midnight Children, her long red hair caked with blood. Alex immediately dashes to shield her, knowing that if she does not act quickly, Danielle is in danger of ending up like Ten. Alex and Ira pull her back into the centre of the room where they are surrounded. Countless blood-red eyes stare at them in amusement. These inhuman mercenaries are getting one hell of a kick out of this.

Above ground, Catherine has watched in horror as the Renegades stormed the tunnels. She watched her comrades fight and die and all the while there was no getting through to the General. She doesn't know what to do; there's no signal down there. She couldn't abandon her post and go in after them, what use was she against a platoon of merciless Renegades? She knows the General had assigned this small squad to the task force to ensure secrecy, but surely even the General didn't expect something on this scale to take place. Knowing she needs to take some sort of action, Catherine checks her weapons and abandons her post in search of General Delin.

Chapter 30

Alex and Ira continue to shield Danielle as much as they can, but they know the situation is helpless if the Renegades attack. Danielle tries to concentrate and remain on her feet, but she has been badly beaten and gravely injured and has lost a lot of blood. However, Alex knows they can't just stand there. She silently plots their escape and is about to make a break for it but just then, the Renegades split apart to create a passage through. Obviously, it isn't a path for Alex, Ira and Danielle to escape through but to let someone in. As the Renegades appear even more smug, the Midnight Children hold their ground. The sound of two sets of heavy booted footsteps echo closer through the chamber.

For the first time, Alex and Ira are actually afraid. They expected Argon but who could the other footsteps belong to? Belial? They hoped with anything left in their hearts that it was not Belial. If so, there was a good chance they could lose this fight right here and now. The Midnight War would be over and Ar Novad's would go up in flames.

The Midnight Children brace themselves, but as the two figures emerge into their view, it is not what they are expecting. The sight stabs them like a knife in the heart. Argon has marched a battered, bloodied but not broken Evelyn Delin into the chamber. Alex had thought that the sight of Argon and what he had become would be the sight that wounded her. However, the sight of her General, her Guardian, being led out like a lamb to the slaughter hit harder that she could have imagined. "General!" Ira cries out. He steps forward, poised to engage but he is stopped in his tracks as Argon draws a thick blade across the sullied Incumbents' neck. He does not draw blood, but the threat is enough. Ira spits on the ground, an uncharacteristic gesture to show Argon his disgust.

"Ira Tallon, it's so nice that we finally get to meet face to face." The words run off Argon's tongue like a song, "I don't think we've been formally introduced."

"Come closer, and I'll introduce myself then." Ira challenges.

"No. Not yet, Tallon. We'll talk later. It's your General's turn to talk." Argon roughly releases the General causing her to fall to her knees in front of him. She looks to the Midnight Children, her eyes so full of pain and sadness like a mother who has failed her children. "I'm sorry," she croaks, "I'm sorry."

"Argon let her go." Alex's calm words cut through the cavern. This is an order, not a plea.

"We both know that's not happening, Valentine." Argon snorts, his deep, dark blue eyes sparking. Argon holds a sliver of revenge in his hands, and he is going to enjoy it.

"Where's the Ankh, Argon?" Alex steps forward trying to distract him.

"Safe." He turns his attention back to Delin, "That's right. I took the Ankh. I took your precious secrets. The Giovanni are going to burn, Valentine, every last one. Stand in my way and I'll take your life too just like you took mine."

"I will not die on my knees." Delin rises, defiant until the last.

"Argon! Don't do this!" Ira screams, but it is useless. There is no way Alex or Ira could make it to her in time. Just before Argon brings his sword down on the back of her neck and through her throat, Delin composes herself. Her eyes meet Alex's. In that moment, as if by telepathy or extrasensory perception, they say goodbye. For a split second, she is the closest thing Alex has ever had to a mother. Only hours before Alex had learnt that this woman had cared for her from a distance her entire life and then in one fatal movement she is gone.

Ira falls to his knees in horror as dark blood gushes from his General's neck. There was nothing we could do he tells himself, or was there?

Alex watches her bleed and die and is revolted as Argon cups his hand to collect the blood from her neck before knocking it back like a shot, "Now, that's what royal blood takes like." He states as blood trickles down his white chin. In that moment Alex understands that while Delin may have been somewhat of a mother figure to her, to Argon she is the mother who abandoned him. It doesn't justify his actions, but it does make Alex pity him even more. I should never have left you.

Alex stands numbly, watching Argon slip the Seal of Incumbents ring from Delin's finger whereby robbing her of all esteem as her lifeless body slumps to the ground. He studies the ring as if it were a disease, "So this, this little thing gives you power over me." He peers down at Delin's blood soaked body, "Not anymore."

"Argon, enough of this!" Ira roars unable to bear the bloodshed and waste of life. Having been a human rights lawyer, he feels completely helpless against these monsters.

"Oh, Tallon, I'm just getting started." Argon pops the ring into his coat pocket and points to Danielle, "Her too." On his command, his two right-hand Renegades march forward to take Danielle.

"Argon!" Alex breaks her composure, "Argon, you can't!"

"Take the Midnight Children," Argon commands the rest of his Renegades who immediately close in.

Alex and Ira raise their weapons and move in to shield Danielle who whispers in defeat, "Alex. It's no use."

"Fight!" Alex urges, grabbing Danielle's wrist and forcing her to raise her sword, "Fight!" Danielle takes a deep breath and accepts Alex's command. Terrified and weakened, she takes on the Renegades. In that moment she decides that she will face death with courage and fight until her last breath.

Again the Renegades are not fighting to kill. Alex, Ira and Danielle face down the swell of Renegades with the odds against them. At first, Alex and Ira manage to hold back the Renegades who merely try to disarm them. However, as they attempt to shield Danielle from their reach, they are overcome. The Midnight Children slash, stab and strike to take out as many of the blood-thirsty bastards as they can, but there are too many. If they were only having to defend themselves, they could have cut through the Renegade wall and escaped, but they could not abandon their comrade.

Suddenly Danielle cries out as she is slashed across the face. Alex turns to aid her, but a brutish Renegade has disarmed her and grabbed her with his thick fist. The Midnight Child reaches to grasp the back of Danielle's coat to pull her back to safety, but she herself is grabbed and dragged backwards. She struggles against her captor and manages to break free, but another Renegade blocks her path. "Danielle!" she screams, "Danielle!" An agonising scream rings out and reverberates around the walls. Alex attempts to fight her way through, unable to see through the mass of mercenaries. Another blood-curdling scream sends shivers down Alex's spine. Terrified for her friend and furious with her enemies this time she fights desperately to break through the hoard when whack! A massive blow to her head renders her immobile. Disorientated and dizzy the last thing she sees is Ira being overpowered. Her consciousness fades. This is it, she thinks, I'm dying and with that, darkness.

Chapter 31

"Alex. Wake up. Wake up, Alex. Alex, please. Wake up. Please, Alex. Please don't leave me."

Still, in her half-conscious haze, Alex hears a voice calling to her. She struggles to focus. Is this real? Her eyes flutter. The voice is not Ira… It's not Julius' voice…

"Rise and shine, sleepy head."

This voice is closer. While similar to the first voice, she heard there is something different, something disturbing in its delivery. Her beautiful blue-green Labradorite eyes snap open, bringing her face to face with reality, or rather, face to face with Argon. It was his voice but his voice trapped in a memory. It was the voice of old Argon, her Argon; her Argon who was gone.

She gazes into his dark ocean blue eyes to find some shadow of the man she loved – the man she still loved. There is something in there, something still beautiful beyond the abyss of hate and heartbreak. Despite what he has done, she can't help but want him. She is the human left in him and he is the monster in her. If he is beyond saving, then perhaps she is too.

Still, after all, that he has done and is about to do Alex cannot forgive him, but maybe, just maybe she can save him.

She breaks his gaze to inspect her surroundings. She is on a wooden stage, worn by decades of performances. Beyond the stage there are rows of dusty red seats and a finely crafted balcony veiled with cobwebs and grime. Cracked and dull, dust-filled lights cast a gloomy glow over the scuffed wooden stage and throughout the room. Clearly Argon is making a mockery of Authorities' Court in the Hall of Vampires. Alex's arms are strung up loosely on a hook which has been strung from the stage lights. To her left she sees Ira hooked in a similar fashion. He remains resilient but silent. Jaw clenched awaiting his fate, Ira's stern expression tells Alex that behind the curtain of defiance lies dread. Seeing her eyes upon him, he nods to Alex to signal that he is OK. Looking to her hip, Alex's sword of course remains in place but her gun has been removed along with her various pyrotechnic devices. Surprisingly her bindings are loose enough to allow her 360-degree movement so, taking advantage of this she swivels around to view Argon's mercenary-like Renegades scattered throughout the auditorium. Each Renegade displays their own satisfied smirk of amusement as if this is some macabre show.

Alex turns full circle, and once again, she comes face to face with her monster. "You've always been one hell of a woman, Valentine," Argon admires her as he runs his hands along her body. His touch is sensual, enticing – seductive. Where once she would have succumb to such a touch instead, she flinches, what is he doing? Her Argon would never have groped or objectified her in front of anyone. He moves around her, hand slipping around the lower part of her waist. Alex remains confused and disgusted but dignified. The Renegades are loving this. Don't give them a show.

She clenches her jaw and grits her teeth as Argon comes to a stop at her side, hands on her waist. He looks to Tallon who watches with disgust and smiles. "Have you had a go on her yet, Tallon?" he plays to both Alex and Ira's revulsion. The Renegades snigger. "Get off me," Alex attempts to shake him off, but he pulls her closer, running a hand up her bodice towards her jaw to force her to look at him, "One hell of a woman indeed…" he lingers. For a moment Argon and Alex's eyes rest on each other and in that moment Alex sees beyond Argon's cold, dark gaze and finds a memory. How has it come to this? Detaching herself from thoughts of the past she studies the cursed Midnight Child's ambiguous expression. His gaze is intense, desirous. A smirk curves the corners of his full lips making it unclear to Alex whether he is looking upon her with love or lust. It unnerves her.

He releases his grip and Alex snaps away from him. As much as she is drawn to him, the display has left her feeling defiled. Argon turns his attention back to Ira, moving closer so that the proximity will provoke him more, Argon smiles, "Did Valentine tell you how she abandoned me? How she left me to die?" all trust visibly vanishes from Ira's face and he turns a paler shade of white. Alex closes her eyes – she knew Argon would do this. She just hadn't prepared herself for how much it would sting. Despite their frequently opposing opinions she has grown fond of Ira. She had come to realise fairly quickly that it was nice to have someone with her to share the burden, however much she wouldn't wish this life on anyone. Now she is in danger of losing Ira. Argon has blood on his hands already. How much blood, Alex can't bear to think, but, if he kills Ira… There would be no going back, Argon would have to die.

Ira's steadfast demeanour collapses. Despite having warmed to Alex and having come to see her as more than an antagonist for the sake of it, the fact that she concealed this connection from him knocks the air from his lungs. His suspicions had recently been aroused by the apparent familiarity with which Argon treated Alex. How he touched her was more than a display of dominance but love. How he looked at her was pure passion, not resentment and a desire to have what he could not. Ira had seen the signs but he had not read them. He was so caught up in all of this mess that he had let this slip right by him. A sinking feeling floods Ira's gut. Alex was content to lead him down this path of destruction but didn't trust him enough, to tell the truth.

With Argon's attention turned to Ira, Alex sees an opportunity to escape. She pulls down on the chains binding her wrists to the hook in order to feel their weight. They are slack but strong. She knows that if she can move quickly, she can break them.

Ira doesn't know what to say. Conflicted, he just leans into his chains. A defeated expression floods his features as he looks to Argon who smirks with success, running his hands over his closely shaved head. It is time for him to play his role. There is no other path for him that he can see. He has come too far to turn back now. He knows too much and he knows he is playing perfectly the role Fate has laid out for him. He had never meant to cause so much death and destruction, but he learned very quickly the power of suggestion. If he played his role in the Prophecy, the Giovanni Authorities would fear him and he needed to even the score. If Fate made him a monster, so be it; if it got him revenge for the life they took from him. He would play the role and win the war; if the Authorities weren't afraid to get their hands dirty, then neither was he.

"Can you imagine, Tallon, can you imagine the one person you love most in the world leaving you to die?" Argon is using his words to sow discord between the two Midnight children, but what troubles Ira most is the honesty in his voice. Argon clearly loved her, perhaps still does but here he is, his mind so bitter and blinded by lies and villainised by a prophecy that he cannot break character. Both Ira and Argon look to Alex. As the cold gazes of these men who once trusted her fall upon her sickening knots of shame twist in her stomach. I never meant to hurt anyone.

Argon moves closer to Ira again, still staring at Alex. "I take it, Alex never told you about the two of us then." Ira refuses to speak, as Argon digs his knife in deeper. Argon is winning and there are no words to argue with him – there is no arguing with the truth and no point in ordering him to stop. Ira knows in this circumstance his best defence is silence. "I take it you don't know much about me, and I don't know much about you, but I know everything about her. Well, I thought I did. You haven't known Valentine for very long, but I bet you thought you could trust her. I thought so too, Tallon. That girl was my world. I'd have given my life for her. When Julius drained the life half from her, I thought my world was ending. How could I live without her?"

Solemn, bitter tears trickle down Alex's face. How dare he? Argon knew she would never have left him if she'd have a choice. He knew she loved him. Despite all that was stake, she had forced Julius to go back for him even when Julius told her it was too dangerous. She risked everything to try to save him and even now she still would.

"I watched as she fled into the night with Julius. I had known her all my life; she was my soul mate, in more ways than one… I never believed she could be so cold as to leave me to die."

Alex has had quite enough. With Argon turning his back on her to taunt Ira further, Alex makes her move. With all her inhuman strength, she slams down hard to break her chains. The Renegades immediately jump to their feet weapons drawn.

Alex directs her sword to her former friend and lover, "Enough, Argon! Enough! Stop this!" Argon gestures for the Renegades to lower their weapons. He knows rightly, Alex has no intention to kill him. "I would never have left you if I thought for a second, there was hope. You know that. I thought you were dead," she pauses carefully choosing her words, "I wasn't trying to protect myself…" her fierce eyes lock on his.

"Then what were you trying to protect?" Argon smirks knowingly.

"The innocent," Alex says no more.

"Then all is lost, Valentine. All is lost," Argon strides towards her as the Renegades remain standing on their guard, "Innocence is long gone. We're killers now."

"You're a killer now," Alex remarks, voice weary with regret.

"And you're not? You've killed many of my men."

"I killed to survive."

"Didn't we all?"

"Elaina wasn't trying to kill you. Danielle, Ten, Trente and Noelle weren't trying to kill you."

"True. But, life is life and blood is blood," Argon shrugs, "I already have blood on my hands regardless so if one life is as important as one hundred, then I'm already stained."

"Those are Belial's words, not yours."

"And those aren't Julius' words coming from your mouth? We may have arrived from different directions, Valentine but we're both on the same path."

"Belial doesn't want you, Argon, he wants your power."

"I don't know what part of 'you left me for dead' you don't understand? Julius waltzed you off to safety. Julius saw a hero in you and a monster in me, so he took you. Belial saw this. He saw how Julius made me a scapegoat. Julius was intent on turning the Midnight Children against one another, so he made up a 'prophecy'. He used it to turn you against me, to sow mistrust. He took you, and he trained you to kill me. Although, Valentine, I don't believe you could. I don't believe you could do it."

"I'll kill you to save you."

"To save me from what?"

"The monster you will become."

"Oh, aren't we holier than though?" He mocks, circling her, "Saint Valentine."

"Oh, don't worry I'll die too."

"And why would you deserve that? Why do I deserve to die?"

"We all deserve to die for the monsters we'll become."

"It's everything we were born to be" he comes closer, "Join me, Valentine. Join me. You know we make a great team."

That is the nail in the coffin for Ira. He can never trust Alex again regardless of what way this turns out. She is too close to the enemy. They have too much between them. Does he think she would betray Julius? Not really… does he really think she would betray her comrades' memories by committing herself to the man who murdered them? Not really… Could he think of a reasonable excuse for why Alex had not told him the truth? Not really…

"What's the difference?" Argon pushes her, "What's the difference if I kill the Authorities or you kill the Authorities? We want the same thing."

Alex pauses before responding, her sadness has turned into self-awareness, "I'll admit I understand your reasoning."

"Alex, no!" Ira gasps in spite of himself. His eyes beg her to be reasonable.

"I'll admit I understand your reasoning. We're one and the same after all. But I won't shit on the graves of those who died for this by standing by your side." Alex steps towards him so close they almost touch.

"So you're abandoning me again?" he whispers.

"No, Argon. I just have a different plan for how this shit is going to play out." Their eyes meet once again in silent understanding. There is a flicker of debauchery in Alex's expression. Argon smirks, flashing a hint of his pearly white fangs.

"You never fail to amuse me, Valentine."

She knows Ira is listening. She knows none of this looks good, but she has to play the game. There is no way to make either trust her but she has to keep the balance right to keep both of them in her hands. However, not content that the wound in Alex and Ira's relationship is fatal, Argon decides to twist the knife. Alex belongs to him. "So, tell me, where does Tallon come into this?" with both Argon and Ira's eyes upon her, Alex rolls hers, she is done with this.

"Argon, if you're not going to kill me, I'm leaving." Again the Renegades raise their weapons. "And they are not going to stop me."

"Maybe not. But maybe this will." He pulls the remote detonator from his coat pocket.

Eyes on the detonator, Alex tries to remain calm while Ira immediately breaks his chains to engage Argon, but he slips away to where he can see and be seen by them both. "It's too late for me. The 'prophecy' damned me. Julius' promulgation of the prophecy made me a monster. He made me a monster. So be it. There's no going back."

"Argon, don't do this. If you do this, you become the monster you despise. You prove them all right," Ira pleads.

"So what? When they're dead, it won't matter what I am."

"It'll matter to me." Alex words momentarily pause Argon. He believes her, but he shakes his head.

"Valentine, you're coming down with me." Their eyes linger on each other mirroring each other's deep-set pain and sorrow. They long for each other, but it can never be the same.

Without warning, Argon activates the detonator. Alex and Ira are horrified. “I want you to see this.” Argon shows them the display, “You have thirty seconds.”

As if there is anything they can do, Alex and Ira race from the dilapidated theatre. The Renegades look to Argon for orders to pursue, but he simply drops the detonator on the stage and shrugs, “Let them go. They’ll come back for me.” As Alex and Ira flee the building, Argon stands like a sombre spectre on the stage. He is alone again.

Chapter 32

The countdown is on.

Breaking out of the building as fast as they can, Alex and Ira race into the streets, into the dying night. The sun approaches. No vampire would dare leave Ar Novad's now.

Realising that they are in a quiet district south of the city but not far from Ar Novad's Alex and Ira dash through the silent, winding streets.

There can't be long left.

Despite their inhuman strength and speed, there is no way they can reach the building in time. Their boots pound the ground beneath them as they race closer and closer.

BOOM!!!

"No!!!" Ira screams.

Time is up. Alex and Ira slam to a stop as the blast bellows through the city. The walls around them shudder as another explosion rips through the night. Debris is blown into the blue, early morning sky. Black plumes of smoke and red burning fire billow from the wreckage. For a moment the city falls silent. Shocked by the violent spectacle, the sparce locals are frozen in fear and disbelief as if unable to comprehend what is happening. Then, all of a sudden sirens and screams wail from every direction.

The Midnight Children creep to the end of a cobbled street and emerge through a stone archway to stand at the edge of the river. They are horrified to their core at the sight before. There are no words. They stare at the blazing inferno before them. The blast has created a massive burning sinkhole that has engulfed Ar Novad's and some surrounding buildings completely like the mouth of Hell. No-one could have survived this.

Crowds of confused and terrified humans quickly gather in the streets as the blaze rages. Police, ambulances, fire engines, news crews and helicopters arrive on the nightmarish scene. Alex is paralysed by the sight as the streets fill with thick, black smoke and ash that falls like snow. She is unable to divert her gaze from the roaring flames ravaging the formerly spectacular building and charring the bodies off all those murdered within.

How could Argon have done this?

Alex stares, unable to look away as the fire rages. How? How could he do such a thing? Surely this act of unnecessary violence had claimed human lives also. Standing by the river wall as the smell of smoke permeates her hair and clothes and the ash settles on her head and shoulders, she realises that Argon has just shed his last thread of humanity. He really has accepted the monster he has become. Sickeningly, she accepts that the only way she can win this war against this monster was to accept the monster in her. She is no hero. Julius wanted a hero to fulfil his prophetic narrative and a hero she will never be. Now, she just wants to get even. Fuck this war, fuck the prophecy, fuck the Midnight Children, fuck the Authorities, the Incumbents, the Renegades, fuck the Ronakites, the Teva and Lanuonin. She will do what she has to do to protect those she loves even if that meant getting her hands dirty and forsaking the humanity left in her. She will embrace the monster in her with open arms and let Ira be the hero.

"Alex, we need to go. We need to get out of here." Alex turns to Ira and realises that they have been drawing attention from the petrified civilian onlookers. These people had never trusted Ar Novads Institute or the soldiers it contained to start with and this incident only reinforced their suspicion. Alex studies the blood on Ira's uniform and blood-splattered skin before looking down to her own blood-stained hands. She nods to him, and they retreat back into the shadow of the archway. Before they flee the scene, Alex spares one last glance at the raging inferno. The war is well and truly on.

Chapter 33

In the crisp early morning light, Alex and Ira, worn and weary approach the solitary road up to San Lorenzo Mansion.

Blood-stained and dishevelled they walk together in silence. The destruction of Ar Novad's has stripped them of all will. Never had they really believed it would come to this. Thoughts race through Ira's mind with the main being, can he trust this woman beside him? Alex just doesn't have the energy to fight with him. Her mind is in too many places. Past, present and future beset her at once and she just doesn't have the heart to argue her case to her companion. She only hopes that someday he will understand her actions.

Suddenly, through the dense trees and foliage of the surrounding forest, the Midnight Children pick up the distinct smell of smoke. Having been rendered numb by the grievous events that had taken place, they hadn't noticed it before. However, something is definitely burning. The Mansion!

With any energy left they take off, sprinting as fast as their exhausted bodies will allow. Taking a short cut through the trees they emerge on to the vast, wild gardens where they stop in their tracks. Julius' beautiful sandstone mansion is smouldering. Police and fire crews are at the scene. Julius.

Alex darts forward but Ira grabs her arm. "Alex, you can't."

"I can and I will." She shakes him off and runs towards the wreckage of the mansion. Ira hesitates. He knows the risk of arriving on a scene like this and dealing with police. They can't risk arousing suspicion, but, it is too late, Alex is already gone.

Ira starts cautiously towards the mansion to where Alex has stopped to absorb and process the devastation. Priceless paintings and sculptures had been tossed from the windows on to the pebbled courtyard below. Books have been torn, pulled apart and burnt. Scattered around the grounds lie tattered and charred pages that the forensic teams collect as evidence. Alex looks around, embittered by the irony of the burning building against the backdrop of such beautiful gardens and the shining sun. As the mansion burns, she studies the flourishing forest, the wild gardens, the flowers, the pond all kissed by the golden morning light. She hangs her head. Everything, everything that they worked for has been lost.

"Excuse me, miss?" she looks up as a plain-clothed detective and a police officer approach her, "Do you live here."

"What happened?" she deflects his question.

"It looks like arson." The young detective appears cagey as Ira approaches. He eyes both Alex and Ira's battered and bloodied appearances warily, "Detective Zane Moriarty." He introduces himself before asking, "Do you know why someone would have done this?"

"Yes." Alex admits to the detective's surprise, "But you'd never believe me."

"You're from Ar Novad's Institute." The detective states.

"No shit Sherlock."

"What happened over there?"

"Gas explosion." Alex clearly lies. Ira can't help but smile. The detective isn't fooled, "And I suppose this is a gas explosion too?"

"The council should probably get those pipelines checked," Ira adds to the lie. The detective rolls his eyes, "I'm going to need you to come in for questioning."

"I'm going to need you to get out of my way." The detective and the officer are taken back by Alex's response. It is glaringly obvious that the two incidents are connected and the detective would like nothing better than to have these two soldiers taken in to custody but he needs to be careful. He knows without a doubt there is something very odd is going on and he doesn't want to do anything to make his suspects take off or perhaps attack. General Evelyn Delin was the go to when shit when down with a whiff of Ar Novad's about it but she had been unresponsive this morning when he called. Of course he considered it being connected to Ar Novad's being attacked but it was not like her. If the police failed to reach her, she would reach them. Had he always believed her story? Not a chance but at least it was some sort of alibi. If the Chief accepted it, his job was done. He can only hope now that Evelyn had not met her fate in the explosion. Looking to Alex, the detective adopts the political approach, "This must all be overwhelming. I'll give you some time to process." With that, he and the police officer return to the crime scene.

Alex strolls towards the fountain where some smart ass has decapitated the statue of John the Baptist. She stares at the headless statue as the mansion burns around her and the papers containing Julius' life's work litter the ground. The only thing to do was laugh. Fair enough, she thinks. I'd have done the same.

Taking a seat at the edge of the fountain, she fishes John's head from the water and holds it in her hands. Ira stares down at her, listening to the water trickle softly. One question burns in his mind, "Why didn't you tell me?" he asks softly.

"I couldn't," Alex sighs.

"You thought I couldn't understand?"

"No."

"You thought I couldn't trust you?"

"No. I thought I couldn't trust myself."

"You still love him?"

"I always will."

"After everything he's done?" Ira is appalled. Alex doesn't answer. Her silence says it all. Ira takes a step back. "Alex, I didn't sign up for this. I didn't sign up to become a monster!"

"None of us did! We got sucked in. The monsters came for us."

"Whoever fights monsters should see to it that in the process he does not become a monster." Ira quotes Nietzsche as a warning.

"Don't give me that shit." Alex sulks, "We didn't have a choice."

"Are you saying 'we' as in you and I? Or 'we' as in you and Argon?"

"Fuck sake. This, is why I didn't tell you."

"You should have! We are a team, Alex. Aren't we?"

"Yes."

Exasperated, Ira puts his hands behind his neck and sighs, "I don't want to become a monster. I don't want you to become a monster and unless you let him go, you will. He'll drag you down with him. I don't want anyone else to die. I don't want this blood on my hands. I don't want to go down that road."

"Too bad, Tallon. You're already on it, and there's no going back."

"You've given up."

"No, I haven't."

"You have. You've given up fighting for your life, for your humanity. Don't leave me the way you left him."

"You believe him? You believe him that I abandoned him?"

"I don't know what to believe any more, Alex."

"I didn't abandon him. I tried to save him, but Belial beat me to it. I thought Argon was dead. I was scared. I thought I'd lost the one person I'd ever loved and the one person who'd ever loved me…and I didn't want to lose my child either." Ira can't believe what he has just heard. The truth is evident in Alex's eyes.

"Where is your child now?" he asks carefully.

"Gone. It couldn't survive in a world like this."

Ira suddenly feels incredibly ashamed. He can see the pain and sadness in Alex's expression. "I am so sorry," he whispers.

"Don't be. I'll get my revenge. I'll follow Argon's bloody footprints through the fire. I'll kill everyone if I have to." Ira is uncomfortable with Alex's forbidding resolution but decides for the sake of sensitivity to let it slide. "Where do we go now?" he asks.

"We continue our search."

"We have a lead?"

"I think we might." Alex removes a bundle of papers from her inside pocket. Ira sighs.

"Alex, perhaps this is an opportunity to abandon this quest. Maybe this is an opportunity to claim our freedom."

"There's no such thing as freedom."

"We could try."

"They will find us." Alex asserts before lowering her tone, "Someone covered up evidence in Ar Novad's."

"What do you mean?"

"There were CCTV cameras in the vaults. Someone, someone would have been able to see the Renegades rigging the tunnels." Alex's statement hits Ira hard – she is right. "And now the evidence is destroyed." He muses discouraged.

They linger a moment watching the firefighters placate the flames. "Do we have a way out of here?"

"Yep."

Ira stands, extending a hand to help Alex up which she accepts. Setting the head of the statue down, she starts off towards the detached garage that is as big as a house in itself. Punching in the code the steel vault-like door slides up, revealing an enviable selection of sports cars. Alex scans the cars to find that

Julius' Porsche is gone. Ira notices the same. "Do you think Julius' made it out?" he questions.

"He better have 'cause I'm not ready to do this without him." Alex moves through the garage, past the cars and arrives at an equally enviable selection of motorbikes.

Moments later, the loud revving of motorbikes and tyres on the pebbled path takes the detective's attention. He and the surrounding police turn just in time to see Alex and Ira zoom down the driveway scattering torn pages, stones and dust into the air. The commanding officer turns to two police officers, "Follow them! Call in support! Do not let them get away!"

It is already too late. By the time the police car races down the driveway in pursuit, Alex and Ira are already gone. As the smoke from Ar Novad's blackens the sky and the flames continue to burn, the Midnight Children slip through the city streets with ease in search of support for their war of the damned.